PHOEBE ATWOOD TAYLOR

GOING, GOING, GONE

An Asey Mayo Cape Cod Mystery

A Foul Play Press Book

THE COUNTRYMAN PRESS
Woodstock, Vermont

This edition first published in 1990 by Foul Play Press,
an imprint of The Countryman Press, Inc.,
Woodstock, Vermont 05091.

ISBN 0-88150-172-7

Printed in the United States of America

10 9 8 7 6 5 4 3 2

One

BIG JOE, the tiger cat, poised for another playful spring at the tangle of cod line Asey Mayo was patiently unwinding in the woodshed of his Cape Cod home, abruptly changed his mind in mid-air. A corkscrew turn left him crouched by the kitchen door with his ears back, his tail twice normal size, and his yellow eyes staring balefully through the screen.

Asey, looking up curiously to see what new game the cat had devised, found that Joe wasn't playing any longer. Joe was in deadly earnest now, and from his throat was issuing his general advance warning to all strangers, a sinister half-mew, half-rumble.

"Stow it," Asey said as he turned to the cod line. "No dogs or intruders in your own kitchen, feller! You got your signals mixed!"

But Joe continued to crouch by the door and snarl, and suddenly Asey heard the unmistakable sounds of the dining-room-entry floor boards creaking. Joe turned around and gave him a disdainful "See-I-*told*-you-there-was-someone!" look, and Asey leaned back against the woodpile and rubbed his chin reflectively.

The only other person about was his housekeeper cousin Jennie, and she couldn't possibly be responsible for that weird creaking. Her passage across those entry floor boards was a stolid plank-plank-plank, like someone pushing a laden wheelbarrow over an old wooden bridge. Besides, Joe wouldn't snarl at Jennie, who had raised him from a kitten, and who gave him the lion's share of her meat ration. It couldn't be any visiting friend or neighbor, either. Any one of them would have knocked, or called out.

Gremlins must have descended on his house, Asey decided, and then he sat up straight as he remembered the stranger he'd seen on the shore road some fifteen minutes earlier, a man in a gray suit, with a bulging, baglike brief case under his arm. Because the Nickersons, farther along up the lane, were expecting an insurance adjuster to call about their boathouse fire, Asey had mentally dismissed the man as the awaited adjuster. Could he have been, instead, a salesman or a peddler who'd sneaked in and made himself free of the place?

"I wonder!" he said softly as he got up from the overturned pail on which he'd been sitting, stepped over the network of cod line, and joined Joe at the side of the kitchen door.

The creaking increased, something rustled, and a broad figure loomed on the entry threshold and hesitantly sidled into the kitchen.

Asey stifled an exclamation of amazed bewilderment.

Then he blinked.

But what he was seeing was no mirage. It actually *was* his cousin Jennie, cautiously creeping on tiptoe across the linoleum as if she were walking on eggs, any one of which might at any instant explode like a land mine.

She came to a halt by the telephone, warily removed the receiver, and asked for a number in low, conspiratorial tones. While she waited for the connection, she kept darting nervous little looks around. Just, Asey thought, as if she had no business being in the kitchen, and rather suspected a King Cobra of lurking in a corner, to boot.

Joe relaxed and focused his yellow eyes questioningly on Asey, who shrugged. *He* didn't know what the matter was, either. He'd never in all his life seen Jennie act like this before. On the whole, he would have been less surprised had he found the gray-suited stranger making off with the silver, or the best Lowestoft cups.

"Nellie? That you?" Jennie gave the impression of having crawled into the mouthpiece of the phone. "It's me. I'm all dressed and ready to go!"

For the first time, Asey noticed that Jennie was decked out in her best flowered-print dress and white pumps, and the broad-brimmed straw hat she'd taken two days to buy in Boston.

"Everything's settled!" Jennie went on in the same excited whisper. "Took some plannin', too—Asey Mayo may be the brainy old Codfish Sherlock they call him in the newspapers, and they can decorate him with medals for improvin' tanks and all, but I tell *you,* Nellie, he can be *awful* stubborn!"

Asey raised his eyebrows and wondered what he'd been stubborn about. To the best of his knowledge, he'd spent the first two days of his current vacation from the Porter Tank Plant amiably acceding to Jennie's every little whim. The spots on his blue dungarees and denim shirt bore witness to the amount of painting and whitewashing and renovating she'd saved up for him to do. He'd even uncomplainingly helped clean the attic on a fine June day meant for fishing.

"I didn't want to *rile* him," Jennie continued, "and I knew he'd *hate* the idea. He wouldn't *stand* for it. He'd just be stub —good gracious, no! I never told him a *word* about it, or about the money sittin' there in that secret drawer! He'd *never*— Nellie, *who* told you it *was*n't there? Oh, her?" Jennie sniffed. "Well, *I* don't believe that under-the-floor story. Think of the *mice!*"

At the mention of mice, Joe got up and hurried away, as if he'd just recalled urgent business elsewhere. Asey, however, continued to stand beside the door and eavesdrop. While he couldn't imagine what in the world Jennie Mayo was talking about, his curiosity was increasing by leaps and bounds.

And after her next words, his curiosity swerved into blank incredulity.

"Wherever that money is," Jennie said firmly, "we've got to take a crack at it—think of laying our hands on all that cash! What? Oh, I don't know what you'd do about that old safe. Blow it up, or smash it, or something, I s'pose."

A paragraph of a letter he'd recently received from Jennie's husband, Syl—now in the Navy—flashed suddenly into Asey's mind and stayed there for a moment, like a printed subtitle in an old-fashioned movie. "Jennie says she's been taking this jujitsu course and some sort of lady commando training," Syl had written. "Sounds to me like it was giving her a lot of wild ideas, and is probably a bad thing. You can't tell what it'll lead to. You know how she always admired Jesse James. Why, she might rob a bank!"

Jennie nodded so vigorously that her hat almost came off. "Sure, Asey's takin' us," she said, "only he don't know what *for*. He thinks he's drivin' me to the dentist to see about that pivot tooth—'course I know the dentist's just next door, silly! So you go stand out in the road, and I'll make him pick you up and take you with us. Tell Etta and Mary to be out, too, and for goodness' sakes, do try and make it seem like you wasn't there on purpose, and hadn't any idea we'd be drivin' by. Hurry, now!"

She replaced the receiver, picked up her capacious knitting bag, gave her hat brim a final pat in front of the mirror, and swung the wooden shed door to without noticing Asey standing outside. He heard the back door slam, and peeked out the shed window in time to see her secrete the key among the petunias in the window box.

Then she marched over to the black Porter roadster parked

in the yard, sat herself on the red leather seat, and stuck her thumb firmly on the horn.

"A-sey!" she called out serenely after half a dozen blasts. "A-sey May-o! Time to take me to the den-tist's!"

Asey found himself grinning at the bland simplicity of it all. Not for one moment, when Jennie had so feelingly discussed her bothersome pivot tooth, had he suspected that it was only a part of a deep-laid plot to induce him to carry her and her friends to some apparently underhanded project which Jennie knew he wouldn't approve of, and which, for all the intrigue involved, sounded as much like robbing the First National Bank as anything else.

"For Pete's sakes!" he said aloud. "That bank *is* next door to the dentist's office, now I think of it!" In the next breath he added, "Oh, but those women couldn't be up to any *harm!*"

Still and all, they were up to something. And Jennie occasionally did let herself get carried away by her enthusiasms. People still spoke in awed tones of the havoc caused by her Women's Defense Committee, a few years back, when they instituted a rifle class. There was her Bond Drive bonfire which had come within an inch of firing the whole town. There had been the affair of the bearded summer visitor whom Jennie had taken for a spy. While no one had ever proved that Jennie's antiespionage measures had driven the poor fellow into a sanatorium, no one had ever disproved it, either.

Asey sighed, looked with regret at his sailboat waiting at the wharf, and strolled out to the car as the horn began blasting again. To be on the safe side, he'd better string along, find out what was brewing, and generally keep an eye on things.

"Tooth hurtin'?" he inquired sympathetically as he got into the car.

"Sometimes it does," Jennie returned, "and sometimes it don't. It isn't so much that something *feels* wrong as it makes me nervous worryin' about it. Let's see, now. The shortest way would be along Mill Road, wouldn't it?"

Asey nodded. Mill Road was where Nellie and the others lived. You had to hand it to women, he thought as he drove off down the lane. They certainly planned out details. If he'd finished winding the cod line in the barn instead of bringing it to the woodshed, he would have taken the Mill Road in all innocence, and been genuinely surprised to find Jennie's girl friends in need of a lift to town.

Having planted in his mind the route she wished him to take, Jennie didn't spoil her act by displaying any undue satisfaction at his apparent acceptance of her suggestion. Instead, she tentatively touched the side of her face in the vicinity of the pivot tooth, and managed a couple of first-rate winces.

At the foot of the lane, Asey slowed down before swinging onto the main tarred road, and then he put on the hand brake and got out of the car.

"Saw a piece of glass I want to pick up," he said in response to Jennie's question.

He went through the motions, too, of picking up something from the sandy rut, and flinging it into the bushes. But his eyes were fixed on the square orange sign, newly tacked on the telephone pole, which had caught his attention.

"AUCTION!" the sign said. "The Estate of the Late John Alden. Sale to Be Held on the ALDEN PROPERTY, Directly Adjoining the FIRST NATIONAL BANK Building on Main Street, on Tuesday, June 22nd, at 2:30 P. M. USEFUL and VALUABLE Articles of ALL DESCRIPTIONS!!! MANY RATIONED ITEMS MAY BE FOUND HERE!!! Also VERY FINE ANTIQUES and COLLECTORS' PIECES. You CANNOT AFFORD to MISS THIS EVENT! Come and BRING THE FAMILY! Quinton Sharp, Cape Cod's Favorite Auctioneer. You Can ALWAYS TRUST SHARP. Also LIVESTOCK."

Asey thought he was beginning to catch on. Jennie's purpose in inveigling him into taking her to the dentist's on one side of the bank building was nothing more sinister than to attend the auction being held on the other side of the bank building. Jennie adored auctions, she knew he hated them, and had rightly assumed he would balk at attending one. As for the money she'd been talking so mysteriously about—the flicker of a smile crossed Asey's face as he returned to the roadster. He thought he understood about that, too.

"Sliver of milk bottle," he said conversationally. "Dangerous. You can't tell whose good tire might—"

"Asey, you're turnin' wrong! I thought we was goin' to take the Mill Road!" Jennie interrupted.

"Thought it'd be a nice change to drive past the fresh ponds," Asey told her blandly. "Haven't seen 'em since I come home. Besides, it's not more'n half a mile longer."

Jennie opened her mouth to say something, thought better of it, and lapsed into a slightly dismal silence.

"Tooth trouble?" Asey inquired.

"N—well, yes," Jennie said. "Yes, sort of. Oh, there's Miss Spry!" She leaned out and yelled "Yoo-hoo" at a white-haired woman who was backing a beachwagon out of a garage, and then turned to Asey. "You never met Miss Spry, did you? Miss Solatia Spry? She's that antique dealer from Orleans who moved over here to the old Hawes house last winter. I guess she's startin' out for the au—" Jennie stopped short. "Guess she must be startin' out for town, too."

"Could be," Asey agreed. Privately, he thought it very probable that Miss Spry was going to the auction of the Alden antiques.

Fifteen minutes later, he drove past the dentist's office, past the First National Bank building, and drew up at the front walk of the estate of John Alden.

"Here you are!" he said. "Have a nice time, an' don't let Sharp pull his old bush trick on you—that's the one where he keeps wavin' his arms at a bayberry bush out of your sight, an' takin' higher bids from it, so you keep raisin' your own bid sky-high. I'll pick you up later—an' I sure hope Nellie an' the girls manage to hoof it over here in time. So long!"

"You—why, you—you—" Jennie was bristling with indignation to such an extent that Asey wouldn't have been surprised to see her back arching into a ridge like Joe's, when he'd heard the floor boards creaking. "I never, I *never* in my life—Asey Mayo, how'd you know?"

Asey chuckled. "They call me Yogi Mayo," he said. "Sees some, knows some, hears some, an' guesses the rest. Get on with your auction. I'm goin' fishin' in the fresh pond to kill time till—"

"Well," Jennie raised her voice till she drowned him out, "all *I* have to say is, if *I* get that money, you won't be so smart and—and so superior! And if you only *stayed,* maybe *you* could get it, too! You and your *guessin',* which some people call *snoopin',*" she added acidly, "you'd be just the person to guess where John Alden's money'd been hid!"

"Jennie," Asey said patiently, "you haven't got into one of your buried-treasure streaks again, have you?"

"No buried treasure about it! It's money, that's what! *Cash* money!"

"I ought to have known the minute I heard you talkin' to Nellie," Asey said with a sigh, "that you'd fallen for buried treasure again. Be yourself, Jennie! They been advertisin' auctions with buried-treasure rumors since—"

"I tell you it's cash money!"

"Same thing. Since I was a kid in knee pants with copper-toed boots," Asey said, "one Sharp or another's been packin' 'em in at auctions with talk about hidden money. It's part of the Sharps' stock in trade. They've auctioned off hundreds of rickety, tumble-down houses at fancy prices because, owin' to a little advance propaganda, someone thought there'd be a tin box stuffed with money an' jewels buried under the parlor floor, or maybe cached in the chimney—"

"You see that crowd?" Jennie interrupted. *"See* it?" She brandished her knitting bag in its direction. "Practically all Barnstable County's here. And *why?* Because they know—*we* know—that John Alden *did* have money, cash money, and it's hid in something!"

"It always is," Asey said gently. "That's just what I been tellin' you."

"John Alden had loose money hid away," Jennie said doggedly, "and everyone knows he did! Everyone knows he never trusted banks after nineteen-twenty-nine, when he lost so much in banks that blew up. All he trusted was money. Paper money, and coins. He always paid taxes and large bills—like havin' his house painted—with big, old-fashioned paper money. And when he dropped dead so sudden, he never had any chance to tell anyone where it was hid, see?"

"Uh-huh."

"So that money's inside of something, and everything has to be auctioned off today. Someone," Jennie said almost dreamily, "is going to take home that old desk of his, or a bureau, or pictures, or a sea chest, and find—"

"An' find the insides stuffed with big, old-fashioned bills," Asey finished the sentence for her. "Uh-huh. I know. I've heard it all before. Now run along, an' have fun buyin' junk, only please, lay off Currier an' Ives, will you? Our house has enough of them anemic children an' sad-faced ladies without any waists!"

Jennie grabbed his sleeve as he reached out for the starter button. "Listen, Asey, I know sometimes it's all talk, but this time it's true! Gordon Sharp, Quinton's brother, was executor of the estate, and he padlocked the place as soon as Alden died. The money *was* here, and it still *is!* The will said everything was to be auctioned off just as it stood, and the proceeds to go to the town's Hospital Fund—the Alden relations are pretty mad about that, too," she added. "They expected to get left the china and the highboy and all the really good pieces, and now if they want 'em, they got to bid 'em in. Come on and stay, Asey! It's goin' to be great fun!"

"Nothin' doin'!"

"Honest, it'll be excitin', with the relations biddin' against the antique dealers for the good things, and all the town tryin' to grab scarce things—there's tins and tins of corned beef, you know. And a car with four fine tires, and yarn in skeins, and —oh, eggbeaters, and an electric iron, and a rubber bathroom plunger—and shellac! You said yesterday you wanted some shellac! And boats and oars and rowlocks—"

"If you see an anchor fit for my sharpie, buy it," Asey said.

"And everyone's goin' to bid high on anything that might be the money's hiding place," Jennie went on, "and lots of people are after the house, because they think that the money's—"

"Under the floor boards. I know. This," Asey said, "is where I come in. Thank goodness, anyway you believe in mice!"

"Asey, please wait! Where d'*you* think he might've hidden it? Tell me!"

Asey grinned as he leaned toward her. "You really want to know?" he asked in a stage whisper. "Inside a tin of corned beef!"

"Smarty!" With an indignant toss of her head, Jennie flounced off up the walk and disappeared through the open front door of the Alden house.

"Aren't you staying, Sherlock?" Asey turned to find the roly-poly figure of Quinton Sharp standing by the side of the roadster. "Big doings here. You shouldn't miss 'em. Alden had a nice dory you'd like. Just the thing for pulling your lobster pots, and the planking's as sound as the day it was bought."

"An' you guarantee a hundred thousand dollars in gold certificates lurkin' between each an' every plank?" Asey inquired dryly.

Sharp laughed. "Guess you've been listening to rumors, haven't you? Matter of fact, Asey, this time it's probably true. I don't think there's any hundred thousand kicking around, but Alden had money, and he did keep it loose around the house. His will said to lock the place up as soon as he died, and then to auction things off just as they were, and that's what we're doing. He had money in the house somewhere, and it should still be here."

"Your father," Asey said, "used to work up a lot more feelin' in his voice, an' he had a wonderful sentence about who could ever guess what fabulous black pearls from the mysterious Orient might have been smuggled into this weather-beaten little house by the late Cap'n So-and-So, who'd plied the China trade so long. If that didn't move folks, he turned the pearls into rubies as big as hens' eggs, from the heathen temples of mysterious Calcutta an' vicinity."

Sharp leaned against the roadster's door and bent nearer to Asey.

"This is the McCoy," he said seriously. "I knew as much about Alden's affairs as anyone, and I'll give you my word that there's a good ten thousand in cash, at least, somewhere among his things. The market crash and the depression hit him hard, but he had money—you know where he got it, don't you?"

Asey shook his head. "I didn't know him. That is, I knew him enough to say 'Hello' to when I met him in the post office. Wiry man with a cane—had a limp, didn't he? An' a kind of pleasant, ruddy face. White moustache, as I remember."

"And a little Vandyke beard. He used to be a ship broker. Gaines and Alden—you knew 'em. Retired—oh, twenty years or so ago. That," Sharp nodded toward the house, "was his grandmother's place. He never put on any airs, and sometimes he'd clerk for a few weeks at the chain store, or help Higgins peddle clams. It gave people the impression he wasn't too well off, but he only did it for fun. Asey, I'm not kidding. I wish you'd stay here. If I'd known you were home, I'd have driven over to your place and asked you to come here this afternoon."

"So? Why?"

"Don't look right now," Sharp lowered his voice till he was talking in a whisper, "but start glancing at the side of the bank building, and then work around to the lilac bush by the front door, and take in that man standing there. Then keep on looking down toward the river, as if you were trying to see Alden's wharf. Go on, while I gabble. Fee, fi, fo, fum. Fee, fi, fo, fum—see him?"

Asey saw him, all right. It was the tall man in the gray suit with the bulging, baglike brief case whom he'd seen earlier on the shore road near his own house.

"Know him?" Sharp demanded as Asey finished his survey.

"I tossed him off as an insurance adjuster, to tell you the truth," Asey said.

"He's nobody to toss off lightly," Sharp returned. "That's Gardner Alden, John's brother—and he hasn't taken his eyes off you and me since I've been standing here. He's a big-shot New York lawyer—Alden, Someone, Someone Else, Somebody and Thingumabob. He's hipped about antiques, and he means to buy up every stick in the place. I've had a bushel of telegrams from him, and fifty million phone calls, since John died. And plenty of words! He tried to bribe me to make sure that he got the best things. Solatia Spry, she means to get 'em, too—she knows choice stuff when she sees it. So does that Pitkin girl, who has the antique shop over in Skaket. And so," he pointed to a Packard beachwagon parked ahead of Asey's roadster, "does Mrs. James Fenimore Madison, of the Shack!"

"The Shack—that's the soap tycoon's place over in Weesit, ain't it?" Asey said. "The one with the forty bedrooms an' greenhouses, an' the private golf course?"

Sharp nodded. "Looks like someone'd thrown an old wedding cake onto a sand dune," he said, "and then stepped on it. Mrs. Madison's been pestering Alden to sell her his china and that highboy for years, and she intends to have 'em. She brought so much money over from the bank, half an hour ago, she's got her chauffeur standing guard over the bag. There's going to be *too* much money here, Asey! I'm worried!"

"Oh, I don't think you'll run into any trouble," Asey said. "It's just a question of whose money lasts the longest, and I wouldn't have any pangs or compunctions about biddin' 'em up. The proceeds are for a good cause."

"I know," Sharp said. "Ordinarily I'd jack 'em up, slam the stuff at the highest bidder, and feel proud to think it was helping the Hospital Fund. But there's a side to this that worries me. I know Mrs. Madison can take the lot, see? I know she's going to. But I also know that even if she buys the whole kit and caboodle, and bangs the cash down on the block, that still isn't going to stop Gardner Alden from trying to get what he wants anyway— I tell you, Asey, he tried to bribe me! He means business!"

"When you come right down to brass tacks," Asey fingered the starter button, "there ain't much he can really *do,* Sharp. If he's outbid, he's outbid, an' the crowd—golly, it's gettin' to be some crowd!—they'll see to it he don't make any fuss."

"Then there's Solatia Spry," Sharp said. "I happen to know she's got a customer, a big collector in San Francisco, who'd pay her all outdoors for John Alden's china. He saw it when he was here on the Cape a few years ago, and took a fancy to it, and Solatia has a standing offer to buy it for him at any price. She's a mighty shrewd woman, Solatia is. She's not going to let that commission slip out of her fingers without a fight—and she knows every trick of the trade! And that Pitkin girl knows the chance she's got on that deal if she can only catch Solatia napping. And then," Sharp's rotund face darkened, "there's that weasel-faced nephew of John's. He's the one who'd really go in for dirty work. I don't trust that fellow half an inch!"

"As long as you sell the goods lawfully to the highest bidder," Asey said soothingly, "I don't see how there can be any trouble. What happens to the buyers or the stuff they buy ain't hardly your problem—"

But Sharp wasn't listening to him. Sharp was craning his neck, looking at the throng.

"I thought I saw that nephew—he's a son of one of John's sisters, and his name's Alden Dorking," he said. "I wanted to point him out to you. He's a bad actor. Up to the time he was drafted, he was here trying to borrow money from John about every other month. He got injured in a training-camp accident, and was discharged as unfit. Blew into town the minute John died—he's after that loose cash, see? Tried to break into the house last night, but my brother Gordon and I've kept watch over the place—we've been sleeping here because we suspected that Gardner or Dorking might try some funny business. We chased him away."

"Whyn't you just hand him over to the cops?" Asey wanted to know.

"We pulled a boner there. We let him hear us while he was jimmying up the window," Sharp said. "We should have let him get in, and then jumped him and had him arrested. We realized that later. We'd ought to have got *him* out of the way, at least."

"I s'pose you're sure it was this Dorking fellow?" Asey asked.

"He beat it before we could see his face, but it was him, all right. Couldn't have been anyone else. Gardner Alden'd never pull a dumb stunt like that, and nobody around town would. They all knew we were sleeping here. So you see, Asey, it's these angles that worry me. I know whoever gets the stuff, there's going to be trouble brewing from it. And I'm going to have my hands full with the rest of the crowd over the canned goods and tires and such. For John's sake, I want to get as much as I can for everything, but I'm honestly worried. Wouldn't you stick around? Nobody'd try anything crooked as long as you were here!"

"I think you'll be able to handle things," Asey said. "Me, I don't like auctions. They had one at my grandfather's place years ago, and it took me years an' years to buy back the family's possessions, in driblets, like. I never cared for auctions afterwards. You know, you could always try your father's trick."

"Which one?" Sharp demanded.

"Sell off the shotguns or firearms first," Asey said, "but leave 'em on the block for delivery after the sale. That always had a quellin' effect, because as your father used to say, you couldn't never tell if they wasn't bombed, an' the *leetlest* jar might set 'em off. Tell me, do you still stop every now an' then an' swallow spoonfuls of Vaseline, an' make jokes about oilin' the pipes?"

"Sure. And I tell the story about the traveling salesman who got snowed in with the old maid," Sharp said, "and all the old summer-visitor ones—remember? Asey, for a man who doesn't like auctions, you know a lot about 'em!"

"I should," Asey said. "It took nearly a hundred auctions with your father officiatin' before I managed to buy back all of my grandfather's possessions. I can sing that 'Going-going-GONE!' chant of his as good as he ever could, an' a whole lot better'n any tobacco auctioneer on the radio nowadays. So long!"

Ten minutes later he was on the narrow, sandy shore of the nearby fresh pond, taking from its case the rod he kept in the hatch of his roadster.

An hour later, he put his rod back into the case and sat down under the pines. Either the pond was fished out or else the fish had swum up the river to view the auction with the rest of the population.

He looked at his watch—it was three-thirty. The auction wouldn't be over for a couple of hours, so he might as well kill the time here, he decided, as anywhere else.

Tilting his yachting cap over his eyes, he leaned back against a log, and filled his pipe. He could visualize Jennie about this time, perched on the edge of her seat, pop-eyed with excitement. All those hundreds of heads would be jerking as one from left to right, as if they worked by strings, while the bid bounced from Gardner Alden to the antique dealers to Mrs. James Fenimore Madison. Probably, to ease the tension and to give the townsfolk a chance, Sharp would ring in a tire or a tin of corned beef every now and then. Long-established friendships would be battered by an eggbeater, a family feud would grow out of an old, rusty lawn mower, and at least half a dozen women wouldn't speak to their respective husbands for several days because of the shellac, which they either had wanted very violently or hadn't wanted at all.

Jennie would be sure to bid in at least one Currier and Ives print. Jennie was a sucker for top-knotted little boys who looked as if they were about to perish from malnutrition—and she couldn't resist pictures of kittens, particularly if they were playing with yarn or dominoes. She'd just as surely buy up some cumbersome, bulky and entirely useless object which would crowd them out of the car on the way home. Something like an old walnut whatnot, with one foot missing. There were three such lame walnut whatnots home in the cellar, right now.

"All it needs, Asey," he could hear her saying defensively, "is a little rubbin' down, and some fresh stain. Whatnots are hard to come by. They're valuable. And I always *liked* whatnots. Mother used to have one—well, and s'pose this does make the fourth? A room has four corners, hasn't it?"

And if someone Jennie disliked tried to buy one of the tins of food, Jennie would bid it out from under her nose, whether or not it was anything she ever used. And under no circumstances would she ever remember to pick him up an anchor for the sharpie!

He puffed contentedly at his pipe and lazily surveyed the fresh pond. While he'd take the salt-water view from his own windows any day in the week, he had to admit to himself that the ponds had a certain charm. The sky above them always seemed bluer, the white clouds hung over them like spoonfuls of marshmallow cream, and the gulls that had swooped over from the back shore seemed to appreciate the quiet, glassy water after the rolling breakers of the outside beach.

As he wondered if it was worth the effort to relight his pipe, he heard the noise of someone coming down to the shore by the path through the bushes behind him.

If there was another person in the county who preferred going fishing to attending the Alden auction, he thought, it would be only fair to break the news to him that the fish weren't biting, and that he might as well go listen to Quin Sharp's story about the summer visitor who tried to eat a quahaug with the shell on.

He raised himself up on one elbow and turned to see a girl trudging down the path, lugging in either hand a wicker picnic hamper which must have been heavy as lead, to judge by her strained neck muscles, and by the way she was bending forward.

She passed by without looking in his direction, dropped her hampers on the sand, sighed her relief at being rid of the load, and flexed her hands, which seemed to have been cut by the wicker handles.

Asey stared at her interestedly, not because she was any raving beauty, or any different from any other young girl to be seen about town, but because she had one of the hair arrangements which always fascinated him in that they disobeyed all the laws of gravity. Jennie had assured him that such pompadours stayed up with the aid of lacquer and a lot of invisible hairpins, but it always looked to him as if the hair had risen on end from fright, and stayed that way in a state of suspended paralysis.

She was probably about twenty, he decided, although her blue middy blouse and short skirt made her seem younger at first glance. Her trip down the path had winded her, and her face was red as a beet from her exertions.

When she got her breath, she dragged one of the hampers to the water's edge, lifted the lid, drew out a book, and casually tossed the latter out into the pond.

She ducked back from the splash, said "Damn!" and experimented gripping the next book before she decided on a two-handed basketball toss. That one went out farther into the water, beyond the lily pads, and Asey heard her grunt of satisfaction.

By the fourth book, the girl was beginning to hit her stride.

After the seventh, she had become so proficient that she was bowling them out one-handed.

Asey sat cross-legged and watched her. Jennie was always saying that there was no accounting for some people's tastes, and adding some pungent comment about the old lady who insisted on kissing her pig. Why anyone should voluntarily choose to spend an afternoon hurling books into a small fresh-water pond, Asey couldn't begin to imagine, but this girl was obviously working very hard at it, and apparently thoroughly enjoying the process.

For his part, he thought, this was a lot more fun to watch than an auction. There was more room for conjecture. Who, for example, was this girl with the elegant hair-do, anyway? Where'd she come from? How'd she come here? There certainly was a limit to the distance anyone could lug those heavy hampers! And whose books were they? Hers? And why, if she had been seized with a burning desire to rid herself of them, should she put them in picnic hampers—very de luxe hampers they were, too—and bring them to this particular pond? Why hadn't she put them in an old carton and taken them to the dump, or presented them to the local library, or even saved them for some future bonfire? Or just kept them to help while away some cold, dull winter evening?

When the first hamper was empty, the girl paused to light a cigarette, and then tackled the contents of the second.

After thirty more books had splashed to a watery grave, she turned around, still beet-red and breathless, but wearing the self-satisfied look of someone who had done a hard job rather well.

Lightheartedly swinging the empty hampers, she started up the path.

Then she caught sight of Asey, and stopped in her tracks.

For a moment, she stared at him without speaking. Her face turned a darker red, and she was clearly embarrassed and taken aback at the realization that someone had been watching her all the while. But there was also a defiant set to her mouth which made Asey wonder if perhaps she wouldn't face a firing squad before offering any explanations for her actions.

"Good afternoon," he said politely.

"Good afternoon." She didn't, Asey thought, sound any too certain about it.

"Nice day." Asey restrained his impulse to add that it was wonderful weather for pitching sixty-odd books into a pond.

"Yes. I hope," she was looking now at the case containing his rod, "I hope I didn't frighten away all the fish."

"Oh, I don't think you did, thanks," Asey said. "If anything, you've probably drawn 'em here. The fish in this pond are so educated that flies don't interest 'em, but I'm sure they'd most likely enjoy some good readin'."

The girl smiled. "They were just some old books. You know, old things." She made a little gesture to show how old and unimportant they were. "Books are *so* hard to get rid of," she added. "I mean, people are always talking about the Nazis burning books, but did you ever try to? You can't. You simply can't. Not unless you have a roaring furnace—and this isn't the weather for furnaces—or unless you rip every volume apart and burn it little by little. This pond seemed—er—it seemed so convenient."

"I'm sure it was," Asey agreed, and knew it wasn't the retort she expected him to make. She'd expected him to ask a lot of questions.

"Well, good-bye." She took a few steps up the path, and then paused. "They really were *my* books, you know," she said suddenly. "I mean, I bought them, and they were my property, and all that. I just didn't happen to want them around any more. They were mine to dispose of, and—well, I just disposed of them."

"It was my feelin'," Asey said, "that you'd never go to all that work disposin' of someone else's books."

"But it must have looked frightfully silly to you, though," she said. "Just watching those books plop into the water. Well, good-bye."

"Good-bye," Asey said.

She picked up the hampers again, and departed.

Asey listened to the sound of her footsteps dying away, and chuckled.

"Wa-el," he said to himself, "if a batch of sixty-odd books is missin', I know where they can be found. Now, for Pete's sakes, *what*—"

On the opposite shore of the pond a figure had appeared, the figure of a tall man in a gray suit, with a brief case cuddled under his arm.

"Is that man tryin' to haunt me?" Asey murmured. "What'n time is he up to—huh, maybe he's plannin' to toss away into the pond whatever it is that's been bulgin' out his brief case so!"

But Gardner Alden set the brief case down carefully on the

sand, and then, kneeling at the water's edge, he proceeded to wash his hands.

If he were washing a particularly dirty frying pan, Asey thought, he couldn't take any more pains, or work at it any harder. He seemed almost to be scouring his hands with sand.

And then, with great care, he washed his handkerchief.

Asey shook his head. To hear Quinton Sharp talk, Gardner Alden was so determined to get hold of his brother John's antiques, he was all set to commit any crime in order to possess them. But here, in the middle of an auction when everything should be at fever heat, when fur should be flying in handfuls, here was Gardner Alden washing his hands and his handkerchief in a nearby pond!

There was absolutely no accounting for tastes, he decided, or for the odd things people chose to do. But compared with Gardner Alden and the girl with the fancy pompadour hair-do, Jennie's old lady who liked to kiss her pig was a piker of the first water!

"I give up!" he said, and leaned back against the log.

It was after five o'clock when he roused himself, walked back to where he had left the roadster, and drove over to the Alden house.

He had fully expected to find a tired, exhausted crowd milling around, talking and bickering and reminiscing, and making involved preparations to lug their new possessions home.

Instead there was only Jennie, impatiently pacing up and down the front walk!

"Where've you *been?*" she demanded. "Asey, I thought you'd *never* come—and you'd ought to have stayed! The most exciting thing happened!"

"You get the hundred millions in loose bills?" Asey asked.

"All I bought," Jennie said, "was a real sweet Currier—just a lithograph of some kittens—hurry, we got to get right home, quick!"

"You mean, all we got to cart away is a picture of a few cats?" Asey returned. "I don't believe it! What else did you buy?"

"Only a little walnut whatnot. A real small one. The upper shelf's sort of broken, but nothin' a bit of glue and stain won't fix up. And a tin of old-time dog food for Joe—see? It's all I'm goin' to take along now. The picture and the whatnot can wait." Jennie got into the roadster and slammed the door. "Hustle home quick as you can while I tell you about the excitin' part! *How* much d'you suppose an old sea chest went for?"

"How much?" Asey asked obediently.

"Three thousand dollars!"

Asey whistled. "Three thousand dollars? For a *sea* chest?"

"Three thousand! *Think* of it! You see what happened, Asey, that rich Mrs. Madison bought up the china and the best antiques. Nobody could bid against her. She just sat there with a suitcaseful of bills. Miss Spry didn't come— I guess she thought she could fool people by havin' someone else bid for her. Anyway, Mrs. Madison walked off with the best things before you could say Jack Robinson. That's why things was over so soon. *I* thought the expensive things would be exciting," Jennie sounded a little regretful, "but they weren't at all. The corned beef and the tires got people a lot more worked up! Why, one tin—"

"What kind of a sea chest was it?" Asey interrupted.

"I'm comin' to that. It was just a plain, ordinary, everyday sea chest—nowhere near as good as any of yours. I guess Sharp or one of his men must've mislaid it, because they brought it in just before the end. Sharp said what was he offered, and Gardner Alden said two thousand—just like that. Just like it was twenty cents. Then Mrs. Madison said twenty-one, and Alden looked at her a moment and said three."

"But *why,* Jennie? What was in it?"

"*That*," Jennie said, "is why I wish you'd drive faster. Nobody knows what's in it!"

"Look here, you can't mean that Gardner Alden paid three thousand dollars for a common sea chest that wasn't opened—why didn't Sharp open it? He always opens everything!"

"Well, he couldn't open *this*," Jennie said, "because it happened to be locked. Had a spring lock—one of the old-fashioned kind we used to have on the buttery, remember? For no reason at all, it'd spring locked while someone was in skimmin' the milk. Anyway, Sharp said it'd been open earlier in the day—'course, he *tried* to open it, and they brought out a lot of keys, but none of 'em fit. Sharp said the chest was full of books—"

"Books?" Asey broke in. "Books? *Books?*"

"You sound like an old parrot," Jennie told him. "He said books. Old books. When they couldn't get it open, Sharp come right out and said, 'Well, it was open, and there's nothing inside but books I wouldn't pay anybody a thin dime for.' He didn't hint around it might be where John Alden's money was, or anything like that, and I'll have to admit he looked more surprised than anyone when Gardner Alden bid that first two thousand! I thought for a minute he was going to tell his men to take the chest away. He was upset enough so he stumbled in his talk—and you know yourself, Sharp never stumbles! Nothin' ever trips him!"

"So!" Asey said softly. "So they brought on the sea chest last, kind of as an afterthought, an' it was locked an' couldn't be opened, an' Gardner Alden paid three thousand for it, smack like that! Huh! I wonder, now, if maybe Quinton Sharp maybe hadn't perhaps sort of succumbed to Gardner Alden's blandishments he was bein' so powerful righteous about when he spoke with me!"

"No blandishin' about it, Sharp didn't *want* to sell it to him!" Jennie said. "He kept lookin' at Mrs. Madison, hopin' she'd make another bid, but she didn't. Honestly, Sharp was lookin' around as if he hoped to goodness someone would jump out of a bush and say thirty-one hundred, so Alden wouldn't get it. You s'pose, Asey, they might've been valuable books no one knew about? Like that Walt Whitman book that schoolteacher once bought over in Harwich for a dime that was worth so awful much?"

"I wouldn't know—didn't Alden make any effort to bid in any of the good antiques?"

"He hardly lifted up his voice. The Pitkin girl did, though. Everyone knows she hasn't a lot of money, but she had her courage with her. She bid. And Mrs. Madison didn't ride her down on things she didn't want herself, either. And a bald man I never seen before, he bid a lot—*I* think he was biddin' for Solatia Spry. I can't *wait* to find out what's inside that sea chest —hurry, Asey! Drive faster and get along home!"

"Why *home?*" Asey wanted to know. "Why should you be findin' out anythin' there? Is somebody goin' to telephone you?"

"I keep tryin' and tryin' to tell you," Jennie said in exasperation, "but you keep distractin' me with a lot of fool questions! Don't you see, I remembered *your* keys! All those keys out in the woodshed! So I went up to Gardner Alden and told him we had keys that'd open the chest. He didn't seem to care a snap, and just thanked me—what did you say?"

"Nothin'—go on."

"But Quin Sharp was there," Jennie said, "and he overheard, and *he* thought it was a fine idea. He said since they had to take the chest away in his beachwagon anyhow, since Gardner Alden didn't have a car here, why then they'd just stop off at our house and get it opened up, so's he could put the contents down for his record. Sharp said considerin' the price Alden paid, he ought to put down in his records somethin' more than 'One sea chest, supposedly containing books.' He said at least he ought to know how many books, and if maybe there might've been anything else inside there. So he and Alden've driven over with the chest to our house, and they're waitin' there for you to get your keys—now, will you hurry up?"

Asey's foot went down on the accelerator.

"They said at the auction," Jennie went on, "that Quin Sharp and his brother've been sleepin' over at Alden's of nights, lately, and that they've been through everythin' with a fine-tooth comb, tryin' to find the money before the auction. You s'pose they might've found it, and put it into the chest themselves, and then somehow Gardner Alden found out, and that's why he bid so high to begin with?"

"If there was any money tucked away, an' if they found it," Asey said, "I don't hardly think they'd stick it into somethin' to be auctioned off to the public. After all, would you? But on the other hand, the Sharps are pretty honest. They're shrewd traders, an' they'd take the rear molars out of their grandmother's mouth on a business deal. Still, I think of 'em as bein' honest. This all seems pretty peculiar to me, Jennie! Three thousand dollars is a lot of money. You don't shoot that much—"

"Look in our yard!" Jennie interrupted as Asey swung up the lane. "There's Sharp's beachwagon, and Sharp, and Alden —look, two other cars, too! Who's that fat woman? I saw her at the auction. And that fellow beside her is that Al Dorking, John's sister that died's son. My, doesn't that fat woman look *mad!*"

Quinton Sharp hurried over to Asey as he got out of the roadster.

"Am I," he said with feeling, "glad to see *you!* Asey, let me introduce you—this is Gardner Alden, John's brother."

Alden nodded perfunctorily.

"And this's Al Dorking, John's nephew."

Dorking put out his hand and said, "How do you do, sir?"

"And this," Sharp went on, "is Mrs. Turnover, John's younger sister."

The plump woman glared at Asey, and didn't make any comment.

"Jennie's probably told you," Sharp said, "that Mr. Alden paid a large sum for a sea chest, and he's agreed with me that perhaps we ought to open it—"

"Gardner knew where the money was!" Mrs. Turnover interrupted explosively. "It isn't *fair!* That money should have been divided up between us three heirs—*should*n't it, Al?"

"I think Uncle John knew what he was doing when he made his will, Aunt Harriet." Dorking might have an oversized nose and a slight squint, but he had a pleasant voice, Asey thought. And his air of quiet amusement was in pleasant contrast to Gardner Alden's tight-lipped silence and Mrs. Turnover's bubbling wrath.

"Gardner never would have bid so much if he hadn't known John's money was in that chest! He knew we couldn't pay any such enormous sum as that, and everyone *knows* John was worth half a million, and I'm going to call my lawyer and have him sue—"

"Uncle Gard bought the chest, Aunt Harriet," Dorking said. "It's his, and everything in it is his—be reasonable! Even if you and I had guessed that there might be money in the sea chest, we never could have outbid him! I don't think," he added quickly, as Mrs. Turnover seemed about to erupt again, "that there's the slightest question of ownership involved, is there, Mr. Mayo?"

"I wouldn't think so," Asey said. "Now, I'll go get the keys—"

"I already been in and fetched 'em." Jennie held out an old-fashioned, hooplike iron ring about a foot in diameter. "I got 'em while you was talkin'—now, for goodness' sakes, *do* get to work and get that thing opened up before I die of curiosity!"

Twenty minutes later, Asey managed to find a key that turned the lock.

While the group clustered around, he raised the lid.

Jennie screamed, Mrs. Turnover screamed, and Quinton Sharp let out his breath in a dazed gasp.

The chest did not contain books.

It contained the body of a small, white-haired woman, and Asey found his eyes focused on the handle of a knife protruding from the region of her heart.

"It's Solatia Spry!" Jennie said in a shaky voice. "It's Solatia Spry!"

Two

THE early evening patients who were waiting in the anteroom of Dr. Cummings' office paid a lot more attention to Asey, sitting in an armchair in the corner, than Asey paid to them.

He was aware that every time the inner office door opened, someone left, someone else jumped up and darted inside, and that the remaining people gravely got up and moved one chair nearer the door, as if they were playing some stilted variation of Going-to-Jerusalem. One or two men had spoken to him, and he had absent-mindedly acknowledged their greeting. But his eyes remained fixed on the painted chest, covered with dog-eared magazines, that stood under the window beside him.

This blue chest of the doctor's was just about the same size as that other chest of John Alden's in which Solatia Spry's body had so incredibly turned up. It was not a genuine "sea" chest. Like Alden's, it was too long for anyone actually to have taken to sea. But it was an old chest, handmade, and probably had been built for the wife of some seagoing man who wanted something in which to store her linen and blankets.

"How in blazes did she get into that chest?"

Quinton Sharp had said that, Al Dorking had said it, Gardner Alden had said it. He and Jennie would very likely have said it themselves, too, except that the plump Mrs. Turnover had fainted before they had the opportunity. Dr. Cummings had said it when he arrived with the dual purpose of investigating the situation in his official capacity as medical examiner and administering to Mrs. Turnover, who stalwartly refused to stop screaming when she finally came to.

And the state police had taken up the refrain. The sergeant, in fact, had been utterly unable to say anything else.

"How in hell'd she get in there?" he had asked plaintively, over and over again. "How'd she get *in* there? How'd she get *in* there?"

While it was a logical enough question, Asey thought, he personally was far more interested in the next step—the problem of who had put her into the chest.

And when.

Particularly when.

It was speculating about that time element which had thrown Quinton Sharp into a state where Dr. Cummings had finally given him a sedative. Sharp had seemed far more perturbed over the possibility that he might have sold the chest with the body in it, Asey decided, than the fact that the body was in the chest at all.

Out of sheer pity, Jennie had made Sharp a cup of coffee. He had sat over in Asey's kitchen and drunk it, occasionally shaking his head, as if he knew the whole affair wasn't real, and that pretty soon he would wake up and find it all an unpleasant dream.

"Was she in it, Asey?" he'd kept demanding anxiously. "Was Solatia *in* it? Oh, she couldn't have been! It was full of books! I know it was full of books! It was heavy—the boys had trouble lifting it!—but it was just as heavy when we moved it this morning. And this morning, I tell you, that chest was full of books!"

Asey stared at the chest under the window until it became a blue blur.

He didn't notice Dr. Cummings bustle out of his office and change his white jacket for his suit coat. He didn't even look up until the chalk with which the doctor was writing a message on the office slate began to squeak mournfully.

" 'I am busy with Asey Mayo,' " Cummings read aloud what he had written. " 'Nobody in this town has anything so serious it won't wait till tomorrow morning. Personal note to Addie Hines: you have *not* got appendicitis. I saw you buying that melon this morning. Personal note to Rosa Silva: if that baby comes before next Sunday night, I'll endow it with a war bond.' There!" he concluded with satisfaction. "I guess that covers everything!"

"Seems to me," Asey remarked, "that you got an awful rushin' business, doc."

"Funny, isn't it?" Cummings lighted a cigar. "All my life I've thought how dandy it would be if I were the only doctor in three towns, and now I am, by George, and it's driving me stark crazy! I've come to the conclusion that if there aren't doctors handy, and people know it, they worry themselves sick over every little thing. If they knew that doctors were thick as flies, they'd just say contentedly that they could always get a doctor if they needed one, and then they'd get well at once. Now, let's get out of this place before I'm pounced on—you don't realize it, Asey," he added, "but this is the equivalent of a leisurely cruise to the West Indies for me. It's the first time I've left this blessed office at eight in the evening for certainly six months. They gave me a lull for a New Year's present—"

The phone rang, and Cummings made a face at it.

"Want me to answer?" Asey asked.

"No." Cummings touched a switch, and the bell stopped ringing. "They can take it at the house, and if we hurry, we can jump into your roadster and leave before my wife starts yelling for me."

They beat Mrs. Cummings out of the driveway by the scant margin of three yards.

"My, what a wonderful evening!" Cummings ignored her shrill shouts as they drove away. "What a treat! I'll have to hand it to you, Asey. Every time you come home, you manage to scare up a little excitement and get me out of my rut—where were we before that infernal crop of minor ailments stormed into the office?"

"We were discussin' Solatia Spry," Asey said dryly. "You know, somebody'd stabbed her an'—"

"I know! I *know!* I mean, how far'd we got?"

"Not very," Asey said honestly.

"Well, at least I'd told you that she was stabbed rather expertly—"

"Uh-huh, with a fish knife, which I'd already sort of gathered from the handle," Asey said. "You summed it up as a nice horizontal thrust between the third an' fourth ribs, delivered by a person or persons unknown, or words to that effect."

"And so it was. The knife was razor sharp, the whole thing was over in a split second, and it was a lot less gory than I'd have imagined such a thing would be," Cummings said. "Her clothes weren't disarranged any more than yours would be if you'd been stuffed into a chest that size. She hadn't struggled or fought with anyone—no marks or bruises on her. I'd say someone stabbed before she had any idea what was happening. And if you open your mouth and ask me *when* it happened, I shall probably scream like a panther!"

"When?" Asey asked promptly.

"Look, if I've said it once, I've said it twenty billion times! Only in books and in the movies do doctors look at a corpse and say something like 'This individual was murdered at sixteen minutes, four and three-fifths seconds past one o'clock!' Solatia was killed sometime this afternoon, and you know it as well as I do. You know perfectly well the only sure way you can tell the time is to place her and follow her movements up to a certain point—say to the auction. After you've lost her, that's prob-ably when she was killed."

"Come on, doc!"

"Oh, from three-ish until five-ish!" Cummings said pettishly. "*I* don't know! Not much before three, not much after five—Asey, how in hell did she turn up there in that locked chest?"

"That," Asey said, "is what I keep askin' myself, only I put it the other way around—who deposited her in it, an' why?"

"Going, going, gone!" Cummings said meditatively. "You know, this *is* pretty average grisly, isn't it? And I think Quin Sharp was telling the truth. I don't think he knows anything about it. I think he thought it was just books in the chest! Did he remember any more when you talked with him, while I was busy with the cops?"

Asey shook his head. "No, an' he told the cops the same thing he told us. I think he was too confused to improvise, even if he'd wanted to. The reason the chest got brought out so late in the sale was that it just plain got overlooked—easy enough to understand that, with all the truckle they had to sell. Sharp re-membered it was unlocked an' open this mornin'—he's got a real vivid picture of a lot of old books. He don't know at what time the lid was closed. Easy enough to understand that, too, considerin' he had a lot more important things like the china an' the antiques an' such on his mind. He even said he thought of that chest as probably the one item in the whole auction that'd never make for any trouble. An', of course, that lock *is* one of those variable things that pops shut any time it feels like it."

"Did Sharp remember if it'd had a key?"

"He thought so. But he'd never had any occasion to use a key because the lock hadn't ever sprung on him. Probably there was one, an'—oh, you can't tell! Some youngster might've swiped it, or it might've get jounced out when the chest was moved. Nope, Sharp didn't seem to know any more'n you'd reasonably expect him to, an' he's still pretty dumbfounded at Gardner Alden's biddin' so high for the chest in the first place."

"So'm I," Cummings returned. "Why *did* he, anyway? Even back in boom days, I don't recall anyone paying much more than fifty dollars for a chest, unless it happened to be a perfect crackerjack, which John Alden's certainly wasn't—where are we bound, Asey?"

"I'm toyin' with the thought," Asey said, "of callin' on Gardner Alden at the Inn, an' inquirin' into that chest price business. When he left my house, he said it'd been his intention to take the late bus back to Boston an' return to New York on the midnight tonight, but that under the circumstances he'd stay over. He sounded like he felt he was makin' a great concession just to stay, an' he didn't murmur any polite suggestions about his willingness to explain anything if he could."

"I suppose," Cummings suggested diffidently, "that you've considered the possibility that if you'd committed a murder, and had thrust the body of your victim into an old sea chest, it might well be worth three thousand dollars to become the legal owner of the chest? Then you could ship it to—well, say New York. Then you could transship it to someone named John Smith in Seattle. Or Timbuctu."

"Somethin' on that order," Asey said, "has been flittin' across my mind from time to time."

"Very ingenious," Cummings said appreciatively. "A lot less hackneyed than just a plain old trunk. How well did Gardner Alden know Solatia, I wonder?"

"Sharp said she was a very good friend of John Alden's, so I s'pose we can assume they'd at least heard of each other through him, an' wasn't total strangers. I was so busy with Mrs. Turnover faintin' an' havin' hysterics all over my back yard, I didn't get to look at Gardner's face after I unlocked the chest. I don't know what his reaction was then. When I had time to notice him, he was just as tight-lipped an' deadpan as he'd been before. You know, doc," Asey said thoughtfully, "about twenty minutes or so before Jennie an' I left for the auction, I seen him wanderin' along our lane."

"The shore lane? Why, you'd think he'd have been at John's! What was he doing way over there on your lane, of all places?"

Asey shrugged. "I don't know, but I seen him. An' then on our way to the auction, we saw Solatia Spry startin' out in her beachwagon—anyway, we took it for granted she was startin' out, though of course she might just've been backin' for practice, or for the pure fun of it. An' when we reached the auction, Gardner was already there. Sharp pointed him out to me. But Gardner hasn't got a car here, an' so I wondered—"

"By George!" Cummings interrupted. "By George, I think you've got something, Asey! He couldn't have hiked that distance from your lane to John's house in—how much elapsed time? Say less than thirty-five minutes? He must have got a lift from someone in a car! Now, if you saw Solatia backing out —why, of course! It's as plain as the nose on your face! She knew him, recognized him, and took him over to John's, where she was going herself—by the way, did anyone settle the time when she actually arrived at the auction? Jennie and Sharp were bickering about that when I left your house."

"Jennie never seen her at all, an' claims she wasn't there. I phoned some of Jennie's friends, an' they agree with her. On the other hand," Asey said, "Sharp's sure he *did* see her before the sale started, an' remembers how surprised he was not to find her biddin' later. He's positive she was there."

"Of *course* she was there!" Cummings said. "She had to be there. She was put into that chest just about two shakes after she was killed, and the chest was there. Therefore she was, too. Asey, I definitely think you've landed on something. It all fits. Gardner's over your way—heaven knows why. He starts out on foot for the auction, either meets Solatia or is overtaken by her, she picks him up, they drive to John's together. On the way, they have an argument about John's antiques—didn't Sharp say that Solatia had some rich client who'd told her to get that china at any cost? Well, she told Gardner that, and he said she was *not* going to buy it for any rich client, because *he* was going to have it himself. Then—isn't this about the way you had it figured out, Asey?"

"Wa-el," Asey began, but before he had a chance to add "No," Cummings slapped his fist against the red-leather seat.

"By George, I like it!" he said with enthusiasm. "It all fits! And the upshot of their argument is that Gardner kills her!"

"An' puts the body," Asey said in a gentle voice, "into a sea chest that seems to've been sittin' around in the middle of a millin' auction crowd?"

"Oh, that's *your* department, thank God!" Cummings said cheerfully. "All you've got to do is figure out how he popped her in, and tie up a few loose ends here and there. A little proof, a little evidence! Then, of course, you can understand why he bid so much for the chest—so he could remove the evidence of his crime. Really, that's a good, solid motive! That's something you can put your teeth into! He murdered Solatia so she couldn't get John's antiques, and *he* would." The doctor paused, and then snorted. "Only he—Asey, why did you let me run on?"

"It'd work out *so* nice, wouldn't it," Asey said sympathetically, "if only Gardner *had* got the good stuff, an' not Mrs. Madison. Yup, if only he'd bought up the good things, we maybe could even pull a little confrontin' act right now." He brought the roadster to a stop in front of the Anchor Inn. "We could say, 'Aha, you done it so's you could get those antiques an' that china!' an' be real dramatic. But as it is, considerin' he didn't hardly bother to bid on anythin' much except the chest, we can only ask him polite-like why he took it into his head to fork out three thousand for a chest whose contents was described as bein' books of no value at all."

"That three thousand," Cummings said, "gnaws at my vitals. I'm not going to be able to sit down to a good meal until I learn why he paid three thousand for that chest. And it hasn't got any secret compartments or hollow boards where any hoard of money could be secreted away, either! I frankly admit I prodded around with a scalpel. Asey, what d'you suppose he'll give us as a reason for buying it?"

Asey leaned back against the seat. "If he deigns to say anythin', it'll probably be somethin' to the effect that a man can pay what he wants for a thing he wants at an auction. An' so he can. Wait a second, doc," he added as Cummings opened the car door. "I want to figger what I'm goin' to say when he asks me by what authority I'm questionin' him. City lawyers aren't used to our informal ways. I'm inclined to think he'll just sniff if I tell him the truth, that Sergeant Riley told me that Lieutenant Hanson said for me to carry on till he could get here, because he's awful shorthanded an' all tied up with some sabotage problem up the Cape—huh, I know!"

He opened up the roadster's glove compartment, pawed around inside it, and finally extracted a small badge.

"What's that thing?" Cummings demanded.

"Honorary Chief of Police," Asey said. "Town of East Brook End, which is near the Porter Plant. It's got all the authority of a handful of salted peanuts, but it flashes good."

"Haven't you got one that's nearer home?"

"I had a bucket of 'em," Asey said, "but Jennie give 'em to a scrap drive in one of her patriotic moments. I'll keep my hand over the East Brook End part. Let's go."

And if the badge didn't work, he thought as he and the doctor mounted the Inn's front steps, he could always fall back on that peculiar hand-washing episode, and snap out some insinuation about washing bloodstained hands in the pond.

"Doc," he paused on the top step, "you said there was mighty little gore involved. Tell me, to what extent would anyone have acquired any stains in the process of puttin' her into the chest?"

"Oh, I should say it could have been done without any at all. Probably was—people are careful about that sort of thing, you know, unless they're the Jack the Ripper type. First thing the average person does with a cut finger is to hold it as far away from 'em as possible. That knife was like a razor, and the thrust was quick. The whole thing was quick, and neat. Don't think your man even got his hands stained—that knife handle was as clean as a whistle. You saw that yourself!"

"In short, no stains?"

"I don't think. Of course, Hanson's experts may be able to tell you differently," Cummings said. "They're bears for stains. After a little of their research, they can tell you if whoever moved her had stained hands at the time, or not—though what use that information'll be to you next week, which is when they'll probably get to it, I don't know. Even Dirtyface Jones, that village nitwit over in Skaket, washes *his* hands once a week, and I'll wager your murderer has slightly higher standards— oh, hello, Martin! How's the leg?"

While Cummings turned to speak to his patient, Asey went on into the lobby and rang the hand bell that stood on the desk.

The ancient clerk, whom Asey recognized as the grandfather of the regular clerk, now somewhere in the South Pacific, shook his head at Asey's request to see Gardner Alden.

"You can't see him, Asey, because he ain't here. He's gone to the movies. Came downstairs here about fifteen minutes ago, he did, an' said he'd expected the police to visit him, but he guessed they apparently didn't intend to, an' so he was goin' to the movies." He nodded toward the movie announcement thumbtacked on the wall by the desk. "I showed him the program there, an' he seemed real pleased with it. Extry long show tonight, you know. He said it sounded like a good show, an' a bargain at that."

Asey glanced casually at the poster, and then he leaned over and scanned it carefully.

The extra-long bargain show was Stinky O'Leary and Bud Mazutto, the Kings of Slapstick, in "My Jungle Love." And the cofeature was Two-gun Blaney in "The Lariat Kid."

"So he's gone to the movies," Asey said. "Huh!"

"I s'pose," the clerk said, "you an' Doc Cummings could go up to his room, if you'd a mind to—pretty terrible thing about Solatia Spry, wasn't it? She was here for supper only last night an' had a good hearty meal, poor woman! Well, I s'pose you could look around, only there ain't much for you to look at. He hadn't no bags except for a little brief case thing, an' he took that along to the movies with him. Made a little joke about it, he did. Said he hoped I wouldn't think he was runnin' out on his bill, but he had valuable papers in his brief case, an' he didn't want us to have the responsibility of 'em. Nice, considerate sort of feller."

"I don't know him myself," Asey said, "but I've got the impression that he's—uh—thoughtful, an' takes what you might call pains. Thanks."

Cummings, still talking with his patient, looked up in surprise as Asey emerged from the lobby.

"Are you *going*? What's the matter? Wouldn't he see you?"

"He's out," Asey said. "Will you be long?"

"I'm right with you now—just take it easy, Martin, and don't try to move brick buildings by kicking 'em, and that leg'll be all right. Well, Asey," he said as they returned to the roadster, "what now?"

"How'd you like to go to the movies?" Asey inquired. "Two-gun Blaney in 'The Lariat Kid,' an' the cofeature is Stinky O'Leary an' Bud Mazutto, the Slapstick Boys, in 'My Jungle Love.' Two for the price of one, an'—"

"Asey, are you deliberately trying to upset my digestive system?"

"Also selected short subjects," Asey said, "includin' Jimmy Simpers, the Hep Cats' Pride—"

"If you're even remotely serious," Cummings interrupted, "just drive me back to my treadmill. I'd rather put whitewash on poison ivy, and lance boils, frankly. You don't *really* want to see those hideous pictures, do you?"

"I wouldn't go if you paid me," Asey told him, "an' I keep wonderin' why they'd appeal to Gardner Alden. But then, I decided once an' for all, this afternoon, that there was no accountin' for tastes."

"He's never gone to that frightful show!"

"Accordin' to Old Man Baker at the Inn, Gardner was practically pantin' at the thought. No," he added as Cummings gave a derisive snort, "I didn't believe he'd gone, either. Just for the record, I think we'll drop over an' find out for sure."

"And how d'you expect to go about it?" Cummings wanted to know. "Borrow the usher's flashlight, and make a face-to-face survey?"

"I thought of askin' Tim—"

"Tim's in the Air Corps. His mother runs the place now."

"Wa-el, maybe I can get her to stop the film an' put the lights on for a second," Asey said. "Bein' as how I've all but spent the day spottin' Gardner's gray suit one place or another, I think it won't take very long for me to locate him."

Ten minutes later, they strolled out of the theater and got back into the roadster.

"Even if you don't know where the man is," Cummings said, "you at least have the satisfaction of knowing one place where he isn't. I give you my word, just that brief glance at Two-gun and his carnival of bullets makes me happy to think I never have time to get to the movies any more. Between the Gila Monster that Two-gun'll kill within the next reel, and the rogue elephant who'll run amok in that jungle epic, there'll be an epidemic of nightmares that'll drag me out of bed a hundred times before morning. And if that *was* Rosa Silva in the back row, I *may* be out a war bond before midnight. Asey, why did Gardner lie and say he was going to the movies? D'you think he's up to some mischief? He ought to have guessed that you could check up on him easily enough!"

"Uh-huh," Asey said, "only when you say you're goin' to the movies, you don't hardly expect anyone to follow you an' track you down—at least, no city person like him would. He'd just take it for granted that anyone huntin' him would drop back later to the Inn."

"Where's he gone, d'you think?" Cummings drummed with his fingertips on the car door. "Not to John's, certainly! There's nothing there. Over to Solatia's house, perhaps? I wonder!"

"I'm wonderin' myself. We might go see if he did—I meant to go there anyway, an' take a look around, an' see if Riley's man was all right," Asey said. "Riley was goin' to send one of his cops there to stay till Hanson could drop by an' shut the place up official. Jennie told me," he started the roadster and backed out of the parking space, "she said that Solatia lived all by herself in that big place."

"She had two maids when she first moved there, but they left to work in a factory. I don't know a lot about her," Cummings said thoughtfully. "Now I think of it, she must have been the only person in three townships who didn't have the first grippe, or that half-grippe that came after, or the throat that came after that. I knew her to speak to, of course. She was on the ration board, and she once had a spotter's shift with my wife. She's done very well in her business, I gather, though of course she made most of her money back in the Cape boom days when all those Middle Westerners surged around paying ten dollars for someone's old chopping bowl with a crack in it."

"No family?" Asey asked. "Jennie didn't seem to think she had any."

"I've never heard any mention of 'em," Cummings said, "and my wife—or Jennie—would probably have known if she had. Women have the most incredible talent for finding out how many relations people have. One woman picks up some mention of an uncle in Milwaukee, another picks up a brother in the soy-bean business, another lands an aged stepmother in St. Petersburg, and then everyone gets together and adds 'em up— bang, a family! *Asey!*"

"What's the matter?" Asey slowed down.

"I've had an idea!" Cummings said solemnly. "It's tremendous!"

"Welcome, idea!" Asey said promptly. "Mayo needs you!"

"Before someone could put Solatia into that chest, someone had to remove the books—"

"No, doc!" Asey said firmly. "No! Don't bring them books up now!"

"But where are they *now?* What became of them? They just flipped into my mind like," Cummings snapped his fingers, "like *that!* You've *got* to think about those books! You've got to bring 'em up! You've got to bring 'em to *light!* Why, those books are your clue!"

"Doc, I'm tearin' my mind to a frazzle tryin' *not* to think of them books!" Asey said. "I'm holdin' them books in abeyance till I can iron out a few dozen other items, like why did Gardner swear he was goin' to have his brother's things, an' try to bribe Sharp to get 'em for him, an' then never bother with anything but that chest—an' pay three thousand dollars for it when he probably could've got it for four-fifty, an'—well, don't let's confuse things any more by thinkin' about books!"

"But if you knew where they were—"

"That, doc, is most of the trouble. I'm afraid I *do* know."

"What? How d'you know? Where are they?" Cummings demanded. "Where?"

"A beautiful girl with a pompadour threw 'em into the fresh pond near John's," Asey said. "Now, please, don't ask me any more, because I don't *know* any more—an' before we start trackin' down beautiful girls with pompadours, let's track down Gardner Alden, an' settle him! I mean it, doc! Don't talk about books now!"

They drove along the dimly lighted highway in a silence broken only by the doctor's occasional peevish mutterings.

"Pompadour!" Asey heard him say under his breath. "Pompadour! Why a *pom*padour? Why not a *wig*? Who in blazes *was* she?"

He squirmed around the seat, slapped his fist against the car door, chewed at the cigar stump parked in the corner of his mouth, and made noises in the back of his throat which Asey decided were meant to indicate his general state of incredulity.

"Hey, Asey!" he said suddenly, "you've gone by! It's the old Hawes house. You've gone by!"

"Have I? No, I didn't see—"

"Yes, you have—look, you're way beyond, Asey. You're clear to the Orleans fork."

Asey stopped. "Golly, you're right! I wasn't thinkin' about the house so much as I was watchin' for the lights—doc, I never seen any lights at all! Did you?"

"I wasn't even looking for 'em," Cummings said. "I didn't notice. Probably the cop blacked out."

"Even the dumbest of Hanson's crew would probably know when he was two an' a half miles from the shore zone," Asey said. "I don't think he'd black out, an' I don't think he'd be sittin' there in the dark, either. I know I wouldn't, if I'd been ordered to go somewhere an' stay till my boss come. I'd make myself to home. Huh! I guess maybe we better drive back slow an' survey this situation!"

He turned around and drove back.

"Asey!" Cummings said excitedly as they passed by the looming outlines of the old saltbox house. "Asey, look! See the—"

"Hush!"

He continued on past the house and around a curve before he finally stopped.

"But, Asey, there was a flashlight in there! No lights, but a flashlight!" Cummings protested. "Blue-hooded, too! I saw it clearly!"

"Uh-huh. I seen it myself."

"A cop would just snap on a light!" Cummings said. "He wouldn't wander around with any flashlight, and a blue-hooded one at that! Asey, d'you suppose that's Gardner Alden prowling around? I bet it is! Turn around quick, man, and go back! Hustle!"

"Wait, now, I want to—"

"Oh, hurry up! If it's Gardner, you want to catch him *in* there!"

"An' if I want to catch him *in* there, doc, I don't think the best way is to drive gaily into that yard with my lights on, an' ask him pretty-please to come out!" Asey returned. "I think I got it. There's an old wood road—yup, I think we'll be able to make an encirclin' action, all right!"

"If you mean that old carriage road—oh, come, Asey! This car is no Porter tank! *Don't* let's go hurtling around back roads, knocking down trees and leaping over bushes! *Don't* always have to take the *hard* way—oh, well!"

As Asey started off, the doctor gripped the door handle with resignation, and closed his eyes.

Five minutes later, he opened them and looked curiously around.

"Is *that* over? The only possible comparison with that hideous experience—"

"Hush, doc! Don't talk so loud!"

"Is the passage of a wounded tank," Cummings went on in

a furious whisper, "trying to creep home to its lair by way of several mountains and a lake—we *did* go through a lake or two, didn't we?"

"Just a bit of swamp, that's all, an' here we are, right behind Solatia's barn. There's the house, see?" Asey pointed through the darkness.

"No, I can't see a thing. And what are we going to do now? Creep like snakes on our stomachs—"

But Asey was already out of the car.

"It's a bit brambly," he warned the doctor as the latter followed him. "Walk right behind me, take it easy, an' make just as little noise as you can. An'—keep your voice down!"

"That I should voluntarily have given up the peace and quiet of my humdrum little office," Cummings said bitterly, "to scratch my eyes out and tear my best suit to shreds—is that a Gila Monster behind that tree, Two-gun? Oh, only a wee rabbit! Hm. If a skunk takes it into his head to join this expedition, I shall—"

"Shush!"

Cummings subsided.

Quietly, Asey circled around the barn, glided along the shadow of a thick lilac hedge toward the rear of the house, and finally came to a stop just a few feet away from the back door.

Cocking his head to one side, he shut his eyes and listened.

Except for the rustle and swish of the leaves in the tall elm trees, and the thumping of the bullfrogs in the swamp beyond, everything about the old place was as quiet as a grave.

There were old house sounds, of course, of creaking shutters and loosely fitting windows and doors. And just above his head, in the wooden gutter of the slanting roof, a squirrel was chattering at something.

"With all this fancy circling," Cummings said in his ear, "you've missed him by six months! He's gone with the wi— ouch!"

Asey's elbow had bored sharply into his side.

Then Cummings, too, saw the cone of light glowing in the corner room, that same eerie blue cone from a covered flashlight which they'd spotted when they'd driven past the house.

The cone moved, slowly.

Then the person holding the light apparently rested it on a table, for it remained in a horizontal position, without wavering.

A few seconds later, it was moved again, this time in such a manner that the beam focused down. Not directly down at the floor, but rather as if someone were aiming at a spot on the wall about three feet above the level of the floor boards.

The fellow must have propped it, Asey decided, for it continued to glow down at that angle.

"Opening a safe?" Cummings breathed the words in Asey's ear.

Asey shrugged, craned his neck in an attempt to see better, and then turned around.

"You stay here!" he ordered, and added emphasis to his whisper by pointing firmly at the doctor and the patch of ground on which he was standing.

Cummings nodded a vigorous assent. Had he been able to state his mind, Asey thought as he started to inch around the side of the house, the doctor would undoubtedly have expressed some sardonic sentiment about Two-gun Blaney about to pounce on his villain, and added something about his own personal preference for staying well in the background on all such occasions.

It had been many years since he had been inside the old Hawes place, but he remembered that it used to have a side door. The side door led into an entry, and the entry led to that corner room. If he could only enter by that door, he could sneak up on the fellow from the rear. If the door was locked, he'd have to climb up the slanting roof to one of the upstairs windows.

But the door was open!

Holding his breath, Asey edged in.

He stepped over the threshold, and the next thing he heard was Cummings' voice.

There was something the matter with it, too. It didn't sound right. It was dim and far off, like a bad telephone connection. And it sounded worried. Asey couldn't remember when he had ever heard that voice sound so worried and unhappy.

If he opened his eyes, he decided, he might hear better.

He blinked up at Cummings, kneeling beside him, and Cummings promptly scowled at him.

"Come to, hey?" he remarked. "Well, my fine Homespun Sleuth, next time don't be so confoundedly fancy! Next time don't pay so much attention to strategy, and worry a little more about your tactics! Next time just you dive through the window and *grab* the fellow—er—you were after Gardner Alden, remember?"

Asey nodded.

"I'm glad you *do* remember," Cummings went on, "because obviously you lost sight of the fact about twenty minutes ago."

"He jump me?"

"*I* don't know what happened!" Cummings said. "*I* wasn't there! *I* was obeying orders, standing exactly where you planted me, out by the back door. Next to the rhododendrons. *I* never heard a sound—oh, I heard a thud, but I just thought that was you, jumping *him!* I wasn't even very moved when the blue light went out. I thought you'd picked it up—and if I hadn't called out to you at that point, I suppose I'd be standing there like a living statue among the rhododendrons even now."

Asey sat up. "You mean—gee, doc, didn't you even see him?"

"After I called out to you, there was this ghastly silence," Cummings said. "I yelled again, and then I rattled the back door —I frankly don't know which rattled more, it or my teeth. When I finally got up enough courage to open it and come in,

I found you here on the floor, and I remember being very grateful that there was no one else—you might as well lie back, Asey. You can't pretend you're not still groggy."

"I'm all right."

"It's a wonderful thing to have a head as hard as yours, you know," Cummings said. "You probably won't have a lump any bigger than a baseball tomorrow, and I'm sure your head won't pain you after Thursday—unless you move your eyes too rapidly. I don't like to appear harsh, but if you'd gone at that fellow more directly, Asey, I don't think he'd have smashed you with that length of lead pipe. At least, not so successfully."

"So he hit me with lead pipe?"

"Well, perhaps it was copper pipe," Cummings said. "Or a sock filled with beach sand. Who knows? Perhaps he even had a formal blackjack—"

"What's that noise?" Asey interrupted as someone in the next room began to moan.

"Oh, that's Riley's cop."

"What's the matter? Did he—"

"Yes, Gardner used him to practice on," Cummings said, "and because his head isn't as thick as yours, he felt the blow more. He feels terrible. I found him in the front room, tied up with his own belt. He doesn't know what happened. He says he was reading Joe Palooka, and something hit him. He just came to about ten minutes ago—when he started keening, I thought pixies had come out of the wall to serenade me. Hm. That fellow could pick up a lot of extra cash from vitamin ads!"

"Who, the cop?"

"No, Gardner Alden, of course! You know the sort of thing I mean. 'I'm a man of sixty, but I don't feel a day over thirty, and I have all the pep and vigor of a lad of sixteen.' Gardner Alden not only gets around like a human jeep, he does things!"

"He certainly does," Asey said reflectively as he touched the lump on his head. "Old Baker at the Inn told me Gardner was a nice, considerate sort of feller—an' he is, when you think it over! It was nice of him to leave that blue light burnin' in the window for us, so to speak, an' considerate of him to do such a neat, businesslike job as he done on my head."

"Just a wee bit more of that neat, businesslike consideration, and you could have had a real vacation in the hospital," Cummings said. "But I appreciate his not bothering to biff me. That *was* considerate. Of course, I admit I'm chagrined to think he rates me merely as someone to elude, or to run away from, instead of a potential danger to him, like you and the cop. What was he after here, I wonder? I looked around, but nothing's been ransacked that I can see. Her desk in the sitting room hasn't been touched."

Asey got to his feet, and found, after his head stopped swimming, that he liked what he could see of Solatia Spry's home. The sitting room beyond had nice mahogany, pleasant curtains, comfortable armchairs, and an air of having been lived in.

"Can you really walk?" Cummings asked. "Oh, I suppose nothing can stop you, can it, you indestructible creature! See, her desk is as neat as a pin."

Asey took his time crossing over to it, because the floor had moments of seeming to rise up and hit him in the face.

"I wish my wife would keep a file!" Cummings said wistfully. "See this little one of hers, here?" He read off the headings. "Ration Board, Business, House, Gas-electricity-oil, Insurance, Car, Taxes, Food. I've always wondered what it would be like to live with an orderly woman. I don't think anything's been touched."

After a tour of the house, Asey agreed.

"I'd say things was as she left 'em—at least nobody seems to have done any large-scale lootin' an' plunderin'." He paused in the doorway of the front parlor, where Riley's man had progressed from a prone position on the horsehair sofa to a semi-upright slouch in a chair. "How's your head? Better?"

"Yeah, a lot. Say, there's a funny thing—I tried to telephone Hanson about it, but the phone don't work. Something's wrong with the wire outside, I think. It's like it'd been cut, see?"

"So!" Asey said. "Huh! What's the funny thing you was goin' to phone about?"

"It's this beachwagon that's here—"

"I was going to ask you about that, Asey," Cummings interrupted. "Who drove that back from the auction? D'you know? Because it's occurred to me if you could find out from them where Solatia'd parked it this afternoon, then you could find out who'd been parked near her, and by checking up with people, you might be able to place the exact time of her arrival. And the identity of any passenger. *You* happen to know who drove the beachwagon back?"

"Me?" Riley's man smiled. "I'm glad it wasn't me," he said. "I'm glad that's something *I* don't have to explain about. Because this beachwagon's halfway into the barn, see, and halfway out. And one wheel's jacked up, and the wheel's off—flat tire, see? And there's a spare laid out, and *that's* flat, and one of the rears—the left, I think—well, *that's* flat, too!"

"In a nutshell," Asey said, "she had two flats an' a flat spare. An' the phone wire seems to've been cut!"

He leaned back against the arm of the horsehair sofa.

He and Jennie had seen Solatia backing out. Apparently the tires had been all right then. Certainly, if she'd been aware of any tire trouble, she wouldn't have been backing at all. Neither would she have let them go by with just a cheerful wave of the hand. She'd have blown her horn, attracted their attention, and asked either for help or for a lift. After all, that auction had been important to Solatia Spry.

But he couldn't remember seeing any lone beachwagon parked in the vicinity of John Alden's house when he had picked up Jennie after the sale. He couldn't remember anyone's mentioning the vehicle. No one had thought of it after the sea chest had been opened. No one had been told to drive it back here.

"In fact," he said aloud, "I plumb forgot all about that beachwagon myself! Doc, this is on the puzzlin' side. Jennie an' I seen her, seemingly leavin' here. But there wasn't any beachwagon left over at Alden's after the auction. Not that I remember seein', anyways. An' even if it'd been parked out of sight somewheres, no one was told to bring it back here! I wonder, now!"

"I'm past wondering," Cummings said with resignation. "I'm bug-eyed. I'm speechless. Three flats and a cut phone—there's something more than the long arm of coincidence there, Asey! That definitely smacks of sabotage!"

"Maybe it's this lump on my head," Asey said, "but I can't seem to reach any other conclusion myself. Now, s'pose we take a look at things—where's that big flashlight I seen a minute ago?"

The phone wire, they found, had very obviously been cut.

"I could do a better job with one hand," Cummings remarked as he peered up to where Asey was focusing the light. "And that roof's so low, you *could* reach up and do it with one hand, too. Hm. Let's get on to the beachwagon!"

Asey surveyed the tires for a moment, and then handed the light to Cummings.

"Hold it, will you? I want to do some pawin' around."

"Well?" Cummings demanded when he finished. "What's the story?"

"I think," Asey said slowly, "we'll take it for granted that her tires was all right when Jennie an' I seen her, else she'd have stopped us an' asked for a lift. I think, doc, that she was just backin' out of the garage, an' that a few seconds after we drove by, she heard a tire go. Well, she's got to get to the auction, an' she hasn't left herself much time—after all, she hasn't any need to go over there early an' paw around John Alden's things. She knows 'em. Now, she's a logical-minded woman, so she eases the beachwagon into the barn, where it'll be easier to work a jack than in the driveway. She gets halfway in, an' another tire pops. She gets out, hurries indoors to the phone— one flat she'll tackle herself, but two she needs help with. But the phone—"

"The phone's gone," Cummings broke in, "so she comes back and takes out the spare, and finds that's gone, too! What happened, did someone tamper with 'em in such a way that they'd pop when she started driving?"

"That cleanest wheel," Asey picked it out with the flashlight, "that's just had the air let out, I think. But the other two—well, it feels like they'd had long, thin nails driven into 'em. I think someone stuck 'em in so's a few turns of the wheel would drive 'em through into the tube."

"In short, the tires were fixed so that they'd go when she started out," Cummings said, "and the phone was cut so that she couldn't call for help. Someone was trying either to keep her away from that auction entirely or to delay her getting there—isn't that the way you figure it?"

Asey nodded. "An' when she found the spare was flat, too, she probably marched out to the road an' prayed for someone to come along an' take her. She must've known that most everyone had already gone—"

"By George!" Cummings broke in. "By George, *now* I see how this works! Gardner Alden was over this way just to pierce those tires and cut her phone! *That's* why he was over here! *That's* how he happened to be on your lane, don't you see? He took the wrong turn at the fork—it's very confusing there for people who don't know their way around! Yes, sir, that's it, he'd taken the wrong turn, and got over to your lane! As for Solatia, someone gave her a lift over to the auction, of course. After the news of this has spread around a bit more— probably by tomorrow morning, at the latest—someone'll turn

up and tell us that they took her. Then—what are you mur-
muring about, Asey?"

"I was just sort of beginnin' to wonder, doc, if she ever *did*
get there!"

"Of course she got there! Why in the world would you think
she *didn't?*" Cummings retorted. "You certainly don't suspect
that that woman in the sea chest was two other people entirely,
do you?"

"No, but—"

"I cannot imagine any conceivable reason why—Asey, you
can't think she wasn't killed at the auction! What could give
you any such notion as that?"

"It's all those people," Asey said. "I seen that crowd. I can't
visualize anyone's stabbin' anyone with all that mob millin'
around, an' not be seen. An' Sharp said the chest was in the
room behind where he was standin', all afternoon. His helpers
was in an' out, all the time—one of the things that seemed to
worry him so was his mental picture of his men hoppin' over
that chest, an' sittin' on it, an' such. But throughout that whole
auction, people were sittin' there with their eyes glued on Sharp,
an' on that room behind him where the sea chest was!"

"You sound like a man," Cummings remarked, "who's forgotten all about Harry Houdini! Maybe *this* was done with
mirrors, too! I'll grant you there seem to be some practical
problems involved—but merciful heavens, man alive, they're
child's play compared to the problems you'll scare up if you
figure things out any other way!"

"Wa-el—"

"Look here, Sharp said the chest was brought over here in
his beachwagon!" Cummings said. "You took that chest out of
his beachwagon, at your house, didn't you? Yes, I heard you
tell Riley that. Now, Sharp and Gardner came over together
—I heard Gardner say so. Therefore, unless Sharp and Gardner
started with a chest full of books, and came here and killed

Solatia, and took out the books, and put her into the chest and took it to your house—" he stopped, and sighed. "D'you vaguely see the point I am attempting to make?"

"Uh-huh."

"And while I'll admit that Sharp is rightly named, I don't think he's a murderer," Cummings said. "And if he were, I doubt if he or anyone else would bring that chest to you—Jennie really inveigled Gardner into it, didn't she? With Sharp seconding her suggestion and egging her on? And why should Gardner have paid so much just for a chest full of books? But if he'd killed Solatia and put her into the chest, then you could see why he'd pay so—oh, we've gone over that before! The point is that Solatia *got* to the auction, all right! She was killed there, and she—where are you going?"

"I want to see if Riley's man is feelin' well enough to carry on here. I got this hankerin' to track down Gardner," Asey said. "He's beginnin' to fascinate me. I'd like to know what other thoughtful an' considerate things he may be preparin'."

Riley's man said that he'd manage all right. "I got my gun out, and I'm going to shoot at the next funny sound I hear, see?"

"I don't know's I'd go quite so far as that," Asey said, "but maybe you might hook the doors, an' perhaps not sit with your back to 'em, or fall asleep. If Hanson sees you before he sees me, tell him there's a few things I think he might look into. So long!"

Cummings sighed as they started back to the lane where they had left the roadster.

"That was such a lovely sequence of scenes I had pictured at first, I rather resent having it destroyed so completely. I could just see Solatia picking Gardner up, and their argument as they bowled along in the beachwagon to the auction, and his determination not to let her get John's things for her rich customer, and her determination *to* have 'em. But this sabotage—Asey,

I never until this very minute got the proper perspective on the sabotage business! Look, Solatia finally gets a lift to the auction, she sees Gardner there, goes up to him, and accuses him of this sabotage. She says *he's* the one who's been trying to keep her from getting things, and she's going to denounce him —were *all* these brambles here when we came?"

"I don't think they've grown any," Asey said.

"Maybe I've aged in the last hour. It's a shock to come upon you lying starkly on the floor of an entry, looking as if you were more material for a sea chest. Well, to get on, Solatia says she's going to denounce Gardner—" Cummings paused. "Am I running on again?" he asked cautiously.

"I think you're doin' a fine job."

"I think it's even better than my first idea," Cummings said with pride, "because it's *got* more. You have this argument between them about John's things, which might have taken place any time, *plus* her anger at his sabotage, *plus* his anger at her turning up there, *plus* their mutual desire to get John's best things—"

"Over this way, doc. Over here," Asey flashed the light at the roadster. "Mind that poison ivy—huh! You feelin' strong, doc?"

"What's the matter now?"

"Our friend must be basically patriotic," Asey said, "because he didn't slash my tires. See? He just let the air out of 'em."

"*All* of them?"

Asey completed a circuit of the car. "All of 'em. Every last one."

"My mother always told me that doctors who didn't stay in their offices and serve humanity," Cummings said, "would meet with evil. Three miles back to town! Of course I know how to walk. I do it every day. From car to sick room, or car to hospital, or car to office. But it's only fair to tell you that I haven't walked three consecutive miles since I was in the last war. Almost anything might happen."

"Maybe a passin' car'll give us a lift," Asey said consolingly. But they had to walk the entire distance.

"It's a judgment on me," Cummings said as they entered Main Street, "for all the times when I've thoughtlessly advised people to take nice long walks—*why* in the world d'you suppose I ever suggested such a thing?"

"Maybe it's like vegetables," Asey suggested slyly.

"*Vege*tables?"

"Uh-huh. You're always urgin' me to eat more of 'em, but I've always noticed you scrape 'em to the side of your plate an' leave 'em there."

"I save them for the last," Cummings said righteously, "so I can get the full savor—what's that yonder, a stampede? Oh, it's Two-gun letting out. Wait, Asey, I want to watch. I want to see what that bill did to 'em. They ought to be in shreds," he added as people crowded out onto the street, "but they look as happy—"

"Good evening, sir." Alden Dorking paused beside them, spoke to Asey, and nodded at the doctor. "Any developments about Miss Spry?"

"Wa-el," Asey drawled, "Doc Cummings's learned how to walk, an' I've learned the value of a thick head. In a nutshell, no, we haven't found—"

He broke off as Cummings clutched his arm and pointed to a man in a light coat and gray trousers who'd just emerged from the theater.

It was Gardner Alden.

"Oh, Mr. Mayo!" he said. "I saw you there in the movies when the lights went on, and waved at you. I thought you might possibly be hunting for me!"

Three

IT was the light gray-and-white-striped seersucker coat, Asey told himself. He had been scanning those movie aisles for a dark gray coat. That was how he had missed the man.

But almost simultaneously, he reminded himself that he had not just been looking for a coat. He'd been looking, too, for that long face with the tight, thin lips, and the bushy gray eyebrows, and the aquiline nose that was almost duplicated, in a larger size, on Al Dorking's face.

Cummings managed to find his voice.

"Quite a bill you sat through, Mr. Alden," he said. "Was there a rogue elephant to go with the Gila Monster?"

"There was even a vengeful native who slashed the straps that kept the howdah on the heroine's pet white elephant," Al Dorking said with a laugh. "There was everything, with custard pies thrown in. We got the works. I stopped by at the Inn for you, Uncle Gard, but you'd gone—I knew when I saw that double-feature announcement that you'd be right in the front row!"

"My brother John and the rest of my family," Gardner explained to Asey, "have always laughed at me because I never miss a Western picture—haven't for years. And if there's anything I like better, it's a good slapstick comedy team like O'Leary and Mazutto. Really, I had a splendid time!"

He sounded more human and was displaying more animation, Asey thought, than he had at any time during their acquaintance. Perhaps it was the seersucker coat, but there was almost a festive aura about him.

"Still carrying the papers?" Al Dorking inquired, pointing toward the bulging brief case.

Gardner nodded. "I almost don't dare let them out of my sight. They're some of the data on the MacDougall estate, Mr. Mayo," he said parenthetically. "You may have read about it. Some of the younger heirs are well known in café society, and they've been rather noisy about their grandfather's will, which they don't like. I brought these along to study on the train. And by the way, will you or the police want me, d'you think? Because I ought to be getting back. I have rather a lot to do with this case."

"I'll be running along, Uncle Gard," Al said. "I suppose I'll see you tomorrow before you go?"

"Yes, I want to talk with you. Good night, Al." Gardner turned to Asey as Dorking strolled away. "I wonder if you and the doctor would care to come into the drugstore and have some ice cream with me? The movies made me hungry, and the Inn fare was rather slim this evening."

"A sundae!" Cummings said. "That's what I've been wanting! No, *three* sundaes! One for each mile I had to walk. Nothing like walking to give you an appetite—now I wonder, *why* do I always tell fat ladies to walk when they want to reduce? If they're at all like me, it'll only give 'em the appetite of a dray horse. You walk very much, Mr. Alden?" he added casually as they entered the crowded drugstore next to the movies. "I have a feeling that you're probably a great hiker. You have the—er—build."

"As a matter of fact," Gardner said with a smile, "I never walk unless I'm walking after a golf ball, and for the last few years I haven't even bothered to walk after them. I have a troublesome cartilage in my left knee—ah, they're leaving that table over in the corner! Let's take that."

There was something bizarre, Asey thought, about sitting down and eating a strawberry sundae with a man whom you'd rather suspected of biffing you over the head, a short while before, with a length of lead pipe. He knew that Cummings thought so, too, but the doctor wasn't letting the situation impair his suddenly developed appetite for sundaes.

"About Miss Spry," Gardner said. "Is there anything I can do to assist you and the police, Mr. Mayo? I might add that the whole affair was a definite shock to me. I quite sincerely believed that the chest contained some old books."

"Why did you pay so much for that chest, Mr. Alden?" Asey asked.

Gardner looked at him, and smiled slowly.

"You're the first person," he said, "who has had the courage to come out and ask me that directly. Both Quinton Sharp and that police sergeant nearly turned themselves inside out attempting indirect methods, and I thought your cousin Jennie would bite off her tongue, trying not to burst out and ask me. To be perfectly frank with you, I came here with the intention of buying up all of John's best things. I knew all about the will, of course. I knew that he had left nothing to the family—one of my partners drew up that will from notes which John gave me."

Gardner finished his ice cream, and pushed the dish away from him.

"My brother and I were very good friends," he went on. "He knew that I wanted those things, and he told me honestly why he wasn't going to leave them to me, and why he didn't want me to have them. He said that I had possessions enough, that I didn't care for what I had, and that I didn't really care about these things of his. That I simply rapaciously wanted them. We had different points of view, John and I."

Cummings held out a crumpled pack of cigarettes, and Gardner paused to take one.

"Thank you. Yes, John retired long ago, and came and lived here quietly," he drew a small gold lighter out of his pocket and snapped it alight, "and he enjoyed himself thoroughly. He thought I was idiotic to keep on slaving in the city, as he phrased it, when I could sit back and enjoy things the way he did. I could never manage to convince him that nothing would make me much unhappier than to bury myself in a little town —even a picturesque little town like this—and putter around all day, trimming a rosebush, or mending a stone wall, or painting a back porch. Well, to get to the point, I came here with the avowed intention of buying John's things. And I changed my mind at the auction this afternoon."

"Why so?" Asey asked.

"It was the faces of people who were fingering the things I'd known." Gardner seemed to be picking his words with great care. "I found myself resenting them deeply. Then I thought of all the things I have in my own collection, things I'd fingered that had belonged to other people. I don't know if I'm making myself at all clear, but suddenly I felt a little ashamed. I began to understand what John had meant—I just wanted possessions. Like those people prying and peering in drawers and cupboards, touching and fingering and lifting things up to scan them more closely, I didn't really *care* about them. So I didn't bid."

"I see." Asey felt that he had attended enough auctions and seen enough auction faces to grasp what Gardner was driving at. "But the chest?"

"Oh, yes." Gardner stubbed out his half-smoked cigarette. "The chest. Well, when that was brought on, I remembered it —though I hadn't honestly thought of it in years. My grandmother used to keep her treasures and little trinkets in that chest. I remembered that on rainy days, she used to let us play with them. She would take out one thing at a time and tell us a story about it—there were brocades and little clay figures and bits of jade from China, and pink shells and odd sponges and carved wooden ornaments from the West Indies, and laces and coins. All the things that grandfather had brought back to her from all over the world. I wanted that chest. It meant something to me. I wanted it more than the really fine things I thought I'd wanted—does this sound quite absurd to you?"

Asey shook his head.

"I bid two thousand for it," Gardner said. "I'd come prepared to bid much more for the other things. Mrs. Madison raised my bid, and then she looked at me—you know how once in a while people look at you, and you suddenly realize that they know what you're thinking and feeling? I bid three thousand, and she turned away. She understood that the chest meant something to me, otherwise I think she would have run me up for the fun of it. I spent less on what I wanted than I should ordinarily have spent on the things I thought I wanted, and didn't bother with. That's all there is to it, Mr. Mayo."

"Then you didn't care what was *in* the chest," Asey said thoughtfully. "You only wanted the chest itself."

"Exactly. I knew that the treasures and trinkets I'd been thinking about had long since disappeared. I simply wanted the chest. Sharp was obviously so upset at the size of my bid, and people seemed so generally dumbfounded, it occurred to me that I should follow your cousin Jennie's suggestion of having the chest opened. Otherwise, the local people would always think I'd known that something of great value had been secreted in it, and feel that I'd bought the thing solely for this reason."

"What *did* you think it might contain?" Cummings asked curiously.

"I had the impression that John had kept some old books of grandfather's in it. When Sharp found it was locked, he made some announcement to the effect that it was full of books of no particular value. I truly didn't engage in any speculation at all about its contents, doctor. They didn't interest me in the least."

"I s'pose," Asey said, "you knew that your brother had a habit of keepin' a lot of cash around loose in his house?"

"John kept all of his money in bills," Gardner returned. "I gathered from a chance remark of Quinton Sharp's that he thought it was an aftereffect of the market crash, but John always *did* keep as much money in cash as he conveniently could, even before he retired. As he got older, he became more obstinate about having nothing but bills and silver. All of us have our peculiarities, and that happened to be John's."

"It's a nice peculiarity if you can afford it," Cummings commented.

"And it isn't really so very peculiar, after all," Gardner said. "I, for example, don't like the sound of clocks ticking. There isn't a clock in my apartment, unless the servants have some out of my sight and hearing. My sister Harriet—Mrs. Turnover—doesn't like the color yellow. She won't permit a yellow flower to grow in her garden, and she goes around wrenching up anything she suspects of having a yellow bloom. Al's mother, my other sister, disliked cats. John didn't like stocks or bonds or savings accounts or first mortgages. John liked cash." He made a little gesture. "You see what I mean. It's all the same sort of thing, really."

"I should say that it *was* the same sort of thing," Cummings observed. "It was just one of those human quirks that doesn't amount to a hill of beans—until John died. Probably no one ever gave a thought to the matter of his keeping money around until then, when the announcement of the auction brought up the possibility of someone's getting something for nothing."

"I meant to ask before," Asey said. "Just when did John die, anyway?"

"Three weeks ago," Cummings said. "He phoned me and asked if I'd stop by with some medicine for his cough, and he dropped dead shortly after I came. He'd had a bad heart for years. I think if he hadn't retired and taken things easy, that heart would have caught up with him long ago. But what *about* that loose money? No one found it hidden inside of anything, did they?"

"Not according to Sharp," Gardner said. "I'm sure that everything was very thoroughly searched, too. I saw one old lady blowing through the spout of a tea kettle—apparently reassuring herself that nothing in the nature of a few bills had been hidden in it. And I noticed that people who bought pictures at once tore the backing off, as if they expected to find money between the paper and the picture itself. No, I personally agree with Sharp. I don't think that anyone found any of John's cash in any of the articles that were purchased at the auction. Why, just a chance fifty-cent piece in the bottom of an old vase would have caused a terrific hullabaloo, don't you think, Mr. Mayo?"

"Wa-el," Asey said, "you also got to consider that the good people of this town ain't dull, especially about money. There's always the chance they might have found some, or maybe even all of your brother's money, but was too smart to let on about it."

"That's an angle that escaped me!" Cummings said. "And it shouldn't have. Because only this morning my wife asked me in a dreamy voice if you'd have to put it down on the income tax if you happened to buy something that had all of John Alden's money in it. When I told her I thought it should be listed under the Windfall Department, she said, 'Oh dear, then no one should *tell* if they get it, should they? Because if nobody *knew* you had it, you wouldn't have to *put* it on the tax!' Now my wife is no Hetty Green, but if she could figure that far, I'm sure that a lot of others at least figured *as* far, if not farther!"

"Jennie didn't," Asey said with a grin. "Jennie would have broadcast it from the top branch of the nearest tree!"

"That so?" Cummings retorted. "It was Jennie who'd first brought up the income-tax problem, at Red Cross yesterday, you'll be happy to know! Well, Mr. Alden, if your brother had money around, and you know he had it, where do you think it went? Where *was* it, anyway? Did you know where he kept it?"

Gardner shook his head. "John's money was none of my business. I did suggest to him, when we first spoke of his will, that perhaps he ought to make some specific disposition of any cash he might have on hand at the time of his death, and he laughed and promptly ordered me to leave all his relations a silver dollar apiece. He added—jokingly, of course—that he'd figured things out very exactly, and that he planned to have his heart and his capital expire at the same time. Then he changed the topic. I think it's quite possible that he may have had some private plans about his money that he didn't wish to discuss with anyone, even with me."

"You think that he may have given it away, or disposed of it, thinkin' that he wasn't goin' to live very long?" Asey asked.

"Well, if he did, Asey, he must have been clairvoyant!" Cummings said. "Because there was a man who certainly didn't know he was going to die when he did! Why, *I* was with him at the time, and *I* didn't know—he simply started across the room to get his tobacco pouch, and fell on the way! He'd been telling me about his garden, and how he planned to buy an almost-new sailboat from someone over in Chatham—and a very expensive boat it was, too! Oh, no, Asey! John wasn't like old Timothy Henrick over in Weesit—remember Tim? Everytime he had a stomach-ache, he used to call all his relations together, and mournfully present each one with what he called a tribute. Next day, when he felt better, he'd march around and collect all the spoons and cups and saucers he'd given away. Indeed, no! John expected to live a good long time, and I'm sure he hadn't done any disposing! Can't you even guess where he might have kept his money, Mr. Alden?"

"I can't tell you what might have become of it, or where he kept it. As I've said, his money was John's own business. He never asked me where I kept mine, and I never asked him where he kept his. I think," Gardner got up from the table, "that the drugstore man rather wishes we'd leave so that he could close up. He's fidgeting around back of the counter—shall we go?"

"Tell me," Asey said as they walked out again onto Main Street, "did you know Solatia Spry at all?"

"I'd met her at John's a number of times. They were good friends. I always thought of her as a woman of charm, and of excellent taste," Gardner said. "She has often bought things for me. Only last month, she got me some really fine pewter tankards I'd been hunting for a long while."

"Did you happen to see her over at the auction?" Asey inquired.

"No, Mr. Mayo, I didn't. I was watching for her, too. I was particularly anxious to see her before the sale began. I—er—I'm sorry to say that she and I had rather a heated argument over the telephone this morning," Gardner said hesitantly, and Asey felt the doctor's elbow nudging him. "She had a client for whom she wished to buy John's china, you see. She told me honestly that she intended to get that china at any price, and I told her just as honestly that *I* intended to buy every piece of it myself. This all happened when I still meant to buy up everything, you understand. The upshot of it all was that she hung up, and refused to talk to me when I phoned her again later."

"D'you mean," Asey was thinking of the cut phone wire, "that she wouldn't talk to you, literally, or that she just didn't answer the phone?"

"Both. After she hung up, I waited a few minutes and called back, and when she heard my voice, she hung up. Later, she didn't even bother to answer the phone at all. I really regret that Solatia and I had words the last time we spoke together." Gardner sounded genuinely sorry. "I had something important to tell her, and because of our argument, I never got the chance to. I—er—" he started to add something, and then seemed to change his mind.

"I seen you over my way, not very long before the start of the auction," Asey said casually. "I wondered if perhaps you might've been droppin' by at Solatia's house, or had maybe happened to've seen her, since her place's more or less in the same neighborhood."

He heard Gardner draw his breath in sharply, and they strolled along the sidewalk in silence for a full minute before he answered.

"It's strange, isn't it," he said at last, almost as if he were talking to himself, "how a tragic incident like this affects you. I'm afraid that I've never really appreciated until now the mental anguish my clients sometimes have suffered even when they, too, were entirely innocent of any wrongdoing. As a matter of fact, Mr. Mayo, I was over on your lane because I wished to consult with you, and it was Solatia Spry whom I wished to consult you about."

"So?"

"At the time, I thought of the situation only as something which might prove disagreeable to Solatia if someone didn't take a firm hand," Gardner said, "and nip it in the bud. I want you to understand that despite our argument as to who was going to get John's china, I wished her to have a fair chance at it—of course, I thought then that the bidding would be largely confined to Solatia and myself. I didn't know then that Mrs. Madison had made up her mind to outbid anyone who dared open his mouth." Cummings nudged Asey again. It was a sly, subtle little nudge, and quite adequately conveyed the doctor's impression that Gardner Alden was trying to pull a little wool over their eyes.

"The instant you unlocked that chest this afternoon," Gardner went on, "I knew I should at once tell you about this, but

I found myself holding back. I knew that if I told you, I should also have to explain to you why I had not warned Solatia, in person. And that explanation would force me to disclose my argument with her, and might very conceivably give you the erroneous impression that she and I were mortal enemies—er—you follow me?"

"Uh-huh." Asey wanted to add that he was way ahead of him, too.

"On one hand, because she was a friend of John's, and a person whose friendship I also valued, I wished to see her murderer brought to justice, and I wished to aid you in every way toward that end. On the other hand, because of these papers," he tapped the brief case under his arm, "because of the work I have to do this week, because I haven't the time to stay here in town, I did not—er—well, I could not bring myself to tell you, as we all stared into that chest, that I had angered her and—er—argued with her—er—I wonder if I make myself clear?"

"Uh-huh," Asey said. "You just don't want to get mixed up in a murder. S'pose we get down to brass tacks, Mr. Alden, an' leave your mental anguish out of it, for the time bein'. Just why did you want to consult with me about Miss Spry?"

It involved a bald man, Gardner told him rather glibly, who had sat in front of him on the bus coming to town that morning.

"A bald man?" Something clicked in Asey's mind. He remembered Jennie's mentioning a bald man who'd bid a lot at the auction.

"Yes, he was talking with another, a younger man, and because I heard the auction and John's name mentioned, I listened to their conversation," Gardner said. "I gathered that they were bound for the auction, and that they expected Solatia to be the principal bidder. And I received a very definite impression that the pair intended, if they possibly could manage it, to prevent Solatia from attending the sale."

"I see. An' you mean to tell me," Asey's voice had a purring note which made Cummings prick up his ears, "that you wasn't goin' to bother mentionin' this either to me or to the cops?"

"Er—as I've already told you, I knew that I should, Mr. Mayo, but—er—"

"You didn't. I see. Exactly what was the plans of this pair?"

"I don't know. At certain points in their conversation, they spoke in whispers," Gardner said. "I can't tell you what they were planning, nor could I swear on oath that they were actually planning any mischief at all. It's only that I got the impression, from some of the snatches I heard, that they meant to keep Solatia from attending the sale."

"What sort of snatches?" Cummings wanted to know. "What did they say?"

"I can't quote them exactly, doctor, but things like '*If* she gets there,' and '*If* she gets there in time,' and 'Unless she has wings, we're all set,' and 'By the time she gets there.' They mentioned specific pieces of John's furniture, as if they'd seen them and were acquainted with them. They referred to John's highboy at least a dozen times."

"What did this pair look like?" Asey asked.

"The older man was bald, middle-aged, rather rumpled looking, and the younger fellow—well, if you had to describe him in a hurry, you might sum him up as one of those undersized fellows you see around race tracks."

"Huh. Did you see 'em at the sale?"

"The bald man was there and bid often, although Mrs. Madison rode him right out of the picture on the best items. You see, Mr. Mayo, when I phoned Solatia, my primary purpose was to warn her that Harmsworth—"

"Oh, so you *knew* this bald man!" Asey interrupted. "A friend of yours, perhaps?"

"I have attended many, many auctions," there was a note of irritation in Gardner's voice, "and I know by sight many, many buyers and collectors. I know Paul Harmsworth by sight, and by reputation. He is not a friend of mine. I have never done any business with him, and never would. Harmsworth is a faker— by which I mean that he goes around and buys excellent pieces of furniture, here and there, and then has them copied so exactly that he's often fooled experts into taking them for the originals. He pays enormous prices for a good piece, and of course sells his copies for enormous prices. His attitude, his point of view, his personality, are all exactly what you might expect to find in a man who makes his living in such a manner."

"Why didn't you call him by name at once," Asey asked, "instead of referrin' to him mysterious-like as a 'bald man'?"

"Because," Gardner snapped back, "I wished to avoid this very situation which has arisen, Mr. Mayo! I didn't want you to jump to the conclusion that I knew him! I wasn't attempting to make any mystery out of it, or to keep you from finding out his name. Sharp could have supplied you with that from the sale records! Do you wish me to go on with my story?" he turned around and faced Asey as they reached the Inn.

"If you will." Asey stepped on Cummings' foot just in time to squelch the sardonic rejoinder he knew was about to roll off the doctor's tongue.

"I phoned Solatia with the intention of warning her that Paul Harmsworth was in town, and to watch out for any tricks. But before I could mention his name, she started to talk about buying John's china, and we got into that argument. I never got a chance to tell her about him, and I felt," Gardner said, "that *someone* should be told about him, or that something should be done about him."

"To a certain extent," Asey said, "it would sort of be to your interest as well as Solatia Spry's, wouldn't it, Mr. Alden? If anything was done to prevent her from gettin' to the auction, people—knowin', of course, that you intended to bid for your brother's things—might maybe think that *you* was to blame, mightn't they?"

"I assure you," Gardner said, "that my primary concern was Solatia. Because I had no tangible proof that Harmsworth and his friend were planning anything, I couldn't go to the police. So I went to you, to tell you, and to ask your advice."

"I see," Asey said. Privately, he wondered why Gardner hadn't told Quinton Sharp, who could have phoned Solatia and warned her in the twinkling of an eye. "An' how'd you get over my way, by car?"

Gardner described in detail the milkman who'd given him a lift. He described the milk truck, and the route.

"He left me at the foot of your lane, and after I'd walked a few hundred yards, a man in a Porter roadster drove by. Since everyone who speaks of you," Gardner said, "always mentions your Porter roadster, I hailed him and asked if he were Mr. Mayo—and he almost bodily lifted me into the car and rapidly drove me to a half-burned boathouse on the shore."

Cummings shook with laughter. "I get it, Asey! He hailed Mayo Nickerson in that old Porter you sold him, and Mayo drove him over to the scene of his fire!"

"He took me," Gardner said, "for an insurance adjuster he'd been expecting, and he poured figures at me until I finally shouted at him and asked if he were Asey Mayo. He was very apologetic and drove me to your house, but no one was there. It had all taken more time than I'd expected, and I was worried about getting to the auction, so Mayo Nickerson drove me there. Someone pointed you out as you were talking with Sharp, but you drove away before I could speak to you. There!" he gave a little sigh. "Now I hope that you understand everything, Mr. Mayo!"

"I think you've explained most all I wanted to know about," Asey said, "except why you washed your hands down at the pond durin' the middle of the auction."

The lights of the Inn porch were dim, but dim as they were, they provided enough illumination to show Gardner's face turning a sickly, chalklike white.

"Oh," he said softly. "Oh, that's easily explained. John's typewriter was sold to an eager youth who asked me if I knew how to change the ribbon, and I showed him. During the process, my fingers got smudged, and I went down to the pond to wash up. And it was not during the middle of the auction, Mr. Mayo. It was during the intermission."

"I s'pose," Asey said, "you always wash your hands in ponds?"

"It's true, Mr. Mayo, that I *could* have used the kitchen sink! Going to the pond," Gardner said, "was a sentimental gesture. I thought I should like to go there once more and wash, as I did when I was a small boy. I do not expect that I shall ever visit this town again, you see. And now, unless you can think of any other points you care to discuss, I think I will leave you. D'you feel, by the way, that it will be quite proper for me to leave tomorrow morning?"

Asey couldn't tell how much irony was in the man's tone. He was perfectly free to leave, and he knew it.

"P'raps," he said, "you'll leave me your address, an' phone numbers where you can be reached—lend me your pen, doc, will you? Oh, haven't you," he added as Cummings passed it to him, "anything but that old drippy one?"

"That's a grateful patient—"

"I know!" Asey cut off his protest in mid-air. "An' it drips. You got anything I can write on, Mr. Alden? I dragged the doc away without even so much as a prescription blank in his pocket." His foot again bore down on Cummings' instep. "Say, p'raps you got a letterhead, Mr. Alden, somewheres in your brief case? That'd save gettin' ink all over us."

"Why, yes." Gardner opened the brief case, holding it carefully so that its contents wouldn't spill over. "I think I have one—yes, I—"

"Oh, the pen!" Asey said suddenly, and kicked Cummings' ankle.

A spot appeared on Gardner's seersucker jacket as a thin trickle of ink shot out of the pen in Asey's hand.

"Look out, Asey, you've pressed that release!" Cummings reached out for the pen, Asey dropped it, both grabbed—and the brief case went out of Gardner's hands, its contents pouring all over the front walk and the lower porch step of the Inn.

"Golly!" Asey said. "I'm awful sorry, Mr. Alden—doc, get that envelope before it blows away!"

He and Cummings zealously helped pick up the papers, the tube of toothpaste, the toothbrush, soap, shaving things, the clean shirt, the silk pyjamas.

"An' here," Asey gave it to him gravely, "is your flashlight. I see you come prepared for our coast rules, too, Mr. Alden. Blue hood an' everything! I'm awful sorry I was so clumsy, but I'm sure we didn't miss anything. You been very thoughtful an' considerate, answerin' all our questions. I appreciate it, sir. Good night!"

To Asey's intense relief, Cummings waited until they rounded the corner before he exploded.

"Asey Mayo, are you going to let that man get away with that? You *know* he never was in the movies all that time! He went in, skipped out, and came back again—that flashlight! You *saw* that flashlight with the blue hood! *He* was the man over at Solatia's who biffed you and Riley's man! You *know* he was! You're *not* going to let him get away with it, are you?"

"The night," Asey said, "is yet young. It's not even midnight. Why trouble his dreams? We can always get him if we want him. Huh, you'll certainly have to admit he *is* a very thoughtful an' considerate man, doc! If that yarn about his dear old grandmother an' the pink sea shells wouldn't wring a heart of stone, his violent consideration for Solatia Spry would! Think of his larrupin' all the way over to my lane in that milk truck, just to ask my advice on her behalf!"

"If Solatia was so mad with him that she refused to talk with him, why in blazes didn't he have Quin Sharp phone her *for* him?" Cummings asked. "I wanted to slap that one right between his bushy eyebrows! Asey, he must think we're damn fools if he thinks we swallowed all that whole!"

"On the contrariwise," Asey said, "he don't think we're fools at all, doc. He explained every last little point—most of 'em, if you noticed, he explained before we asked him, even. Then he bounced everything off into the lap of an antique faker who'll roar with laughter an' deny it all, because there ain't a shred of evidence against him. You can't hold anyone for talkin' in a whisper in a bus, an' that's just about what that part amounted to."

"You think he thinks we believe him?"

"I don't know what he thinks," Asey said, "but I'm willin' to bet that feller can prove everything he claimed. I bet he *did* show someone how to change a typewriter ribbon. I bet his old grandmother *did* keep pink sea shells in that chest. An' his description of that milk truck was a gem. I bet if I'd asked him, he'd have known just how many empties an' how many cream bottles there was. 'Course, the fact remains that he had plenty of time before he went dashin' off in the truck to have gone to Solatia's an' sabotaged her tires an' phone. Yup, I hand it to him, on the whole. Tossin' suspicion at Mr. Bald Harmsworth —why, even the name sounds villainous! I think he only made one real error that I'd call bad."

"What's that?"

Asey chuckled. "He never asked me when or if we could send him his dear old grandmother's treasure chest that he paid three thousand dollars for, an' practically couldn't bear livin' without. He plumb forgot it. Otherwise, he was good."

"I didn't notice that," Cummings said. "He had me so convinced of his feeling for that chest—you know, in spots he *was* pretty convincing, Asey!"

"You might recall," Asey said, "that he's made a lifework of convincin' judges an' juries, an' if he wasn't reasonably successful at it, he probably wouldn't be the head of Somebody, Fiddle-de-dee, What's his name, an' so on. Don't yawn so vigorous, doc, you'll get me started, an' I still got to get back an' get my tires pumped up. I wonder if Eddie's still open."

"If you refer to Eddie at the garage, you're living in the past," Cummings said. "Eddie's on a submarine, or was, the last I heard."

"Who runs the place for him?" Asey inquired. "His kid sister, or his aunt?"

"Both of 'em," Cummings returned, "and they run it better than he did."

"Wa-el, if the girls have a tire pump kickin' around," Asey said philosophically, "I guess I can manage from there. I'll call you if anything turns up."

"Okay. Oh, Asey!"

"Uh-huh?" Asey turned back.

"Oh, what's the use!" Cummings said. "I've warned you before, and you always do just as you damn please! But if *I* had that lump on my head, *I*'d go to bed. In fact, I'm going to bed without one. But if you do any more prowling around, you might bear in mind that there is more than one sharp fish knife on Cape Cod, and that they're occasionally employed as a lethal weapon. I'll even go a step farther and point out that had that lead pipe been a fish knife, you would not now be worrying about four flat tires, my fine Codfish Sherlock! You'd have no more worries than Solatia Spry. Consider that gruesome thought at regular intervals, please!"

He marched off down the road toward his house, and Asey turned back to Main Street.

The street lights flickered out as he paused on the corner. The quickest way to the garage was across lots, he knew. But the back yards of Main Street were now a maze of Victory Gardens, and he had no desire to tread on anyone's Victory Radishes, or to become entwined in anyone's Victory Pole Beans.

Perhaps the long way around the block was better after all, he decided, and started off along the still, elm-shaded street.

He was nearly abreast of the Inn when he heard the sharp metallic slap of a bicycle stand being kicked up.

A second later, a bicycle shot out onto the street from a patch of darkness beyond the Inn, and whizzed away in the opposite direction.

Asey turned and stared after the bicycle. Gardner Alden's light seersucker coat, he thought, was almost as good for identification purposes as a glowing neon sign.

"A thoughtful an' considerate man," he murmured. "You relieve our worries about your bein' much of a hiker, but you wouldn't for worlds upset us any by mentionin' how snappy you ride a bike. Huh! Well, there's nothin' I can do about you now!"

Doubtless, he thought as he hurried on toward the garage, doubtless Gardner Alden had thought of some other sentimental gesture in connection with his dear old grandmother, or his far-off boyhood days. Perhaps he'd remembered where he could locate one of those pink sea shells. Perhaps he was going to look for the last time at her initials burned in the bark of a tree!

At the garage, he found Eddie's aunt, a tall angular woman with glasses, fighting a tire which wouldn't come off its rim.

She looked up at him a little belligerently.

"Go on, say it! But it's not in the book!"

"I know," Asey said. "It's the one they don't tell you about, with the hump, an' you use brute force. Gimme that iron, an' you hold the other one here. See?"

Between them, they conquered the rim.

"Now," Asey said, "my cryin' need is a tire pump. If you could spare the gas an' the time to drive me back of the woods by Solatia Spry's—"

"Say, what's going on in those woods, anyway? I went there about half an hour ago—was it *you* who called me in such a rush, Asey?"

He shook his head.

"Well, someone did. I had a call to fix some flats, quick, and I went whooping over there, but I couldn't find any car anywhere near Solatia's."

"Who'd they say was callin'?" Asey asked. "Was it a man or a woman?"

"Man. I had an engine running, and I couldn't hear any too well—the name might've been Smith or Pumpernickel, I wouldn't've known. I wouldn't've gone," she added, "if I hadn't thought it might maybe be you, or someone else doing something about this business of Solatia Spry. She was a nice woman, Asey. Before I took over here for Eddie, I used to drive her around a lot, to auctions and sales and such. Driving tired her —you get in," she nodded toward the wrecker, "and I'll take you over to your roadster. Yes, there was a time when I'd seen so much Sandwich glass and old mahogany and old china and such, I was something of an antique expert myself."

She backed the wrecker out, juggling it between two parked cars, two school buses, and the gas pumps.

"Nice work—how'd you pick up the garage business?" Asey asked. "Didn't you work at the library, Ellen?"

"Mm. But this is lots more fun, and ten times the money. I was always handy—father used to be a watchmaker, you know, and I used to help him. Then I took a course last winter. Sometimes I get stumped, but I've got by. Asey, Old Baker from the Inn stopped for gas, and he said you'd been there hunting Gardner Alden. Probably everyone's told you, but I can tell you again—and I *know*—that Solatia always mistrusted him. She never liked him a bit."

"Huh!" Asey said. "Is that right?"

"Of course, John Alden never had any use for him either," Ellen went on. "John didn't like any of his family except Al Dorking, anyway. He said they all had too much ambition for their own good. He and Solatia used to have a lot of fun with poor Gardner!" she added with a laugh. "Gardner thinks he knows so much about antiques, but I tell you, Solatia's fooled him more than once—and didn't it make John laugh! She stuck him with some tankards not very long ago. She told me all about it while I was doing her valve job."

"I'm beginnin' to be glad," Asey said, "that Eddie's on that submarine. Tell me, Ellen, while you was drivin' Solatia around, did you ever run into a man named Harmsworth?"

"Paul Harmsworth, the bald-headed man? Oh, sure! He makes those reproductions of old furniture, and Solatia used to say they were more beautiful than the originals. He's a lot of fun, he is. He hired a car from me this morning to go visit Solatia, just after he and his helper came on the bus. He always goes to visit Solatia if he's within fifty miles of here."

"Would you call him a faker?" Asey asked thoughtfully. "Did Solatia call him that?"

"No, never," Ellen said. "A faker's someone who sells fakes for the real things. Harmsworth doesn't. He reproduces old things and sells 'em for reproductions. Everyone I ever met up with in the antique business always seemed to have a lot of respect for him, Asey. He's real jolly and friendly. Once I remember his lending Solatia money when she ran short at a sale in Boston. And he'd like as not phone her from Chicago or somewhere, if he'd happen to've run into someone who was after something that he knew she had for sale."

"You know," Asey said, "your picture of Harmsworth an' Gardner Alden's picture of Harmsworth are so different, you'd hardly guess it was the same man except for the name."

"From what I've seen and heard of Gardner, I guess he and I'd be inclined to paint different pictures of the same person. For example," she said shrewdly, "I don't think he and I'd describe *you* in the same way, either!"

Asey chuckled. "The roadster's on the back lane," he said. "The old carriage road. I forgot to ask, but you *did* bring a tire pump, didn't you?"

"Suspicious of lady mechanics, like all the rest," Ellen said. "Well, I *didn't* bring a pump. But I've got a gadget that hitches to the exhaust that'll blow you up in two shakes."

Five minutes later, Asey gravely informed her that Cummings was right.

"You're better than Eddie. How much do I owe you?"

"I'll trade you the air for the rim you helped me with, and charge the trip up to good will. Who killed her, Asey, do you know?"

"I don't even know," Asey said with a sigh, "who let the air out of my tires!"

"You better keep the air gadget, then," Ellen told him, "till you get done. I liked Solatia. Anything I can do, you let me know. Like gasoline. I could maybe siphon some out of the lawn mower for you, or something."

"I'll bear that in mind," Asey said. "There's one thing you might tell me. You get to see people—who's a girl in town, around twenty, brown hair, who wears a pompadour?"

"Oh, who's a girl around town, around twenty, brown hair, who *doesn't?*" Ellen retorted. "I counted nine at the auction.

That's why I'm working late tonight, you see. I sneaked off to the auction. But then Eddie used to sneak off for the ball games!"

She turned the wrecker skillfully on the narrow lane, and departed.

Asey sat quietly in the car for a moment.

Then he shook his head impatiently and pressed the starter button.

Perhaps it was because he'd been biffed with a piece of pipe, or a brick wall, or the side of a tank, perhaps it was because he was tired and his head still throbbed at intervals, perhaps it was because he just was dumb. But his thoughts kept reminding him of the soap operas, the radio serials Jennie kept blaring in the kitchen all day long.

"*Did* Gardner kill Solatia?" he murmured. "*Did* he sabotage her car an' phone? *Did* he put her into his dear old grandmother's chest? *Did* Gardner really sit through Two-gun an' the Slapstick Boys? Was it *his* blue-hooded flashlight Mayo seen glowin' so eerie-like? *Was* it the wicked Gardner who biffed him an' Riley's man?"

It was so easy just to *ask* the questions! No wonder they rolled so easily off announcers' tongues!

"*I* could do it all night, myself! *What* is Gardner up to on that bike? *What* evil does he have in store? *Does* Quinton Sharp, the honest auctioneer, know more than we suspect? *Is* the bald Paul Harmsworth a nice dealer or a nasty horrid faker? And *who* was the girl with the pompadour?" Asey sighed as he started the roadster sliding down the lane. "Kiddies, Old Man Mayo wishes *he* knew, too. An' let me whisper this one to you, kiddies! Uncle Asey won't even let them books enter his mind, so if *you* been thinkin' about 'em, you stop it, *quick!*"

He hesitated when he came to the main road, and then he turned and drove back along it toward Solatia's house.

"Let's be fair," he said to himself, "an' not call him Gardner, in spite of his blue flashlight. Let's call him the biffer. Now, the biffer skipped when Cummings yelled out my name, an' he skipped before he got to touch anything at Solatia's. Why shouldn't he return? After all, he wanted whatever he was after badly enough to lay two of us out cold!"

And if by some rare chance the biffer's name was Gardner Alden, where would he be calling at this time of night, and on whom would he be calling?

"Huh! He hardly bothered noticin' his sister even when she had hysterics, an' he didn't pay as much attention to his nephew, an' it'd have been easier for Sharp to call on him at the Inn. An' if he was on callin' terms with anyone else in town, the doc or Jennie would've told me so. Yup, let's be fair as can be, but let's guess maybe perhaps Gardner come back!"

He stopped the roadster some distance from the house, and approached it on foot.

Although the shades had been drawn, the place was alight from the front parlor to the woodshed. At least, this trip, no one was creeping around with a flashlight. And if a car or two had been parked in the yard, he'd suspect that Hanson and his police had finally arrived. Only there weren't any cars.

But there was a bicycle, parked by the bushes at the corner of the house. He'd have missed seeing it entirely if a streak of light at the side of the shade curtain hadn't happened to fall on the chrome handle bars.

Asey grinned as we walked up to the machine, unscrewed the valve caps of the tires, and let out the air.

As he got to his feet, he became aware of something else in the shadow of the bushes.

Riley's man was there, neatly bound and gagged and blindfolded.

And Riley's man was still there, five minutes later, when Asey himself, also neatly bound and gagged, was placed beside him.

Four

It was one of those things, Asey thought, that you did with a rope.

He knew all about it. During the past months, the Porter Tank Plant workers had been regaled during their lunch hours with any number of demonstrations of what lethal work you could accomplish with a rope—providing, of course, that you happened to have a rope handy, that you had it poised and ready, and providing that your intended victim was as much of a credulous, unsuspecting and generally gullible dupe as he himself had proved to be.

Most of the demonstration victims hadn't begun to be as co-operative as he'd been, either. Not one of them had gone so far as to get caught just after they'd bent over to take the air out of bicycle tires, when they were completely off balance, and thinking only what a pleasant relief it was to flatten some-one else's tires for a change.

Red Cross workers had displayed the rope trick, air-raid wardens had done it, high-school girls had gaily romped through it, Cub Scouts had worked at it with such vicious enthusiasm that their small victim had had to be revived with a bucket of cold water. Once a couple of genuine commandos, visiting heroes whose chests were bright with decorations and campaign ribbons, had shown their version. That had been the least interesting and the least spectacular to watch, he recalled, because before anyone had guessed that it was the rope trick again, it was all over.

Yes, he knew just what had happened, and just how it had been done. But he had to admit scant consolation in the knowledge now.

He remembered, too, Bill Porter's often-repeated comment on the trick.

"It's a wonderful combination of jujitsu, the Indian rope trick, and black magic. It's very, very neat. But unless they use that stick to tighten it up, I bet I could get out of it, and I bet you could too, Asey. We know too much about rope tied in a hurry, and most of these people aren't seagoing. They're lubbers. They overestimate the power of their little rope!"

They hadn't used a stick on him, and Asey bet with himself that he probably could get out of it, too. This wasn't any official demonstration rope. Unless he was vastly mistaken, this was some of Solatia Spry's old clothesline. And he'd been perfectly conscious when the man jerked out that final, dandy little hitch they always gave at the end. He'd strained against that hitch as much as he possibly could, and it had given him a little leeway.

As Bill Porter said, that hitch worked two ways. It caught someone quickly and lashed them quickly, but once you got the right pressure on the right rope, you could unhitch yourself. Not in any twinkling of an eye, but it could be done.

He wriggled his wrists experimentally.

Why, he asked himself, if a good biff had been so successful before, should someone now bother with a lot of old clothesline?

The answer seemed simple enough. This time it was two other people. The first man had liked a blue-hooded flashlight to work with, and he biffed with smart precision. This one went in for full lights and the rope trick.

Or was someone shifting his methods so that it would appear to be someone else?

Asey wriggled his ankles.

He stopped wriggling as he heard the sound of footsteps coming around the house from the direction of the back door. And he almost cut his right shoulder in two, trying to prop himself up enough to get a look at the approaching person.

If his mouth hadn't been stuffed full of a cheesecloth gag that tasted of furniture polish and had apparently been wrenched off Solatia's clothesline, Asey would have expressed his feelings in a long-drawn-out whistle of amazement.

For it wasn't Gardner Alden!

It wasn't Gardner in his light coat who'd walked past the window whose shade let out that convenient little streak of light!

It was a young man with a brisk, springy step.

Was it—could it be Al Dorking?

Asey nearly choked himself in his effort to sit up a little higher. If only the fellow would return this way and walk through that streak of light again!

"Give me a break!" Asey muttered wistfully into the cheesecloth. "Come on back this way! Come back this way! *That's* it, feller, come on! Keep comin'!"

A minute later, he leaned back on the ground, and relaxed.

It wasn't Dorking. This young man had light hair, he was taller, and he walked with a noticeable limp.

Asey worked away with renewed vigor at the rope, and found as he tugged and strained that the fellow wasn't any landlubber. He'd thrown in for good measure a bunch of sea-going hitches that had never turned up among the high-schoolers or the volunteer firemen.

The streak of light at the side of the window suddenly disappeared. Apparently the house lights were being turned off.

Asey stopped tugging.

If the young man was preparing to leave, he would certainly come and have a look at him and Riley's cop before departing. Under the circumstances, it might therefore be wise for him to appear as inert and helpless as possible. A lot of energy would have been expended in vain if those knots got tightened up again!

After a survey of his victims, the fellow would have to come to some decision about his bicycle with the deflated tires. Asey grinned widely at the thought. He couldn't ride it away; he probably wouldn't be unwise enough to leave it behind as evidence of his presence at Solatia's. He'd be forced to walk off and wheel it along with him.

And that, Asey decided with satisfaction, might just possibly be his undoing. Because those knots were coming. With luck, he could be after the fellow in ten minutes. And ten minutes of trundling a bicycle wouldn't put him exactly at the other side of the world!

The young man left by the back door—Asey heard it slam. But he never bothered to come and check up on him and Riley's man.

And he never went near the bicycle, either!

Instead, he marched off into the woods at the rear of the house. Asey could hear the crackle of the underbrush as he plunged into it, and the slightly uneven pad of his footsteps as he limped away.

The cheesecloth gag got a hole bitten through it as Asey went at the remaining knots with everything he had.

He freed himself just in time to hear the noise of a car engine starting somewhere in the lane where he had previously been parked.

"I'm leavin'!" Asey tore off the gag and spoke rapidly to Riley's man. "He's in the lane, I'll miss him if I wait to untie you, an'," he started to run and called the rest back over his shoulder, "I ain't got a knife with me to cut you free!"

He wondered as he raced along to his roadster if this young fellow could possibly be the person who had called Ellen at the garage. He might have been. And then again he might also have been the person responsible for the deflating job.

"*Is* the man with the limp the Deflater," he murmured as he slid in behind the roadster's wheel, "or was he one of the Deflated? *Whose* gent's bike in good condition, with chrome handle bars an' a bell, is now parked outside the residence of the murdered woman? *Does* it belong to Gardner Alden? Oh, for the love of soup, I never thought of that angle before! Maybe Gardner's all tied up in a neat bundle under the rhododendrons! Or the lilac hedge. Who knows? Maybe that's why I didn't rate a blindfold, like Riley's man. Maybe he'd run clean out of blindfolds by the time I come along!"

He kept his eyes glued on the hill beyond Solatia's. The fellow might be headed toward town, or away from it. But either way, he could catch him now. Just one flash of his headlights was all that would be necessary!

"Just one little flash," he said. "Just one little sniff of your headlights, son, an' I'll pull you as good a Paul Revere as you ever seen—oh, come on, you! I hope you ain't gone an' changed your mind at this point! *What* is the man with the limp doin' in them woods? *What* evil is he up to? Mayo heard him start his car. *Did* he vanish into a puff of smoke? *Will* time tell? Huh!"

He waited impatiently.

He could have undone Riley's man a hundred times, he decided. He could even have dropped into Solatia's kitchen and fried himself an egg.

Finally, he shook his head.

"Foxed, I guess," he said with regret. "I guess I underestimated you, feller, on account of your seemin' youth. I didn't guess you'd be so foxy, havin' no earthly reason to suspect that Uncle Asey was loose an' waitin' to pounce on you! Huh! I don't know's I ever seen so many thoughtful an' considerate people in all my born days! Whoever'd have thought you wouldn't bother to use up your battery by wastin' it on old car lights for nonessential drivin'!" He considered a moment. "I guess you must've been headed toward town, so you just coasted quiet down the slope. I'd have heard your engine racin' if you'd climbed them uphill ruts. Yessir, I bet you sneaked out on me, an'—yessiree, by golly, there you go now!"

The long roadster shot forward as if it had been fired from a gun.

Asey still couldn't see any car headlights. But above the insistent hum of the telephone wires, his ears had caught another hum, the hum of a car motor, and he was following that elusive and receding sound.

He probably couldn't have heard it before, anyway, he told himself. The fellow had coasted, without lights, down to the main tarred road ahead of him. Still without lights, he'd eased himself over the little rise, and only now, at the foot of the hill beyond, would he have had to put his foot down on the accelerator.

"Must know your way around pretty good," Asey said, "to keep on in this unlighted fashion!"

He leaned over to snap off his own headlights, and found he'd never remembered to put them on.

"I wonder, now, if you're a native, too! Huh, someone with a limp who might have somethin' to do with Solatia Spry! Golly, if only I'd paid more attention to Sharp's helpers at the auction!"

They had been dragging pieces of furniture around John Alden's yard while he'd been talking with Sharp before the sale. Was it his imagination, or hadn't one of them been light-haired, and walked with a limp?

"Wa-el," he increased the Porter's speed, "we can try an' find out!"

He could see the car now, a black blob ahead. And on the outskirts of the village, he saw its red taillights suddenly flash on.

A sissy, Asey thought. That's what the fellow was, a sissy. He could follow the white-striped highway without headlights, but he didn't dare to tackle the winding curves of the village streets.

But as far as he was concerned, those streets were a cinch without lights. He had driven the first Porter car there, some forty years ago, before headlights had even been thought of. He could drive those streets blindfolded. Once, on a bet, he actually had!

He grinned as he slowed down to match the pace of the car ahead.

It turned up Main Street in second, passed the First National Bank at a crawl, and started to swerve to the curb by John Alden's house. Then it jerked to the opposite curb, only to pick up speed and swerve once again back toward Alden's.

Asey chuckled. The whole affair somehow reminded him of two people trying to make up their minds as to which side of each other they were going to pass on.

He snapped off his ignition and waited in the shadow of the elms while the car jerked rather reluctantly away from Alden's, as if it personally didn't want to leave the place at all, and proceeded at a tired snail's pace up the street.

"I get it," Asey murmured. "You really mean to go to John Alden's, but you've thought it over an' decided to park in the lane an' walk back, so's your car won't attract any attention from the neighbors, or maybe upset their slumbers, or perhaps even wake up their dogs. Golly, but you're thoughtful!"

All this thoughtfulness and consideration was beginning to leave its mark on him, he decided. It was inspiring him to be thoughtful, too.

"Yessir, it's only right an' proper that someone should be

there to welcome you!" he said. "It ain't nice to go visitin' a house this time of mornin' an' not be greeted by someone. Might make you lonesome an' blue. Surprise, surprise, feller! I'm goin' to be waitin' over on the porch for you!"

And he was.

But he wondered, as he heard the soft pad of footsteps on the flagstone path, and peered out from behind his hiding place of an empty packing case, if the surprise part wasn't perhaps back-firing a little.

The fellow wasn't alone!

Somewhere en route, he had picked up a lady friend.

Asey nearly gave his presence away entirely as the pair approached the porch, and he realized suddenly that this wasn't even the fellow with the limp!

He bore no relation to the man with the limp. He was shorter, he was dark, and he wore white flannels and a dark coat.

This *was* Al Dorking.

And his companion, looming up behind him, was his plump aunt, Mrs. Turnover.

"Have you got the keys? The keys? Where are the keys?" the sibilant whisper was so penetrating that it seemed almost as if she were talking through a loudspeaker. "Have you got the keys?"

"Yes, Aunt Harriet."

"Well, hurry up! Do hurry up! I don't want anyone to see us standing out here!"

"Yes, Aunt Harriet."

Al Dorking unlocked the door, the pair slipped inside, and closed the door behind them.

Their first gesture was to pull down all the window shades.

All except one, which apparently had a recalcitrant roller and refused to be pulled down more than halfway to the sill.

Asey sighed as he saw the blue beam of a flashlight flit across the small panes.

No question about it, the whole Alden family must own stock in a battery concern, he decided! Or else they'd all given each other blue-hooded flashlights for Christmas presents.

He listened for a moment at the door, satisfied himself that the pair had moved to another section of the house, and then slipped indoors.

They were in the small front parlor, he discovered. Mrs. Turnover had barked her shin, and was considerably annoyed about it.

"I don't know why anyone should leave a small walnut what-not in the middle of the floor!" she said pettishly. "Just one stick of furniture left in the house, and it has to be in the middle of the floor—what's that tag on it say?"

"Jennie Mayo," Al told her.

"Well, why didn't Jennie Mayo take her walnut whatnot home? Why did she leave it here for me to stumble on? Why, I might have broken my leg!"

"I'm sure she didn't leave it here for that purpose," Al said soothingly. "She was very kind to you this afternoon, Aunt Harriet! No one could have been any kinder to a stranger than she was to you!"

Mrs. Turnover rather grudgingly admitted that Jennie had been kind enough.

"Kinder than my own brother, I must say!" she added with a sniff. "What do you think of that cousin of hers, Al? That Asey Mayo?"

"I don't know any more about him than you do," Al said. "I never saw him outside of the rotogravure or the newsreels until today."

"Is he *good*? You know what I mean, is he really any *good* at solving things like Solatia Spry?"

"He's supposed to be. I think," Al sounded amused, "that he has his eye cocked toward Uncle Gard. Mayo doesn't know Uncle Gard like you and I do, so he probably never would have guessed—Uncle's got a pretty bland face, you know. But the old boy was worried about things tonight. I saw 'em in the drugstore eating ice cream, after the movies, and I'd have said Uncle was on the ropes."

"Serves him right!" Mrs. Turnover said promptly. "Gardner bought that sea chest expecting to find all of John's money in it, and what happened just served him *right!* He thinks he's so clever, pretending that John's money doesn't matter one bit! But it *does.* He needs money just as much as the rest of us do, for all he's so hoity-toity! Now, Al, where's that paper? You haven't gone and forgotten to bring that paper, have you?"

"I have it right here in my wallet, Aunt Harriet. Here it is."

"I must say that you're the first person, Al, who's shown me the slightest bit of thought or consideration in this affair!"

Asey winced.

"It's not entirely a charitable gesture on my part, Aunt Harriet." A rather harsh note seemed to have crept into Dorking's ordinarily pleasant voice. "We agreed that because I found the paper, half of whatever money we may find is mine. You haven't forgotten that, have you?"

"We put it in writing, didn't we?" Mrs. Turnover returned acidly. "Or maybe you for*got* that we put it in writing!"

"Of course I haven't forgotten!" Al sounded amused again. "Not after all the trouble and grief we had drawing that agreement up! No, I just wanted to make sure that we understood each other, Aunt Harriet. If the directions on my paper work out, if there *is* money where the paper says, half of it's mine. Right? Now, let's get to work. You hold the flashlight, will you? The first direction is about the third—"

"Where's east?" Mrs. Turnover interrupted.

"East?"

"East."

There was a little silence.

"Er—why east, Aunt Harriet?" Al asked after a moment.

"Because that's what it says on that paper of yours!" Mrs. Turnover said with asperity. "I read it right over your shoulder when you held the paper up! The third brick from the 'E.' That means east. At least, it meant east when *I* went to school. I don't pretend to know what it may mean *now*adays, of course!"

"Oh, I see. But I think you'll find that isn't an 'E,'" Al said. "It's an '*L*.' That means the third brick from the *left,* see?"

"'*E,*'" Mrs. Turnover said firmly. "East!"

"'*L,*'" Al told her with equal firmness. "Left!"

"*I* know my own brother's handwriting better than you do," Mrs. Turnover said. "That was the way he made a capital 'E.' East. E-a-s-t." She spelled it out. "*East.* And east is *not* left. East is right. It makes a great deal of difference."

"But, Aunt Har—"

"You certainly can't claim it doesn't make a difference whether or not you start finding something from the third brick from the right," Mrs. Turnover said, "or the third brick from the left! If you wanted to go three blocks *east* of Fifth Avenue, you wouldn't start by going three blocks *west* of Fifth Avenue, would you? No, you wouldn't! Not if you had any sense! It certainly makes a difference, and you can't say it doesn't!"

"Oh, it does, and I agree with you entirely, Aunt Harriet." Al was obviously making a tremendous effort to keep the peace. "But this is an 'L'—"

"Alden Dorking, you listen to me! The sun rises over there, doesn't it?"

"Er—well, rather more over *this* way, I think, Aunt Harriet."

"Are you trying to tell me I don't know where the sun rises in my own grandmother's house that I slept in as a child? It rises right over *here!*"

The wall against which Asey was leaning was given a terrible thump.

"Do you *dare* say it doesn't, Alden Dorking?"

"I'm sure you know best, Aunt Harriet. If you say the sun rises there, that's where it rises. That's east. But I point out to you," Al added slyly, "that's left, and you said east was right!"

"If you wanted to go three blocks *east* of Fifth Avenue, would you go three blocks *west* of Fifth Avenue? Of course with everything topsy-turvy the way it is *now*adays, perhaps *you* would! If I've said it once, I've said it a million times, not since the days of poor dear Mr. Coolidge has *any*one done *any*thing that *wasn't* topsy-turvy. Now, *east*—"

Asey slid down on to the floor of the little room next to the parlor, and stifled his laughter by stuffing his handkerchief into his mouth. If the cheesecloth gag had only been handy, he would willingly have stuffed that in, too. Furniture polish and all.

"And over here," Mrs. Turnover continued inexorably, "is *west*. And here is *north*. And here we are back at *east* again." The wall behind him was thumped once more. "Now, east is *east*—"

He ought, Asey told himself weakly, to be putting a stop to all of this nonsense. He ought to be pulling himself together and sending this pair packing home. He ought to be getting on to his job of finding out who the man with the limp was, and where he had disappeared to.

"There!" Mrs. Turnover said. "North, south, east, *and* west. That is not an 'L.' That's an 'E.' EAST! Now, Alden Dorking, for goodness' sakes *do* get started, and *don't* waste any more time arguing about *east!*"

"I—er—I—" Al paused, and Asey wished that he could see the expression on his face. "All right, Aunt Harriet," he said brightly. "Let's get on." He paused again, rather as if he were afraid to continue. "Well, the next direction is the third brick down."

"Would that be the third brick down from the *first* third

brick, or the third brick down from the top row of bricks? Now, let me think! If it's the third brick from the third, then—one, two, three—then it's this! But if it's the third brick from the top, then it's this other one, over here. And," Mrs. Turnover said acidly, "*I* don't like *either* of them!"

"Why not, Aunt Harriet?"

"No wiggle."

"No what?"

"No give," Mrs. Turnover said. "No wiggle. They don't even *wiggle*. If there was anything behind either of them, they'd wiggle. And they don't. You can try them yourself. I'll bet *you* can't make them wiggle, either! The trouble is, Al, you didn't start out right."

Asey heard Al Dorking's sigh.

"Aunt Harriet, I tried—"

"Al, I never thought! They changed it!"

"Changed what?"

"East!" Mrs. Turnover said with triumph.

"Who changed east, Aunt Harriet?"

"John and that mason. Not a capital M Mason, but a little one. The fireplace used to be over there, and something was wrong with the chimney—it always smoked. So they took all the bricks down and tore it out, and then moved it over here! Don't you see? That would make east left. Not right. Try it that way, Al. The third from the east, and the third down—now, count, Al! You don't want to get it wrong again! One, two, three—"

If by some streak of fate this pair actually should happen to stumble on a cache of John Alden's money, Asey decided that Al Dorking certainly would have earned his right to his half. He, personally, wouldn't care to take on Mrs. Turnover for less than eighty-five percent of any possible buried treasure in which she also was involved. And not even then, if he could avoid it!

"I never understood *why* John should want to keep his money around loose in the house, behind a lot of bricks or something," Mrs. Turnover said. "Why he couldn't have had a box in a bank vault, like anyone else—on the other hand, you wouldn't be bothered with going to the bank, and you wouldn't lose keys, I suppose. I'm always losing my vault key, and everyone's always so tiresome about it. You have to have that man with the drill come, and sit there while he drills away. It's worse than going to the dentist's, because you have to listen to that horrid sound, and there's nothing to show for it when you're through. No fillings or anything, I mean—why, Al, *isn't* that smart!"

Asey pricked up his ears as he heard her appreciative tongue cluckings.

"Tch, tch, tch! Of course it doesn't wiggle, the way I expected. *I* was sure it would wiggle. One brick would, I mean. *Isn't* that smart, those *three* bricks all coming out together on that thing!"

Asey got to his feet, and hurriedly tiptoed to the door.

"They've been halved and put on a wooden backing that's hinged like a door on the end, see?" Al said excitedly. "But you'd never guess, would you, unless you happened to know just which bricks! Uncle John's mason must have been a honey. You just swing it aside—"

"And there's a *real* box *in*side! Why, it looks just like my own vault box! The same size and shape and everything—how much? Quick! Look in, Al!" Mrs. Turnover's voice was shrill, all of a sudden, and very high. "Look in! How *much?*"

Neither of the two noticed Asey as he slipped quietly into the parlor. They were so thoroughly preoccupied with the long, flat tin box that Al Dorking had just extracted from the side of the old brick fireplace, Asey decided, that they wouldn't probably have paid any attention to anything short of a large block-buster bomb.

"It's empty." Al's disappointment was plainly written all over his face, and his tone was flat and expressionless. "It's empty, Aunt Harriet. There isn't a damn cent in the thing."

"Empty?" Mrs. Turnover pushed him out of the way, and peered into the box herself. The odd bluish beam of the flashlight made her seem even larger than she was, Asey thought. She appeared to be on all sides of Al Dorking at once. "Isn't there *any*thing in it? Not even *one* bill? Not a *dollar?*"

"You can see for yourself, can't you?" Al said. "It's empty."

There was a little moment of silence.

"I know! *You* took it!" Mrs. Turnover said triumphantly. *"You took it!"*

"I? But I—"

"You took it!" she repeated. "When you found those directions on that paper in that book of John's you bought, you rushed right over here and opened up that door thing, and you took it, every cent!"

"But, Aunt Harriet—"

"Don't you Aunt Harriet me! You took it all, and then you came and told me about the paper with the directions you'd found, and made me sign my name to that agreement about sharing with you! I see now why you did that! You did it so if *any* money is found *any* time, you'll make me give you half! It was a trick!"

"Aunt Harriet, will you listen to me, please?" Al said. "Just let me—"

"A trick, *that's* what!" Mrs. Turnover was practically panting with anger. "Gardner *told* me to watch out for you! John always *said* you were a tricky sort! And your own poor mother told me before she died that sometimes she wondered if you wouldn't go *too* far with your tricks, one day, and disgrace the family's good name! Your poor mother told me about the checks you forged—"

"See here, I never forged *any* checks, and let's leave mother out of this!" Al was beginning to lose his temper. "I found those directions in one of Uncle John's books that I bought at the auction. I brought that paper over to you in good faith, and I told you what I thought it was—why, I broke my neck getting it to you, because I felt you had a right to know! And if I hadn't, Aunt Harriet, you never would have known about that fireplace safe in a million years! Why you should suddenly take this attitude, I don't know! Ten minutes ago you were calling me the only thoughtful and considerate relation you had!"

"But then I thought you were being honest," Mrs. Turnover returned, "and now I realize you've tricked me into signing an agreement so that if *any* money's *ever* found, you'll claim—"

"Aunt Harriet, I never tricked you into anything! I explained where I'd found the directions. I told you I thought it might mean that this fireplace was where Uncle John had kept his money. I said if the directions actually worked, didn't you think that I deserved a share—and believe me," Al said bitterly, "you were glad enough to say 'yes'! *You* suggested the fifty-fifty arrangement. *I* didn't!"

"You bullied me into signing that agreement, and now if any money's ever found, I'll have to give you half! If *that* isn't a trick, then *I* don't know what a trick is! And *you're* a tricky, deceitful swindler, that's what you are, Alden Dorking!"

Before Asey could guess what was coming, Mrs. Turnover's right hand swung up and smashed Al full across the face.

"There!" she said. "That's what I think of you! I've been wanting to do that to you for years, and if your poor dear mother'd done it a few times, you'd have been a lot better off now!"

Al gripped the tin box, raised it slowly, and for a moment, Asey thought he intended to bang it over his aunt's head.

Then he lowered his arm.

"You're not worth it!" he said. "You're not worth the effort, and—"

"An' besides," Asey interrupted, "it ain't polite to hit ladies, particularly if they happen to be your aunts. Mrs. Post says not even if they hit you first."

Al swung around and stared at him blankly, but Mrs. Turnover seemed to take his presence as a perfectly natural and proper thing.

"You see, Mr. Mayo?" she said. "He's a greedy, grasping, avaricious thing! He's money mad! That's the trouble with young people these days—they're money mad! They *won't* work. They don't *want* to work. Why, Al never put in an honest day's work in his life! He's *borrowed* money, he's *scrounged* money, he's tried to *marry* money—as if any girl in her right mind would marry someone with a nose like his! No, he's like all the rest of his generation, and they *all* just expect money to be handed out to them on a silver platter!"

"The trouble with *you* and *your* generation," Al told her, "is that you're just as greedy and grasping and avaricious, but *you* expect everyone to *leave* you money on a silver platter! We know you in the family, don't forget! We've seen you at funerals and will readings, and we've heard your comments! I wish you could have heard yourself, a few minutes ago, asking 'How *much* in the box?' I wish you could have seen your face in a mirror! No, don't you talk about greed, Aunt Harriet, because you—"

Asey stepped between them as Mrs. Turnover prepared to wade into battle with both fists swinging.

"S'pose," he said, "that you two stow all this! You can finish it up tomorrow when you're fresher an' not quite so stewed up. *No,* Mrs. Turnover!" he caught her right wrist and gave her a little push away from Al. "No! We had enough troubles today without addin' mayhem at this hour in the mornin'! Now, if you think it's safe for the pair of you to drive in the same car, get along! Otherwise, Mrs. T., I'll take you back to wherever you're stayin' in the village. Come on, now. You get goin'—"

"*Why?*" Mrs. Turnover demanded explosively. "Just *why,* I'd like to know?"

"Why what?" Asey asked.

"Why are *you* ordering *me* to leave this house?" she said. "Just *why?*"

"Wa-el," Asey said, "for one thing, this don't happen to be your house, an'—"

"Oh, is that so! Is *that* so! It was my own brother's house, and my own grandmother's, and her mother's before her, and—"

"Uh-huh," Asey said gently. "I know. It was your brother's an' your grandmother's an' her mother's an' grandmother's. But there was an auction, remember? An' it ain't your brother's an' your grandmother's an' so on, any more. It's been sold."

"Perhaps," Mrs. Turnover said, with rising inflection, "no one told you that *I* bought it?"

"Uh—*you* bought it?"

"This house," Mrs. Turnover said, "is *mine.*"

"That's true enough," Al added. "She *did* buy it, Mr. Mayo."

"Huh," Asey said. "I didn't know that. It's a point no one enlightened me on." He suddenly felt a little foolish. "Wa-el, even if it's your house—"

"I should *think,*" Mrs. Turnover said with triumph, "that a de*tec*tive, who's *supposed* to know *ev*erything, would *cer*tainly be *able* to find out a *little* thing like *that!* This is *my* house! I bought it, I paid for it, and it's all *mine*—every stick and stone of it is *mine!* Do you *dare* to deny that, Mr. Mayo?"

"No, ma'am!" Asey said promptly. "But—uh—in the interests of harmony, couldn't we maybe perhaps call it a day, like, an' continue this treasure hunt tomorrow? S'pose we just sort of wander along home—"

"This," Mrs. Turnover made a sweeping gesture, "is **my**

house. My home! And if I want to come to my own home in the middle of the night and pull bricks out of my own fireplace, I certainly shall! If I want to pull up the floor boards and tear out the plaster to find my own brother's money that I should have had my just and due share of, then I shall *pull* up the floor boards and tear out the plaster!"

"Ma'am," Asey said as she paused for breath, "nobody's goin' to stop you from rippin' off the roof, one shingle at a time, if that's what you want to do! But right now—"

"If I want to pick up something," Mrs. Turnover got her wind again, "and throw it out of the window, why, I most certainly and assuredly *will!*"

She reached over suddenly, picked up Jennie's little walnut whatnot from the floor, and hurled it at the nearest window. The fact that the window was closed didn't seem to bother her in the slightest.

"There!" she said with satisfaction as the sound of breaking glass ceased. "There!"

"Feel better?" Asey inquired.

"There's nothing the matter with the way *I* feel! I never," Mrs. Turnover assured him vigorously, "felt any better in my life! Now, this is my house, and nobody's going to order me out of it! If I want to stay here till—till *doomsday,* I shall stay! Al, where's your copy of that agreement about dividing John's money if we found it anywhere in this house?"

"I have it in my wallet, Aunt Harriet. Don't worry about it. It's perfectly safe."

"I want you to show that to Mr. Mayo. I want him to see my copy, too!" She fished around inside her capacious pocketbook and finally drew out a sheet of notepaper. "Mr. Mayo, you take this, and take his, and compare them! I want someone to see both copies, in case Al should try to make any changes on his."

"But I don't want—" Asey began.

"Read this!" She forced her paper into his hand. "Al, give

him yours! Go on, now, *read* that! Al, give him your paper!"

"But, Aunt Harriet, he doesn't want—oh, well, all right! If it'll quiet you down!" Al removed a paper from his wallet and held it out to Asey. "Here, Mr. Mayo. Take it. It's a simple enough document, and for my own protection, perhaps you'd better assure yourself that no coercion was involved. Frankly, I'm not a bit crazy over her use of that word coercion!"

Asey waved the paper away.

"I can't see," he said, "that any agreements between you an' your aunt on the division of any of your uncle John's hidden money—always providin' you bring it to light, an' providin' that there *was* any in the first place—can have any particular bearin' on the solution of the murder of Solatia Spry. Which, in case you've forgot, is the thing that I'm tryin' to get on with. 'Course, a fly sittin' on the wall for the last half hour might have some doubts as to whether or not *I* hadn't lost track of the fact myself, but I haven't!"

"I wish you would read 'em, just the same, Mr. Mayo," Al said. "Here, at least compare them, and see if you can find any evidence of coercion!"

He held his paper out again.

Mrs. Turnover promptly snatched it from his hand, almost simultaneously snatched her own paper from Asey's hand, and with a quick motion, she tore both papers in two.

Then she tore them again and again.

Finally, with a little crow of satisfaction, she let the shreds fall like snowflakes on the floor.

"There!" she said. "What's sauce for the goose is sauce for the gander! *You* tricked *me* into signing that, and now *I've* tricked *you* into giving it up, and *that's* the end of *that! There,* Alden Dorking! Put *that* in your old pipe and smoke it! And now, both of you get out of my house—go on, get out!"

Al looked at Asey and grinned.

"Aunt Harriet," he said, "you're superb. And as mother always used to say after you'd tried her beyond endurance, you really mean very well, at heart. Now, look! You've had your fun. Come along back to Mrs. Sanford's—you truly *can't* stay here, you know! There aren't any beds, or—"

"It's my house!"

"But don't you think," Asey said tactfully, "that maybe you'd be more comfortable if you was to go back to Mrs. Sanford's for the night? You *won't* be very comfortable here without—"

"Who wants to be comfortable?" Mrs. Turnover demanded. "What business is it of yours if I'm comfortable or *un*comfortable, I'd like to know!"

"None, ma'am. It's your business entirely, an' if you got a burnin' urge to sleep on bare, cold wooden floors, probably with mice playin' tag around you, why just you go right ahead an' do it. *I* should," Asey said, "if *I* wanted to, an' it was *my* house. Comin', Mr. Dorking?"

"Oh, yes," Al said. "I'm one who likes a bed to sleep in— you may keep my flashlight, Aunt Harriet. You ought at least to have a light."

"Good night, ma'am," Asey said politely. "Pleasant dreams!"

Followed by Al Dorking, he left the parlor and strolled back to the porch door.

At the foot of the flagstone walk, Al hesitated and turned around.

"We can't let her stay there alone, can we, in that empty house? Oughtn't we to *make* her go back to Mrs. Sanford's?"

"Probably," Asey said. "But the Lord's endowed me with just so much energy, an' if I go wastin' any more of it tryin' to sway your aunt Harriet, I'll turn into somethin' that my cousin Jennie could pin up on her clothesline with the dish towels. You get your car out of the lane, an' run along. I'll wait around for a few minutes an' see if maybe she don't change her mind— oh, by the way, tell me somethin'. Do you always drive a car without any headlights, Mr. Dorking? At night, I mean?"

"Why, I never do!" Al said in surprise. "And will you tell me something, also by the way? How did you happen to find us here?"

"You two," Asey said, "somehow materialized out of a man with a limp."

"A man with a *limp?* Who? I don't understand what you mean!"

"The car I was followin' that supposedly contained a young feller with a limp," Asey explained, "became a car containin' you an' your oversized aunt. An' you *was* travelin' without any headlights when I first spotted you on the highway!"

"Oh," Al said with a laugh. "Now I see what you're talking about! I'm not in the habit of driving without any lights at night, but something's wrong with mine—the battery cable's on the blink, or something, and the lights come and go. The lady garage mechanic here in town told me philosophically that if she tinkered with 'em, she'd probably only make 'em worse, and that in her experience she'd found that one day you'd go over a good jouncey bounce, and never have a speck of trouble again. She added that she *hated* batteries, always had, and was fresh out of new cables, anyway, and hadn't any idea when she might expect to get any new ones."

Asey chuckled. "That sounds like Ellen. Wa-el, I think I get what happened, now. I picked up the sound of your car motor when you turned onto the highway from the road leadin' away from Mrs. Sanford's. N'en I followed you over here. Well, I'll take care of your aunt, an' then go back an' rescue Riley's man from the hydrangeas—I hope Mrs. T. won't keep me hangin' around too long!"

"The old girl—"

"I'm right here, and I can hear every word you say, Alden Dorking!"

They swung around to find Mrs. Turnover standing behind them.

"*I* heard you mention my name," she went on, "and so I came out the other door—what's he been tell you about me, Mr. Mayo?"

"We've largely been discussing battery cables, and a man with a limp, Aunt Harriet," Al said. "I don't think your name ever came up at all."

"Let me tell you, Mr. Mayo," Mrs. Turnover said, "if he's going to go around talking to a de*tec*tive about his own *aunt,* his *aunt* can tell a detective something about *him!* Calling me a jouncey bounce!"

"*What?*" Al said.

"A *what?*" Asey echoed.

"A jouncey bounce! I assume," Mrs. Turnover said with dignity, "that he prefaced it with other equally uncomplimentary remarks about my size! *I* remember some of the nasty names you used to call me, Alden Dorking, when you were younger, and I suppose your vocabulary's increased since then! But why you should see fit to make insulting remarks about me to a de*tec*tive—well!"

"Look, Aunt Harriet, I was telling Mr. Mayo what the lady garage mechanic said about my car's battery cables—something about the first jouncey bounce would whack whatever was wrong back into place, as I remember! I wasn't talking about you at all!" Al said. "This lady garage mechanic in the village—"

"I never heard of a lady garage mechanic in my life, never! I've heard of lady everything elses, but *never* a lady garage mechanic, and furthermore, I certainly don't believe that one exists in this town! You can't crawl out of things that way, Alden Dorking!" Mrs. Turnover was beginning to breathe hard again. "Mr. Mayo, I wasn't going to say a word against him to you—any more than I intended to say anything against my brother Gardner. I had my own suspicions, but I kept them strictly to myself. *I* don't go around *making* trouble! I'm not that sort."

"I can imagine," Al said, "that the men who invented bomb racks and poison gas and nitroglycerin probably have all been guilty of making equally self-righteous remarks. And meaning them deeply. But I'm not going to let you get away with this jouncey bounce business, Aunt Harriet! I was quoting this woman at the garage, and Mr. Mayo will back me up."

"Mr. Mayo," Mrs. Turnover turned to Asey, "that boy can't be trusted as far as you can shake a stick! He's in debt—he was head over heels in debt before he was drafted into the Army, and he's spent borrowed money like water since he was let out. He's been down here, snooping around for John's money, hoping he'd find it so he could get himself out of this whirlpool of debt!"

"Mr. Mayo isn't interested in my financial problems, Aunt Harriet," Al said wearily. "And you'll wake up everyone on Main Street if you don't lower your voice!"

"I shouldn't *think* you'd want anyone to speak above a whisper of your financial affairs—financial affairs!" she repeated with a scornful sniff. "Your debts, you mean! That's all *your* financial affairs ever amounted to! *I* knew you were here, snooping around for John's money. Ever since he died, you've been snooping around for it! Everyone in town knew you were. And they all knew that you came here and borrowed regularly from him when he was alive, too! I wouldn't be a bit surprised to find *you* killed Solatia Spry yourself! You had a motive, and you can't deny it!"

"This is going too far, Aunt Harriet!" Al sounded as if he wanted to knock her down, Asey thought. "I hardly saw Solatia Spry half a dozen times in my life! *I* don't know the woman! She was old enough to be my grandmother!"

"You're twenty-seven, and she was fifty-six, and that's *not* old enough to be your grandmother, because I'm younger than your own mother was, and *I* certainly couldn't be your grandmother, and I'm fifty-six, myself! And how *old* she was hasn't anything to do with it! You were furious with her because she told Polly Madison about you!" Mrs. Turnover almost smacked her lips with pleasure. "She told Polly Madison *all* about you!"

"In the first place," Al was rigid with anger, "I don't know *what* Solatia Spry knew about me to tell Polly Madison, or anyone else! In the next place, I can't imagine any tidings she *might* have told Polly that would make me furious, because I don't know what she *could* have told Polly! I didn't even know that the two knew each other! In short, my fine fat aunt, you're talking through your silly hat!"

"You've been running after Polly Madison—you knew Polly would make you a wonderful wife! After all," Mrs. Turnover said, "even with the world in the state it's in *now,* people always have to wash!"

Asey grinned as he followed her oblique method of setting forth the fact that Polly Madison, obviously a daughter of the rich Mrs. Madison and the late soap tycoon, Mr. James Fenimore Madison, was well endowed, and would in all probability never want—at least, as long as dirt existed and had to be removed.

"Solatia warned Polly about you, Alden Dorking, and you know she did, because Polly dropped you like a hot cake, the very next day! Everyone in town knew it, Mrs. Sanford told me. Polly went right back to her old beau, Christopher Bede!"

"I never knew Polly Madison very well, and I can't think why she shouldn't drop me for Chris Bede, any time," Al said. "I'm afraid Mrs. Sanford and the rest of the local gossips forgot to give you the whole story. Polly's engaged to Chris, you know —oh, you didn't know that? Well, he's been in China, he came home last week on leave, and they're planning to be married very soon because the doctors think it'll be several months more before his ankle's well enough for him to go back to active service. So you see, my dear aunt—"

"Hey!" Asey said suddenly. "Bede! Chris Bede! I remember

him as a tow-headed kid—he *has* got light hair, hasn't he? I thought so! An' he's a little taller than you, ain't he, Dorking?"

"Yes. He was at the auction today with the Madisons. Sharp was shorthanded," Al said, "and Chris drove Mrs. Madison crazy because he insisted on spending most of the afternoon helping Sharp's men shove furniture around, and stuff her new purchases into one beachwagon or another. Mrs. Madison thought he should just sit and watch, and rest his bad ankle. She almost missed the highboy because she was so busy trying to shove him into a chair. I think Bede's family have been here for years in the summers," he added. "I've heard Uncle John mention the name—have you any more direful and foreboding things to tell Mr. Mayo about me, Aunt Harriet? Because if you haven't, I'd like to get back to my little spool bed at Bluebell Cottage by the Sea."

"Oh, you can try to pass it all off lightly!" Mrs. Turnover said. "But just the same, I *know* you were furious with Solatia Spry for telling Polly the sort of person you are! And if Mr. Mayo wants to know something *else,* I wouldn't wonder if you and Gardner hadn't cooked up some plot between you to find John's money! *I* wouldn't be surprised if the *two* of you hadn't killed Solatia because she wouldn't tell you two where the money was either!"

"Just what do you mean 'either,' my good aunt?" Al asked softly. "Did *you* by any chance happen to ask Solatia Spry if *she* knew where the money was, yourself?"

"Well—uh—well, I—"

For a moment, Asey thought that Mrs. Turnover had finally been deflated, but she picked up almost at once.

"Well, yes, I did drop by and talk the money situation over with her this morning, but she wouldn't tell me a thing. She said she didn't know anything about John's money, although, of course, I'm sure she *did!*"

"I keep thinking of words," Al said. "Like greedy, and grasping, and money mad, and avaricious! So you, too, made your little effort to find out where the money was! I did, and never made any bones about it. Uncle Gard did, but he pretended he was only interested in Uncle John's antiques—and got himself stuck with that sea chest! Yes, we all tried. And we all got stung. And that's that! And unless you want a few illuminating and instructive thoughts from me on the topic of people who live in glass houses, and of the moral requirements of those who cast the first stone, I am going home, dear aunt!"

"But *I* didn't buy the knife!" Mrs. Turnover's voice rang out jubilantly.

"Knife?" Asey said. "What knife? You don't mean—"

"The knife she was killed with, of course! *I* didn't buy it. He," she pointed to Al, "*he* did!"

Five

"*He* bought it, and it was a clump!" Mrs. Turnover concluded.

"A clump? What was a clump?" Asey wanted to know. "You mean that the knife was a *clump?*"

"Yes, a *big* clump."

"I'm afraid, ma'am," Asey said, "that I don't quite understand this!"

"Why, Al bought it, and it was a clump! A *clump!* A batch. A packet—oh, what *do* you call it when things won't sell by themselves, and so auctioneers stick them all together into a stack?"

"A lot, you mean?"

"That's it! A clump. A lot. Well, it was a lot. It had pails with holes in the bottoms, and old fish lines, and fishhooks, and a clam hoe without all its teeth—or was it that other thing? I don't know *why* I can't remember," Mrs. Turnover seemed annoyed with herself for forgetting, "if it was a clam hoe *or* a quahaug rake. Anyway, it's teeth were missing. And some of those wooden bird things, too."

"Er—decoys?" Asey felt that he was beginning to catch on to her sudden mental leaps. "Duck decoys, perhaps?"

"Three big ones, and two little ones. Then there were some of those things you put into a hole in the side of a boat to rest your oars in. And then that fish knife, with a leather case. And Alden Dorking bought the lot!"

"No, dear aunt!" Al said. "He didn't *buy* it, either! He *bid* on it. Because Sharp threw in half a dozen of Uncle John's books—for good measure, and to read while you fished, as he put it—and they were books I recognized and would have liked to own. So I bid, but I did *not* buy the lot!"

"You did, too! Because I *know* you bought books!" Mrs. Turnover said. "You told me you got those directions for finding the money box on a slip of paper in some books you'd bought at the auction!"

"I did. But that was two other books." Al turned to Asey. "I *did* bid on that lot that had the knife. It was going at—oh, at around fifty cents, as I remember. Then Sharp threw in a Currier and Ives print of some kittens—what did you say, Mr. Mayo?"

"Nothin'. I just coughed," Asey told him. "Go on, please."

"Well, then the bidding jumped to six or eight dollars," Al said. "That woman antique dealer, Miss Pitkin, wanted the print, and Mrs. Madison bid, too. Sharp apparently thought he could run them up, because he horsed around and told a story about a cat in Truro who always had striped kittens and brought home large fish for the family dinner, and then he threw in a little walnut whatnot—why, it was the same little one that Aunt Harriet pitched through the window a while ago!"

"Uh-huh," Asey said. "An' then the biddin' took another jump?"

"Miss Pitkin and Mrs. Madison and someone else got it up to eleven or twelve. I didn't want the books that badly, so I dropped out. I didn't go beyond four—Mr. Mayo, that little whatnot had a tag with your cousin's name on it! *She* must have bought that lot!"

Asey nodded. He had come to that conclusion a full minute before.

And he was willing to wager he could guess what had happened after Jennie'd bought the lot, too. Jennie had called out that all she wanted was the picture and the whatnot, and for the men not to bother bringing all that other junk to her.

That meant that anyone at the auction might have asked her for the remainder of the lot, and that Jennie'd probably told them she'd consider it a pleasure to have them take the stuff off her hands.

The chances were that she wouldn't even remember who had made the request. If she could remember, it would turn out to have been someone like her dear friend Nellie, who wanted the old cod line to tie up her Victory Tomatoes with, and who never guessed that a knife was in the lot, too.

The chances were that Jennie herself hadn't known that she'd purchased the knife. She couldn't have known, he decided. If she'd had any contact at all with fish knives during the previous week, let alone that afternoon, she'd have been sure to have mentioned the fact about thirty seconds after he had unlocked that sea chest and brought to light the body of Solatia Spry.

In a nutshell, anyone could have asked her for the rest of that lot.

Anyone at all.

Or anyone could have taken the infinitely simpler way of just reaching out and helping themselves to it!

"Are you sure," he said suddenly, "that the knife actually was in that lot?"

"It certainly was! I saw it just before the sale started," Mrs. Turnover said promptly. "It was just sitting there in one of the old buckets. I heard someone who wanted to buy a bucket say that it was just like Quinton Sharp to cover up a hole with a nice-looking knife in a case."

"But did you see it when Sharp was actually *sellin'* the lot?" Asey persisted. "Did he hold it up for people to see, or make any comments about it? There's a Sharp family joke about sharp knives that he'd've been sure to pull when he sold that one, seems to me!"

"He told that over Uncle John's carving set," Al said. "I keep feeling that he held up the fish knife, but I can't remember, can you, Aunt Harriet?"

"Well, to be utterly frank and honest with you, I *can't!*" Mrs. Turnover said with what, for her, was amazing candor.

"I remember noticing before the auction that the knife was over a hole," Al said. "It made me laugh, because I'd just noticed that a chair with a torn cane seat had an aluminum pan sitting over the tear. Sharp had marked the two as one lot."

"Uh-huh, I recognize the Sharp technique," Asey said. "Who cares about a little old piece of loose cane, when this genuine prewar aluminum pan is also offered! Thrown *in!* Why, you can pick up a bit of cane and mend that seat in less than five minutes—but *where* can you find a genuine aluminum pan? The pessimist looks at the hole, ladies and gentlemen, but the optimist looks at the pan!"

"Why, that's just exactly what Sharp *did* say!" Mrs. Turnover told him. "Were you there this afternoon, Mr. Mayo? I didn't see you!"

"Nope, I wasn't there, but I been to other auctions. When was this fish knife an' duck decoy lot sold?"

"Just before intermission, I think," Al said.

"That's right," Mrs. Turnover for once agreed with him. "I remember being thirsty, and someone said there'd be an intermission in a few minutes, so I waited for it before I went to get a drink of water."

It flashed through Asey's mind that Gardner Alden said he had gone to the pond during the intermission.

"How far from this house *is* the pond, I wonder," he said thoughtfully.

"Oh, I didn't go *there* for a drink!" Mrs. Turnover said. "I went to the kitchen tap! I'd never dream of drinking that pond water—grandmother never would permit us to, but she always sent us there to scrub our hands if we'd got too dirty. The water's very soft, you know. The soap used to froth like whipped cream. Gardner always loved to watch it, I remember. He often got grubby so that he'd be sent there to clean up, just for the fun of frothing the soap."

"Huh," Asey said. "An' did your grandmother keep pink shells in that sea chest your brother bought?"

"Why, those shells!" Mrs. Turnover said. "I haven't thought about them in years! You really are *good,* aren't you, Mr. Mayo?"

"Why so?" Asey asked.

"To have found out that grandmother kept those pink shells in that old chest, of course! You must have gone into things," she said, *"much* more thoroughly than I'd suspected! I suppose you found pink slivers in the cracks of the chest, or in the corners, and put them under a microscope, and discovered it that way?"

"Er—not exactly, ma'am." She seemed so awed by what she thought was his discovery that Asey didn't feel like disillusioning her. "I used a sort of a different method, like. Al, how far is the pond from this house, anyway?"

"Oh, a three-minute walk, I'd say. There's a path down through the woods."

Asey nodded. "I see. It was a good drive for me in the car, but I was takin' the long way around the far end. Huh, I don't know's I ever realized the lay of the land here before. I always thought of that pond as bein' a lot farther away—Mrs. Turnover, the church clock's strikin' three. Are you about ready to come along back to Mrs. Sanford's with me?"

"Certainly *not!*" Mrs. Turnover said hurriedly. "I'm staying right *here!*" She sounded, Asey thought, like a small child who'd forgotten for a moment that she was mad. "Right *here!*

And," she added as she started to flounce back up the walk toward the house, "you're making a big mistake in not arresting *him,* even if your cousin *did* buy that knife! If *I* were you, *I* should arrest him! Even if I'd bought that knife *myself!*"

The door slammed behind her with a resounding bang, and Asey saw the blue flashlight's beam moving toward the back of the house.

Apparently Mrs. Turnover really intended to remain there.

"Well, I *guess,*" Al said in a creditable imitation of her voice, "I guess you've been *told!* And I certainly don't know why a detective who's had the *whole* thing *told* him, simply thrust at him on a silver *platter,* can't understand when he's been *given* the *solution!* What," he added in his natural voice, "do we do about her now—let her stay there with the mice?"

"I think I got just about enough energy left," Asey said, "to go untie Riley's man, an' get home to bed. I don't think I want to tackle her again. Bein' with her is sort of like watchin' the tanks out on the Porter provin' grounds. After a while you feel terrible tired in a vicarious sort of way—perhaps you'd like to stay an' look after her?"

"Unless you want me to, no. I'm tired myself. My car's in the lane, and if I don't fall asleep before I get to it, I can probably manage to get back—Mr. Mayo."

"Uh-huh?"

"I don't quite know how to say this, but seriously, I'm sorry you heard—well, I suppose you'd call it a family spat, wouldn't you? I'm sorry it was your introduction to Aunt Harriet, unless you count her hysterics this afternoon over at your house. She's really a well-meaning and good-hearted soul. I'm sure she had a lot of fun nosing around for Uncle John's money, and I'm just as sure she never expected to find it. And she doesn't need it, either. Uncle Gilbert Turnover was a very successful engineer, and he left her very well off. I think she bought this house not to hunt for money she still thinks is in it, but because she likes the place. Her son, who's the apple of her eye, adores it—he's in Iceland—and I think she largely bought it as a present for him."

"I s'pose that's all true," Asey said. "I mean, I don't doubt that her heart is pure gold an' a yard wide. But on the other hand, she's a peppery sort. She admits she went to see Solatia Spry this mornin'—an' I can just imagine the sort of peppery snit of a temper she'd hurl herself into if she thought Solatia knew where John Alden's money was hidden, an' wouldn't tell her."

"You're thinking of her pitching that little whatnot through the window!" Al said. "Aren't you?"

"Nope, I'm thinkin' of some flat tires an' a mutilated phone wire," Asey told him. "I don't feel your aunt's capable of what you might call a deep an' sustained passion. She boils, an' unboils, an' then boils over again. But while she's at the boilin' point, she don't care two whoops what she does or what she says."

"I agree with you, while she's erupting, she can be very harsh with words," Al said, "and she's very tough on inanimate objects, too. She's a vase thrower by nature. But she'd never hurt anyone physically. She couldn't possibly have killed Solatia Spry, if that's the idea you've got in the back of your head. Aunt Harriet is one of those persons who wouldn't, in the vernacular, hurt a flea."

"She give *you* a good whack," Asey reminded him.

"Oh, but I'm one of the family!" Al said. "That doesn't count! She's really very fond of me, and just as soon as I get a job, she'll go around beaming with pleasure and saying that she always knew I had it in me, that I was just one of those boys who didn't get *started* easily, and she'll never mention my financial problems again, ever." He laughed. "It's simply fate that she should somehow have discovered that I owe a car dealer one hundred and eighty-nine dollars and sixty-three cents!"

"Is that—er—the extent of your financial problems?" Asey inquired dryly.

"I'm afraid so," Al said. "But if you refer to that as debts, in the plural, you can make it sound pretty terrific, can't you? And—well, there's one more thing I want to tell you. About that sea chest. And Uncle Gard."

"Yes?" Asey said encouragingly, as he hesitated.

"I'm not too anxious to tell you this, but I suppose you should be told. I tried to touch Uncle Gard for a job this morning," Al said. "Before I was drafted, I'd rather laboriously got through law school—in a year, out a year, back again. That sort of thing. I'd passed my bar exams, and all. But for all that Uncle Gard's practically carrying on the firm with two elderly stenographers and a couple of charladies, he wasn't too crazy about the thought of hiring me."

Al paused to light a cigarette.

"I can understand why," he went on. "After all, I'm not his ideal of a bright young lawyer, and he's used to taking the pick of the brilliant boys as his clerks. But just the same, I got a bit sore. After all, I'd done my best in the Army. I'd got to be a corporal before they discharged me as unfit. I haven't any returned-soldier-should-have-the-best complex on the basis of my service, but I did feel he could at least have given me some letters to take around, if he wouldn't give me a job himself." He paused again. "So I got sore, and—well, the long and short of it is that I decided to play a little trick on him."

"So? Like what?"

"I'll admit to you frankly that I did hope I could lay hands on Uncle John's money. I *have* been snooping around for it," Al said earnestly. "I've *worked* at it! Uncle John didn't care about money for its own sake. He didn't care who got it after he died—if he had, he'd have done something about it in his will. I thought I had as much right to hunt for it as anyone else, and I certainly need it a lot more than either Uncle Gard or Aunt Harriet! So I've been snooping around, and—"

"Did you, by any chance, break into the house here last night?" Asey interrupted.

"No! Did someone? I didn't know that!" Al said in surprise.

"Sharp told me so," Asey said. "He seemed to think it was you."

"Sharp doesn't like me. I think it's because of my nose," Al said. "I don't know why it bothers him so, but I've caught him looking at it often, with distaste and with suspicion. *I* wasn't the one who broke in, Mr. Mayo! I was at the Madisons' last night, helping to paint their kitchen purple."

"Er—purple?"

"Purple. Mrs. Madison," Al said, "decided at dinner to see what their kitchen would look like if it was purple instead of blue—they used to have a dozen servants there, and Mrs. Madison said she hadn't even known what color the kitchen was. But now she's down to one butler-chauffeur-handyman, and she and Polly do the cooking, and they found they didn't like that blue in the kitchen. So she and Polly and Chris and I mixed up some paint, and proceeded to purple the kitchen till three in the morning—Chris drove me home then. I mean, you could check up on it easily enough, if you wanted to!"

"Sharp's evidence," Asey said, "wasn't what you'd call over-powerin'. He just felt in his bones that it must be you."

"The trouble with having a nonphotogenic face," Al said, "is that everyone always suspects you of everything. As a child, I took the rap for everyone in the neighborhood. But to get back, I'd snooped around the house and asked a lot of questions about the money. I haven't much working capital, but I thought if I could get a clue as to what object Uncle John might have hidden his money in, then it would be worth the effort of shooting the works to buy it at the auction."

"I see." Asey found himself wondering why all the Alden family were so fond of involved explanations. "An' did you dig up any clues?"

"Not one."

"Those directions about the fireplace bricks," Asey said casually. "Did you know the box was there an' make up them directions to fit, or was they bona fide?"

"They're genuine enough. I found them in a book I bought this afternoon. After I came back from the movies, I sat down and looked at it, and the slip of paper dropped out on the rug. I'm not laying any wreaths on my brow, but I do think it was decent of me to go tell Aunt Harriet," Al said. "I could have crept into the house tonight without anyone's being the wiser, and I admit the temptation to do just that was very nearly triumphant. Can you understand how it would have been?"

"Perfectly," Asey said.

"If I'd found that money in the bottom of the old well yesterday, or in the birdhouse the day before, or in the barn, or the attic, or any of the places I've rapped and sounded and gone over with a fine-tooth comb, I wouldn't have considered telling Aunt Harriet, or anyone else. Not then. But now the house is hers. Anyway," Al said wearily, "*I* couldn't find the money. Or any clue to it. I've decided either Uncle John ran out of money before he died, or else he's put it in such a bizarre spot that no one will *ever* find it. Or else someone's already found it and quietly made away with it. I've personally given up all thought of it."

"An' what's all this got to do with your Uncle Gardner?" Asey asked.

"I'm getting to that. I was sore with him for being so sniffy about getting me a job," Al said. "I knew damn well *he'd* like to have that money—he's a lot more interested in money than he is in antiques!—so I decided to play a little trick on him. I hovered around that sea chest before the auction, never moving more than a few feet away, and looking at it anxiously every now and then as if I thought it didn't feel very well. And the old boy bit!"

"Oho!" Asey said. "I see! He figgered you'd located the money, an' it was there in the chest!"

"Exactly. I hovered around until I felt I had his suspicions all nicely aroused," Al said. "When I found I had him going, I worked my fingers to the bone to convince him. If I saw him looking my way, I moved away and stared fixedly out the window at the raspberry bushes. If he moved away, I moved back. Once or twice, when I was sure he was watching me, I very surreptitiously lifted the lid and peeked inside!"

"An' what was in it all this time?" Asey wanted to know.

"Books, of course. There always were books in that chest, as long as I can remember. I—er—" he hesitated. "I sprung the lock. I might as well come clean and tell you that before you find it out."

"*You* sprung it? *You* locked that chest up, with books in it?"

"That's right. The spring was caught so it wouldn't lock, and I wiggled my pocketknife around till I got it springing again, and slammed the lid down. Then I went away. And two minutes later, Uncle Gard was there, tugging and prying at it, trying to get the lid up. I guessed then that I had him going good, and I certainly did! He never bid on a single item—he sat there waiting for the chest, you see, that he thought I'd found a false bottom in, or something. And when he opened his mouth and bid two thousand dollars for the thing," Al concluded, "tears of laughter started to trickle down my cheeks. And when he finally took it at three thousand—well, I was too limp to leave my seat!"

"You feel pretty sure," Asey said, "that he bid only because he thought you'd found out that the money was hidden in the chest, huh?"

"I certainly don't think he paid three grand for it out of

sentiment!" Al returned. "I thought you'd be sure to ask why he paid so much—everyone else at the auction was crazy to find out—and I thought you might like to know the real reason."

Asey had to admit to himself that it sounded a lot more like the real reason than the memory of pink sea shells did. But Mrs. Turnover had remembered those shells, too. And he didn't think she'd been prompted into remembering them either.

"So it was *you*," he said thoughtfully, "that sprung the lock an' slammed that lid closed. An' at that time, the chest was full of old books!"

"No one was more surprised than I to find Solatia Spry in the thing when you unlocked it!" Al said. "I knew then that I should tell you I slammed the lid. But with Uncle Gard standing there—well, I honestly didn't have the nerve to come out and say I'd hoaxed him into making that bid! I still hope he may turn up a job for me!"

"You know," Asey said, "first off, this afternoon, everyone kept askin' 'How'd she get *into* that chest!' An' I kept thinkin' perhaps that wasn't so important as who'd put her into it. N'en I sort of went so far as to tell myself that maybe who'd put her there wasn't so important, even, as who slammed the lid an' sprung the lock. You might almost say, as a matter of fact, that you're the person I had in mind as huntin' all this time!"

"However incriminating it may all seem to you, Mr. Mayo, I can only say I hardly knew her! She's simply a person," Al said earnestly, "whose name I recognized when it was mentioned!"

"Uh-huh. But people have sometimes been known to kill other people," Asey said, "that they hadn't even been properly introduced to. In my experience, you don't always have to have known someone a long, long time an' been often to their house for dinner in order to be inspired into erasin' them from the face of this earth."

"I suppose," Al said, "that if someone had walked to the auction with me, had seen me slam the lid on those books, and knew that the chest contained nothing but books at that time, had sat next me throughout the auction until I left—if you knew that such a person existed, if he were a reputable and honest citizen whose word is generally accepted as gospel truth, perhaps you might feel more secure in your mind about Mrs. Dorking's boy Alden?"

Asey nodded, and allowed that he guessed he most probably would.

"Call up the minister of the white church up the street to-morrow morning, then," Al said in his most amused tones. "He lives just beyond where I'm staying at Bluebell Cottage by the Sea. He'll be delighted to reassure you. Good night, Mr. Mayo!"

He turned, walked up toward the lane where his car was parked, and Asey strolled slowly back to his roadster in the shadow of the elm trees.

The three members of John Alden's family with whom he'd come in contact, he thought, were probably not very different from any other trio you might pluck at random from any other family. Families might be clannish, but they weren't necessarily unanimous. He, his cousin Jennie, and her husband might all contradict one another just as much as the Aldens seemed to.

When you came right down to it, he decided, such variations in opinion were like snapshots taken by a family, as opposed to more formal pictures taken by a regular photographer. While the latter wouldn't perhaps pretty people up, he would soften Gardner's thin lips and take the hardness out of his long face. He'd drape something about Mrs. Turnover's neck so that her chins would seem like only one chin, and the self-indulgence of her massive girth wouldn't be so obvious. He'd tone down Al Dorking's big nose, do something to an eyebrow to make his close-set eyes appear wider apart, and play up his pleasant smile.

But when a family took snapshots of each other, they didn't care how the results might look to an impartial outsider. The thin lips became thinner, the chins multiplied, the big nose became almost comic. Nobody worried about the focus, or the film, or the proper lens. Nobody pulled any punches. It was only the family!

Gardner Alden had given pink sea shells and sentimental memories as his reason for paying so much for that sea chest; Al Dorking claimed he'd hoaxed his uncle into making the purchase; Mrs. Turnover seemed to feel her brother was after the hidden money. If you believed Gardner, you felt sympathetic toward him. If you believed Al and his aunt, you felt that Gardner was a hard, greedy, rapacious man, slightly on the evil side.

If you accepted Gardner's obvious opinion of his nephew, Al didn't count one way or another. If you took Mrs. Turnover's opinion of her nephew, he was a tricky, loutish spendthrift—and Quinton Sharp hadn't held any high opinion of him either. But if you took Al at his face value, he was intelligent, apparently honest enough about his shortcomings and his desire to get John Alden's money. And he was pleasant. And patient. Nobody could have been much more patient with Mrs. Turnover. And he alone of the Alden family seemed to possess some proof that he had nothing to do with the murder of Solatia Spry.

Gardner accepted his sister the way he might have accepted —Asey tried to think of a suitable simile as he climbed into the roadster. The way he might have accepted someone else's sister, say, had he met her hurrying through a crowded railway station. To him, she was worth a perfunctory half-smile and a perfunctory tip of the hat. Al's assessed value of his aunt seemed higher, and was certainly more charitable. He'd been almost insistent in pointing out her good qualities, her good intentions, and her good heart. But all the pleasant adjectives with which he'd tried to whitewash the lady couldn't wipe out her violent little gestures, like smacking Al across the face, and tossing the whatnot out the closed window.

He couldn't get it out of his mind. Asey thought as he turned the roadster around, that the telephone wire at Solatia's had been cut the way that an angry woman might have hacked at it. Both that and the flat-tire job were mean, scurvy little acts of sabotage, and the person who'd conceived the idea hadn't logically thought the situation through. If you really wanted to stop someone from going somewhere, you should stop them— not their vehicle, or their means of communication.

"Let's see," he murmured. "When you go plannin' things against people to hurt 'em or thwart 'em, you most usually base your plans on what'd hurt or thwart you. The average man would be mad an' hurt enough if his phone was cut an' his tires flattened, but would he feel thwarted enough so's he wouldn't go to an auction where he intended to buy things for a rich client, an' make himself a big hunk of commission? Huh, if it was me, I'd be mad as hops. But I wouldn't be thwarted none! On the contrariwise, I'd get over to that sale if I had to walk barefoot, an' through hot coals!"

But how would Mrs. Turnover figure it? How helpless would she feel with her tires flat, and no way of calling anyone to fix them for her?

He chuckled at the hilarious vision of the vast Mrs. Turnover attempting to bend over and change tires in a hurry. Getting out a tire pump and blowing up flat tires was probably a task she'd never lifted a hand to, or even remotely considered undertaking. And he doubted, also, if she would seriously think of thumbing rides, if her own car were out of action.

"I don't hardly think," he said aloud, "that she is the hitch-hikin' type! Nope, she wouldn't have contemplated hitchin' as an alternative way of gettin' over to that auction!"

And is was a sure bet that in her wildest dreams, she'd never think of setting out to walk from Solatia's over to her brother's.

Asey couldn't even visualize her getting beyond the first hill.

"Yes, if you flattened Mrs. Turnover's tires," he told himself, "an' cut her phone, she'd retreat into the livin' room, plunk herself down into the widest chair, an' weep with rage at havin' been thwarted. Yessir, if you done that to her, that'd be enough sabotage to thwart her, all right. Partly because of the way she'd figger, but mostly on account of her size, an' her not bein' physically too active. Now, then, I wonder if it wouldn't be just exactly the sort of thing *she'd* do to thwart someone else, particularly if the someone else was another woman!"

He sped along the outskirts of town toward Solatia's house again. He'd have to return and free Riley's bound-up cop, if Hanson hadn't arrived and already taken care of the fellow. He'd have to find out if the bicycle whose tires he had deflated was still there, and if the cop had any inkling of who its rider had been.

Tomorrow, steps would have to be taken to locate the bald Harmsworth man whom Gardner had talked about. That would be a job for Hanson and his men, since Harmsworth was probably miles away from Cape Cod by now. He'd have to be found and questioned.

Tomorrow, too, he had all that knife business to look into, and the thought depressed him. It stood to reason that if anyone at the auction might have taken the thing, and if everyone for miles around had come to the auction, he had considerable ground to cover.

And tomorrow, he'd finally have to face the problem he'd been endeavoring not even to consider tonight.

Those books!

"Ugh!" he said. "Go on an' say it, Mayo! Whoever put her into that sea chest had to take those books out of it first!"

And no one had stumbled on any heap of books left over at Alden's.

There weren't any unaccounted-for books anywhere, except over in the fresh-water pond.

"An' Ellen said there was nine girls at the auction that had their hair done up in pompadours. Nine! Nine of 'em!"

He sighed. He could always make out a list, he supposed, and go from pompadour to pompadour until he found the right girl!

"*Who* was the girl?" he said in radio-announcer tones. "*Who* swiped the fish knife of John Alden from Cousin Jennie's auction lot consisting of duck decoys, fishing tackle, Currier and Ives kittens, and a little walnut whatnot, now in very, very poor condition? *Which* Alden should Mayo believe and trust? And wouldn't *you* get a minister for a witness, if you were a really *bright* murderer? Yes, kiddies, I think you would! And *who* was the man who biffed first? *Who* did the rope trick? And *who* was the man with the limp? *Could* it have been Chris Bede, whose ankle presumably had been injured in action?"

After all, the fact remained that the person who might most have wanted to keep Solatia Spry away from the auction wasn't Gardner Alden, who hadn't bothered to bid except for the sea chest. Nor Mrs. Turnover, who might have been annoyed into venting her spite after Solatia disclaimed any knowledge of where John Alden's money might have been hidden. Nor Al Dorking, who hadn't apparently cared about the antiques, and didn't have the money to buy them even if he had.

The person who cared most was probably Mrs. James Fenimore Madison, who had actually got the things.

And Chris Bede was engaged to Mrs. Madison's daughter, according to Al.

Could Chris, acting on Mrs. Madison's behalf, have been making away with something from Solatia's house?

It was possible, of course.

It was even likely. For there was something about a murder, as Cummings often remarked, that was inclined to inspire people to retrieve their possessions from what the doctor summed up as the more or less immediate vicinity of the corpse, including the late domicile. Letters, for example, whether or not they were particularly incriminating documents, suddenly loomed in people's minds as something to be recovered at all costs. Pieces of wearing apparel, trinkets, jewelry, sometimes miscellaneous objects like rubber plants or umbrella stands or cuckoo clocks; things that hadn't been thought of in years, all at once acquired a new meaning for the original owner, who wanted his property back instantly, in a rush. Not usually for any specific purpose, as Cummings never failed to add. But the relief that people felt at rescuing their things seemed to outbalance the effort—and oftentimes the danger—involved.

On the other hand, Asey told himself, Mrs. Madison shouldn't have had any problems with Solatia, ever, or have feared her presence at the auction. The Madison money could always have outbid Solatia, any time.

The thing that really bothered him most, he decided, was that while everyone seemed to want to tell their story and their ideas, what they'd done and said and thought, and why, nobody ever mentioned that they'd seen Solatia Spry at the auction!

If Mrs. Turnover could remember the missing teeth of a clam hoe, if Al Dorking could recall the exact bids on a lot of worn-out pails and fishing tackle, why hadn't either of them remembered Solatia? That everyone spoke of the items sold, and not of seeing the murdered woman at the sale, was significant in itself.

Jennie was ordinarily very accurate in her observations. Jennie had said flatly that Solatia wasn't there.

But the chest *was*.

And if the chest was there, Solatia Spry must have been there, too!

Perhaps, he thought, Cummings had been right. Perhaps it had all been done with a lot of mirrors!

"My trouble," he murmured, "is that I shouldn't take vacations. I ought to have stayed right there where I belonged in the Porter plant!"

Something seemed wrong with the highway, and he realized that he had absent-mindedly been driving with only his parking lights on.

He pulled out the light button, and as the long beam flashed on, he at once swerved to avoid the object—probably a skunk, he thought—which he saw lying in the road ahead.

He passed to one side of it, then braked quickly, and backed up.

It wasn't a skunk.

It was a book.

"Huh!" he said, and climbed out of the car to investigate.

It wasn't just *a* book, he found, as he held it up to the car headlights.

It was a fat volume of Harper's Magazine, bound in three-quarter blue morocco. On the marbled board opposite the fly-leaf was an engraved armorial bookplate which bore the name of John Alden.

After studying it for a moment, Asey closed the book and thoughtfully surveyed the rather ornately tooled backstrip, and the stamped date—1892.

Then he tossed the book into the roadster, and looked around.

There was no fog, but the night air was definitely on the damp side, and there were little curling mists rising from the meadow beyond.

Yet that morocco binding was quite dry. The book hadn't been lying on the road long enough to pick up any of the dampness.

"Huh!" he said as he got into the car and started up again. "Huh!"

A hundred yards ahead, he found another volume.

That was bound in three-quarter red morocco, and bore the date 1899.

At the fork in the road below Solatia Spry's house, he found a third.

That was green, vintage of 1896.

On impulse, instead of continuing along the main highway, he took the side road that led to Weesit.

Before he reached Weesit Center, he had an even twenty volumes of old, morocco-bound Harper's Magazines in the car beside him. All were from the library of the late John Alden, and bore his bookplate.

At the Weesit Four Corners, he stopped and considered.

Twenty volumes was a nice round number of volumes, and just about as many old bound Harper's Magazines as anyone might be likely to have around a house. Yes, twenty volumes ought to be about the limit!

But a little practical detective work with his flashlight proved that he had many extensive gaps in the eighteen-nineties. If John Alden had a full run or a complete set, there should be plenty more of those fat volumes lying around in the middle of one road or another.

Eighteen wooden arms, each one of them designating a possible route, stuck out from the Four Corners signpost.

Which road should he take?

He had, Asey decided, too wide a choice to leave his decision to anything but fate. So he said "Eeny, meeny, miney, mo" at the wooden arms, and came out with the West Weesit shore road.

And drew a blank.

The East Weesit road was also bare of books.

But on the South Weesit road, universally known as "The-through-the-woods-one," he picked up the trail once again.

By the time he reached the South Weesit post office and general store, he had harvested the thirty-sixth volume of John Alden's Harper's set.

Continuing on into West Skaket, he found the forty-third. Just to be different, that was bound in three-quarter black morocco, instead of colors.

After driving on three miles without finding any trace of the forty-fourth, Asey turned the roadster around and started back home.

"Wa-el," he drawled, surveying the books with which he was virtually surrounded, "it's a nice way to have got rid of 'em, I'll grant that! Easy, restful—just drive along an' toss one off as the spirit moves you. A lot less labor involved than throwin' 'em into ponds. An' I s'pose if you happened to change your mind, you could always backtrack an' pick 'em all up again!"

Most of the books had been found between Weesit and South Weesit, even though the trail had started over by Solatia Spry's. He wondered if that meant anything more than that someone's arm had been more active around the Weesits than elsewhere.

One thing he was sure of, the books couldn't have a lot of significance in themselves. If John Alden's old Harper's Magazines meant anything as books, they never would have been left out in plain sight for the world to find. While the value of old books was a little out of his line, he was willing to wager that the cost of the fancy rebinding job was more than the original cost of the magazines, and that their probable current value would be based not on what the bindings had cost but on

their worth as magazines. Plenty of them had been printed.
They couldn't be considered rare. And as reading material now
—Asey shook his head. They were nothing he'd personally
choose to while away an evening with. Probably their greatest
value at the moment would be to someone who wanted to fill
up a lot of empty bookshelves with books that had pretty bindings.

Even if Quinton Sharp had a record of the purchaser—for he
assumed that these books must have been sold with the rest
of Alden's possessions that afternoon—that record still wouldn't
help a great deal. Whoever had bought them had only to protest stoutly that he hadn't seen the volumes since he took them
home and stuck them in the shed. If Asey Mayo had found
them strewn like autumn leaves around the roads, why then
someone *else* had filched them and done the strewing, not
them! And unless anyone had actually witnessed the book-
tossing process at some point, all of Hanson's experts probably
couldn't prove differently.

He chuckled as he thought of what a fine story Gardner
Alden, for example, might make of it, had *he* only been caught
in the act of disposing of the volumes. "My dear little old white-
haired grandmother," Asey murmured sardonically, "she always used to throw books hither an' yon on the Weesit roads,
every spring. When I was a wee lad, I used to help her. So
tonight, I was doin' it—such a silly, sentimental gesture as it
must seem to you, too—for the very last time!"

He knew one other thing. None of the books had been on
any of the roads very long. At least, not long enough to have
succumbed to the dampness. They were all comparatively
freshly strewn.

"Huh!" he said. "Forty-three fresh-laid tomes, an' all—golly,
I wonder!"

He stopped the car suddenly, snapped on his flashlight, and
poked around among the books until he found both the last,

black-bound volume, and the first, red-bound copy of 1892.

Because he'd spotted the first book over near Solatia's, he'd taken for granted the fact that the book trail began there. But if the black book were appreciably damper than the red book, then the former and not the latter might have marked the beginning of the trail.

He found, on comparing the two copies, that there was practically no difference to the naked eye. It was probably stupid of him to hope that he could tell if one book had been outdoors in the open fifteen minutes longer than another book, he thought as he snapped off the flashlight. If Cummings couldn't tell how long Solatia Spry had been dead when they found her in the chest, who was he to go making any wild speculations about inanimate objects?

"But if you dropped off the black book first," he said aloud, "an' ended up with the red, then you'd be over by Solatia's when you finished. I don't think you'd come home the same way. I know I wouldn't. I think you'd be pretty sure to avoid the books you'd left behind you, more or less on general principles. If people seen you swervin' around them tomes, they might be suspicious of such an uncurious person. An' if you found someone else pickin' 'em up, the temptation to toss 'em back again might be too great for you to overcome. Yup, I think you'd be comin' back to where you started by some different route."

And if the person was like everyone else, his gasoline problems would have prevented him from driving too far before starting to carry out his book-disposal project.

"On the other hand, you wouldn't have wanted to keep the books with you in your car any longer than you had to," Asey said, "an' still you wouldn't have wanted to start in strewin' right outside your own doorstep. Now, I wonder! If you started from this end, with the black-bound book I picked up last, an' if you run out of books with the red one over by Solatia's, an' if you had to come back by devious an' sundry ways, would you have had the time to be back here now? I wonder!"

Mentally, he traced all the possible routes from Solatia's to a point beyond the spot where he'd found the black book.

Then a grin spread over his face.

To an outlander, to someone who didn't know those curving roads, the thing would seem incredible, he thought as he turned the roadster around.

But in order to avoid bumping into any of the books he'd dropped behind him, someone would have to weave and circle and detour about eight times his original mileage from black book to red book!

And a false turn or two would run it up to ten or even twelve times.

Even he, himself, Asey thought, for all he knew of the roads, would probably make a mistake or two unless he'd thought it all out very carefully beforehand. And just one mistake would more than make up in time for his own forty-three stops, and his flounderings around the Four Corners in Weesit Center.

Three minutes later, he was slowing down at a fork in the road several hundred yards beyond the point where the black book had been lying.

Probably it was just a wild stab in the dark, and a lot depended on how nearly he and the book tosser had missed each other over by Solatia's. But according to his calculations, anyone who'd gone as far as the red book would have to return by this fork if they hadn't returned by the book-lined route.

There simply wasn't any other way!

He parked the roadster square across the road, got out, strolled over to a stone wall, and sat down.

He had just finished lighting his pipe when he saw the dimmed-out headlights of a car approaching up the fork to his right.

A beachwagon arrived at the barrier, and stopped.

It was an elegant and very de luxe beachwagon, and he recognized it even before the door was opened, when an inside light flashed on and provided enough of a glow for him to read the name lettered on the side.

"The Shack," it said.

It was Mrs. Madison's beachwagon.

And at the sight of the driver, leaning out and peering impatiently ahead at the parked roadster, Asey got up and gravely kicked himself.

He should have figured out that one!

For the girl in Mrs. Madison's beachwagon was the girl with the pompadour, the original book thrower!

"An' *who* is she, kiddies?" Asey murmured under his breath. "*Who?* Miss Polly Madison, of course!"

Six

"CHARLES!" the girl said.

Asey craned his neck to catch sight of the person she was speaking to. He turned out to be a wizened little man in a chauffeur's uniform sitting beside her.

"Charles, do you see anyone?"

"No, Miss Polly."

"Recognize the car?"

"No, Miss Polly, but it's a good car. And I'm sure it ain't the cops."

"Charles, see what's inside it, will you?" she said. "If there's anyone, I mean."

Charles had been a coachman or a groom, Asey bet, as he ducked behind a clump of bushes and watched the bow-legged little man march over to the roadster and play the beam of his flashlight around it, and then over the contents of the seat.

Then—a little wearily, it seemed to Asey—he marched back to the beachwagon.

"Miss Polly, I hate to say this. I hate to break it to you. But it's *them!*"

"*Them?*" the girl said blankly. "*Them?*"

"Yessum."

"*Again?*"

"Yessum."

"Oh, Charles, honestly? *All* of 'em?"

"Yessum, I'd say the lot."

"Charles, I could eat *worms!* I could positively sit down on the ground and eat *worms!*"

"To think of them books," Charles said in wondering tones, "here, *ahead* of us!"

"Wouldn't you think that people could leave 'em alone, at least until we get our plans working?" the girl demanded. "At least for the night! Where do they come from, all these millions and millions of people with nothing to do but go out and pick up books just as fast as we can manage to put them *down!*"

"It's really only the second time, Miss Polly," Charles said comfortingly. "We ain't been foiled but once before. Though," he added, "it sure gets to *seem* like a lot oftener!"

"Charles," she said hesitantly, "do you—do you think it's that bald man again, this time?"

"No," Charles said with finality. "No, Miss Polly, don't you worry about him! *He* won't bother us again tonight. He won't bother *any*body again tonight. I fixed him good and proper."

Asey found himself wondering just what Charles had done to Paul Harmsworth.

"Can we get by that roadster, Charles?"

"We could, Miss Polly. It'd either mean taking off his fender, though, or ours. Miss Polly."

"Yes?"

"You know, Miss Polly, we could always take 'em out again."

"Charles, you're wonderful! And then lay them down again, and *this* time we'll be smarter about *where* we lay them down, too!" She got out of the beachwagon. "That's just what we'll do; we'll lay them down again—have we gas enough? I'm *wor*ried about that gas, Charles. It's the only way mother'll ever find out, by the gas. She's so damned gas conscious!"

"There's the power mower," Charles said. "I can always break that again. I'll tell her it's broken, I mean. That'll help some. And then there's still some gas left down in the boathouse she don't know about, from last year. I hid it away from her, for an emergency. We can somehow eke it out, Miss Polly. I'll manage."

"If only mother'll realize it's all for her own *good,* Charles!" She paused to light a cigarette. "That is, when she finds out."

"Yessum. I hope so." Charles sounded as if he had private doubts.

"She thinks Quinton Sharp's such a perfectly wonderful man, it's going to be tough convincing her what a lousy rotten trick he played on her, and what an utter jerk he is! She's so sold on that man—Charles, people take advantage of mother so!"

"Well—"

"Oh, they do! You know they do!" Polly said. "Everyone's always sticking her a few dollars here or a few dollars there, and then making some crack about as long as cleanliness is next to godliness, Mrs. Madison'll never miss a few dollars— Charles, I get so *sick* of soap!"

"Yessum. But you can't say, Miss Polly, that soap ever done you any *harm!*"

"Can't I! It's blighted my whole life!" Polly said with a touch of bitterness. "Chris still worries about people thinking he's marrying me for the soap business. If he was really bright, of course, he'd go into a nailbrush cartel, and then we could play it both ways—Charles, I almost can't face those books! Don't you have that feeling, if you have to touch them again, you'll simply break out into a rash and start screaming?"

"No, Miss Polly, I can't say as I do," Charles returned. "But I know what you mean. No variety, as you might say. Books are all so much of a sameness, like."

"It's not the monotony of the books that's got me down," Polly told him. "It's the monotony of what keeps happening to them! Well, let's get to work and get them out of this Porter—*Charles"*

"Yessum? Is it another snake you think you see?"

"Charles, we're dopes!"

"Why's that, Miss Polly?"

"Polly and Charles, the Original Lame-brains! *Porter,* Charles! Porter roadster! You know, that Mayo man! Asey Mayo. That's what *he* drives!"

"Oops!" Charles said.

"Double oops! Charles, this is the place in books where people say with feeling that they're Undone—oh, no, I don't mean it literally! Don't worry about where you tore your sleeve on the bald man—we'll get it fixed up before mother sees it."

"Miss Polly, what do we do now?" Charles sounded desperately unhappy.

"You probably know as much about detectives as *I* do, and I never saw one in my life, except that man who trailed Aunt Bernice when she was getting her divorce. I don't think you can count him," Polly said. "It wasn't the same sort of thing. Charles, I bet Asey Mayo's lurking around here somewhere!"

"If he's seen us, Miss Polly," Charles said sadly, "if he's seen us and found out about us. And about all of *them!*"

"I know."

"Miss Polly, he'll think—why, he'll think *we*—he'll think it was *us* that took them books out of the sea chest Miss Spry was in, and then he'll find out about the row the Madam had with her, and the row *you* had with her. And the row *I* had with her—ooh!" Charles said in anguish. "Ooh, it'll be awful, what he'll think!"

"He'll be bubbling over with false thoughts," Polly agreed. "I know. Well, let's find out the worst—I wonder, how do you call a detective?"

"You could whistle," Charles suggested, "and ask if he's here—"

"Oh, you can't call him like a dog, Charles! 'Are you there, Mr. Mayo?' Oh, that's silly, too! It's all so silly, Charles! Because if he's been sitting behind a bush listening to us, we wouldn't even need to call him mister. He'd be practically an old family friend, by now—come out!" she raised her voice. "Come out, Asey! Come out, come out, wherever you are!"

Asey, grinning broadly, emerged from the bushes.

"Good evenin', Miss Madison. Or maybe it's good mornin' now."

"Undone, I called it!" Polly recognized him as he walked into the path of the beachwagon's headlights. "And with what brutal truth! *Undone!* Triple oops, Charles! Will you promise faithfully to visit me on the proper days, and maybe bring me files and saws and things inside of chocolate cakes?"

"*What,* Miss Polly?"

"He's seen this picture before, Charles. Or one just like it. Of course, he's come in a little late, this time, but he knows the plot thread. You do, don't you, Asey? And you don't mind if I call you Asey, do you, either? I keep feeling we may be going to see a lot of each other, probably separated by thick iron bars."

"You can adopt me," Asey said, "an' make me an honorary uncle, if you'll just be good enough to straighten out some of this. Why do you?"

"Play book toss, you mean? I never did before," Polly told him honestly. "I've always treated books with intense respect, until today. I used to help father rub gooey stuff on his leather bindings once every year. Then you rubbed it off. It was like shining thousands of pairs of shoes."

"Where'd you like to begin?" Asey asked. "Back at the pond, durin' the auction, or with this?"

Polly thought for a moment.

"On the whole," she said, "this is going to make more sense to you, I think. You see, Charles and I—this is Charles, as you've doubtless gathered," she added parenthetically. "When Grampa Madison first sneaked into the carriage trade, Charles arrived with the first carriage, and he's been with us ever since. The Madison family hasn't any secrets from Charles. He knew us when. And I *must* make it clear that Charles has no part of all this. I dragged him in by the scruff of his neck. Because of snakes."

"Two-legged snakes?" Asey inquired. "Or the regular kind that glides around?"

Polly laughed. "Both. Anyway, Charles isn't any—what d'you call it? Accessory after the fact? He's not one of those. He's not an accomplice. He's just been an unwilling chaperon, haven't you, Charles?"

"No, Miss Polly, it—"

"You mean *yes!*"

"No, Miss Polly, it was my idea, and—"

"You mean yes, and it *wasn't* your idea. It was mine. You see, Asey, we had a plan. I mean, *I* had a plan, but we haven't been able to start it percolating. To begin with, it took simply ages to make mother take the allonal."

"Er—why?"

"To make her sleep soundly, so she wouldn't find out what we were up to. We simply *couldn't* take the chance of letting her get mixed up in this. Because the minute anyone found out about her and Solatia Spry and their fight, it would be too ghastly. They had such a terrific row about that stove!"

"Stove? You mean some antique stove?" Asey wanted to know.

"No, no, a *new* stove. We really wanted a new refrigerator, too, but we've put ice in the old one, and only asked for a new stove. And Solatia refused to give us the permit thing. She was on the ration board, you know, and ran it with both hands. She told us to send the old one away and have it repaired, but we can't, because the company that made it is making antiaircraft shells, and doesn't care about its stoves now.

Then we had a run-in with her about gas for the boat, and oil for the hot-water heater, and a bicycle. But it all started from that infernal stove."

"You mean," Asey said, "that your mother and Solatia quarreled, but it wasn't about the auction, or John Alden's antiques, or anything like that."

"Oh, *that* was where we all went to *town!*" Polly said. "That's when it got utterly virulent, after John died and this business of the auction reared its ugly head. It probably all could have been settled quite amicably if we hadn't started in on this hostile basis, after the stove and the other rationed stuff. Mother and I knew John well and loved him dearly, you see. We didn't want some old collector in San Francisco to have his things, but Solatia was simply determined to buy them for him —you really can't blame her, of course. She'd have made a pot of money. We'd rowed about the stove and the other stuff. Many bitter words had been bandied and flung about. But John's things almost brought us to blows. Mother simply couldn't afford it."

"Miss Polly means," Charles said, "the Madam couldn't afford to outbid Miss Spry, see, sir?"

"I mean," Polly said, "the Madison money isn't much different from anyone else's. There's just so much of it, and principally taxes. With what we've got left, we can't go around casually competing with West Coast millionaire collectors, especially when we didn't know how much they were willing to blow. If it hadn't been for this stove and all, mother and Solatia could have sat down and got together. Solatia could have let mother have the highboy, say, and then mother would have bid her up on the china so that her commission would have been astronomic. And so on. But because of that damned stove—well, you see what I'm trying to say, don't you?"

"You're sayin' that your mother an' Solatia wasn't on any

such terms that they could have settled any division of John Alden's things in a friendly manner," Asey said.

"More than that. They were on such lousy terms that it would have been to the advantage of either of 'em to keep the other away. Charles and I dallied with the thought, yesterday," she added. "We had a couple of ideas about Solatia, but Chris almost spanked the two of us when he found out. Chris—that's Chris Bede, and I'm engaged to him—even he hadn't guessed that they were at swords' points. Nobody knew. I'll bet even *you* didn't know. I'll bet you never even suspected!"

"I didn't," Asey said. "But if nobody knew or suspected, why would you have worried about your mother's bein' involved with the murder at all?"

"The letters—look, let's get into the beachwagon and sit down, shall we? I was ready to drop into a heap after the auction, way back there yesterday afternoon, and I haven't sat down since. You see," she opened the door, "Solatia was a lady, and so is mother, and they weren't the type to screech at each other on Main Street, and pull hair, and all that. They were really good friends. That's why the stove problem really arose. Solatia knew perfectly well we couldn't repair our stove, and how foul it was, but she was leaning over backwards refusing mother the permit, because mother *was* a friend, and she didn't want to be accused of any favoritism. No one in town would ever believe that the Madisons had an old, broken-down stove. They'd say Solatia would give the Madisons a stove, because the Madisons were her dear friends, and all that soap, and so on. If Solatia hadn't known us, we'd have had a new stove like a shot. D'you understand, Asey?"

"I think so," Asey said. "But what about the letters? What letters?"

"I'm coming to them—look out for your foot, please, Charles. I'm going to shut the door. Mother didn't really feel very annoyed with Solatia at first, because she thought she understood what was running through Solatia's mind. So she wrote letters to the ration board, formally protesting being turned down on the stove. And I might add," Polly said, "that mother writes a particularly masterful letter of formal invective. You know, the 'I-fail-utterly-to-grasp' kind. And the minute those letters come to light, people will be right at mother's throat. They'll say that ration board business is part of a motive, and the antique fuss the rest of a motive for her killing Solatia."

"Why haven't the letters come to light before?" Asey asked.

"One ration board woman's having a baby, two men were drafted, two are out west, visiting sons in camp, and Solatia's been being the whole works, all by herself. It was she who read mother's letters, in her capacity as chairman, and she simply rejected the protest, and the request for a rehearing, or whatever you'd call it."

"An' she never showed the letters to anyone, or mentioned 'em to anybody?"

"Not as far as we've been able to find out. We assume they're still in her possession," Polly said. "You see, she entirely missed mother's point in trying to switch the stove issue from her, personally, to the board as a whole. Those letters infuriated her, and then mother got infuriated because Solatia was infuriated, and so on and so forth. One of those cumulative things. Anyway, when she didn't show up at the auction this afternoon—"

"Whoa!" Asey interrupted. "Didn't she show up there at all? Didn't she *come?*"

"If she did, she was wearing a cloak of invisibility," Polly said. "Or a false beard and a red wig, or some sort of disguise. Mother and I got popeyed from watching for her. When she never came at all, we were naturally delighted, and mother had a field day—she just snapped up everything we wanted. But as mother said, she hoped to heaven that nothing awful had happened to keep Solatia away, because we might be blamed for it. Well, that's a lengthy little preamble, but it brings us up to the auction." She paused. "I suppose you know all about auctions, don't you?"

"Some."

"Well, there's a point where auctioneers go berserk—at least Quinton Sharp does. He starts throwing the most utterly idiotic things together, and calling them fancy lots. Completely unrelated things, like ten live chickens and a carpet sweeper that won't sweep. Or half a dozen lobster pots and a cakebox."

"I know," Asey said. "The theory is that you'll pay more for the items together than you would have for either if it was offered separate. You get a chicken lover an' a carpet-sweeperless householder biddin' like mad against each other. It swells the total sales, an' it perks up the crowd. The less connection the things have with each other, the more the crowd enjoys it all."

"I never thought that out," Polly said, "but I suppose it *is* the reason—anyway, Sharp outdid himself this afternoon. He mixed more bizarre items than you'd ever believe possible. And then the rat went and dragged out those Hitchcock chairs!"

Charles sighed lustily at the recollection. "Them chairs!" he said. "Them chairs!"

"Mother is a sucker for Hitchcock chairs," Polly went on. "The minute Sharp put those chairs up, there was mother, bidding her silly head off! And for no reason at all—she never *meant* to bid on 'em! And besides, we've got dozens in the garage loft, haven't we, Charles?"

"Twenty-six, Miss Polly. And nine more in the storeroom. And three more in the attic. And five in the shed. It's not she *means* to buy 'em, sir," he said half-apologetically to Asey. "It's just the Madam can't seem to *resist* buying that kind."

"My cousin Jennie," Asey said, "buys little walnut whatnots an' Currier an' Ives prints of kittens in just the same way an' for the same lack of reason. I know all about that sort of thing!"

"And mother got so worked up, she bid against herself!" Polly said. "Sharp pretended he had another bidder on the other side of the crowd who was bidding furiously, but he never did! And mother went soaring up!"

"It was a bush he was waving his hand at," Charles said sadly. "Not a person. I kept trying to tell the Madam so, but she just bid and bid and *bid!*"

Asey grinned. Apparently the Sharp family's bayberry bush trick still panned out.

"And then," Polly said, "just as Sharp got to the second 'Going!' he stopped short and threw in this old trunk. And *that* is the crux of this whole mess. Mother kept on bidding like a woman possessed, and of course she got the chairs, *and* the trunk! Well, we took the best pieces home first, of course —we had to plot out how to make the fewest possible trips with the biggest loads we could manage, because mother's awfully gas conscious. Charles and I brought over the Hitchcock chairs and the trunk and some other odds and ends on the very last trip, after dinner. And we got to wondering what was inside this old trunk."

"For Pete's sakes, didn't Sharp tell what was inside *any*-thing?" Asey demanded.

"Oh, he called the trunk a pig in a poke. He was in one of those pixie moods," Polly said. "You know, where he'd been selling covered wash boilers and closed laundry hampers full of junk he wouldn't show you. People who hadn't opened their mouths suddenly started bidding like maniacs—not because they *wanted* a wash boiler or a laundry hamper, but just out of curiosity, to see what was packed away inside 'em. Oh!"

"What's the matter?" Asey asked.

"I never thought *that* one out before, either," Polly said. "Another trick of the trade, isn't it? Well, with all the excitement of Gardner Alden's paying so much for that sea chest, and fat Mrs. Turnover's paying so much for the house—and

wouldn't it have done John Alden's heart good to see his relations shelling out! Well, with all that going on, I forgot about
the trunk until we brought it home. And then Charles and I
opened it—it wasn't locked, or anything—and it was full of
books. *Those* books." She waved a hand toward Asey's roadster. "Those damned three-quarter morocco bound Harper's
Magazines!"

"And right away," Charles said, "I said to Miss Polly, I said,
'Miss Polly, if Miss Spry was found in that sea chest that'd
been full of old books, then someone had to take them old books
out to put her into the chest, and *these* is *those* books!'"

"What Sharp had done was obvious enough," Polly said.
"He'd put the books into an old empty trunk—and sold the
works to *us!* The good old Madisons. The fall guys. Sell 'em
anything as long as you throw in a few Hitchcock chairs—Sharp
knows mother's weakness for them, heaven knows! He's sold
her all the others. So we get the chairs, with this old trunk
casually thrown in as a humorous afterthought—and all the
books from the sea chest carefully planted inside! Sharp is no
fool. He knew that sooner or later, someone would get to
wondering what had become of those sea chest books. And
when someone finally got around to questioning him—you
probably would have, wouldn't you?"

"Uh-huh," Asey said.

"Well, Sharp would have a mammoth brain wave and remember that old trunk he hadn't opened publicly because he
was selling it as a pig in a poke. He *knows* that trunk was
empty when he sold it—"

"*Does* he?" Asey interrupted.

"Oh, he'll say so, anyway! He'll say that was his little joke,
ha ha ha, selling the *empty* trunk! Then he'll suggest that
maybe someone better take a look at it, just the same, and bang!
The Madisons have the trunk, but it isn't empty, it's full of
books! The books! D'you follow?"

"I think so," Asey said. "I—"

"The Madisons, therefore," Polly continued, "must have killed Solatia Spry. Because gee whiz, *these* are the books from the sea chest someone had to take out before they could put Solatia in. It's all the evil work of those Madisons! They hid the books after they stuck her into the chest, and then tried to sneak 'em away in that old empty trunk Mrs. Madison bought. Yessir," she said with a broad Cape twang, "it was them as killed her afore the auction so as they could buy up all of John Alden's antiques! Let's have a necktie party, fellers, an' string the old Madisons up to a phone pole—who ever *liked* soap, anyways?"

"But it wouldn't be just the Madisons, sir, you see," Charles said quickly. "It'd be the Madam. She'd be the one they'd blame for it all. And Miss Polly and I, we didn't feel the Madam ought to be mixed up in it, so we thought we'd just get rid of them books, see, sir? And—"

"And we couldn't tell mother, because she's so damn honest, she wouldn't think *any*one would ever do a thing like that to us," Polly said, "and besides, she thinks Quinton Sharp is such a marvelous man. She wouldn't believe it of him. And she wouldn't go to bed and give us a chance to get out and get started—she was so excited about her new things, she kept twittering around and feeling them! Finally, I convinced her she looked as if she had a headache, and practically stuffed an allonal into her mouth, and got her to bed—usually she falls asleep the instant she looks at a pillow, but tonight she simply took forever. Wasn't it *awful* waiting, Charles?"

"Yessum!"

"But she finally fell asleep, and Charles and I got the books out of the trunk and into the beachwagon, and then we took 'em and strewed 'em around the East Weesit road. We wanted to go farther away, but we had to be *so* careful about gas!"

"Why?" Asey asked.

"Why? Because mother is so awfully gas conscious, she watches every *spoonful* of gas—"

"I mean, why did you strew 'em at all?" Asey said. "Not just in East Weesit, but what in the world made you think of strewin' 'em anywheres?"

"That," Polly said with pride, "was our *plan!* It took an hour to figure it out, too, didn't it, Charles? You see, if anyone had known the books were in that trunk, they'd have been after us at once. But nobody was after us, so nobody *knew!* That is, nobody but the person who put them in it, in the first place. See?"

Asey nodded.

"We decided if we were to put the books somewhere else, where they'd be found easily—*that* was our Waterloo," Polly said. "We made it too damned easy! Anyway, we decided to strew 'em. Then if whoever found 'em claimed that we'd done the strewing and that they'd come from the trunk, why, we'd know they were the persons—I mean, that he was the person —who'd put the books in the trunk in the first place. We'd know who was guilty!"

"But s'pose he didn't bite?" Asey suggested. "S'pose he didn't care where the books was, as long as they didn't involve him?"

"Then we'd have drawn a blank on finding the murderer," Polly said, "but *we* wouldn't be burdened with all those incriminating books ourselves! They'd be out of *our* hands!"

"We had another angle, too, sir," Charles said. "We thought after we got through getting rid of the books, we could wait around a little while and see if anyone hit the trail of 'em and sort of tried to do anything about 'em. Like if someone had been watching our house to see if we'd find the books in the trunk, and what we'd do with 'em. We thought maybe we might trap someone."

"An' did you?" Asey inquired.

"We never got the chance, sir," Charles said sadly. "You see, we—"

"We got trapped ourselves," Polly interrupted. "We never realized we were being followed, but as soon as we finished laying the books down—this was the *first* time—then this car drove up, and out popped that bald man. Paul Harmsworth. He made us pick up every one and put them all back into the beachwagon again."

"Why?"

"Harmsworth's a great friend of Solatia's—mother knows him, too. She's bought things from him. It turns out," Polly said, "that Harmsworth's violently upset about her being killed, and he's going to find out who did it if it kills him, and he's violently suspicious of mother and me."

"And me, too, sir," Charles added. "He was once at an auction where I took away something Miss Spry'd bought—quite by accident, it was. But he knows Miss Spry never trusted me again, and she always picked on me if she got a chance."

"And he knew I'd quarreled with Solatia occasionally—she took an inordinate interest in my love life," Polly said, "and sometimes she goaded me into resenting it verbally. And he knew that mother and Solatia had quarreled about John's things—and he brought it all up. In his agitation, he even denounced us as the dastards who let all the air out of his tires!"

"So!" Asey said. "Then it was him who called Ellen, an' it means he was somewhere around Solatia's, earlier in the evenin'. Go on!"

"There's nothing much more to go on about," Polly said. "He just seemed convinced that we were two of the most guilty people outside of the Rock."

There was a little silence.

"Just what did you do to him, Charles?" Asey asked.

"Well, sir, he was very hasty, sir, see? And he never give

Miss Polly a chance to explain anything, and he was all for making us take those books to the cops, and such like, sir, and so—well, sir, I just tied him up and left him in the woods, sir. I mean, sir, the way I figured it, nobody knows him much around here, but they know Miss Polly and me, and they know *we* don't go kiting around in the middle of the night, and Mrs. Madison and my wife'll swear we wasn't out, anyway, and he can't prove anything. It's only his word against ours, and ours is better."

"What Charles means," Polly said, "is that we rationalized the situation that way afterwards. For a few minutes there, after we'd disposed of him, we were just a wee bit panicky. We lit out for home so quick! Then we thought, who *was* this Paul Harmsworth but a bald man, and what could *he* prove?"

"So," Asey said, "havin' pulled yourselves together, you went an' laid the books down all over again, huh, over a longer route?"

Polly nodded. "But we were too excited to think it out first, so in order to get back here without running into the books, we had to weave drunkenly around on side roads, all over the place—after the Harmsworth incident, we weren't too anxious to have anyone else connect us directly with those damned Harper's! And we got as far as here—and this time, if *you* hadn't gone and picked 'em up just as fast as we'd laid 'em down!"

"I see," Asey said. "I see!"

"If we'd only known what a swell person you are," Polly said, "we'd have come straight to you and told you the truth, and not bothered with all this malarkey. Wouldn't we, Charles?"

"Yessum!" Charles said with sincerity. "Yes, sir, we would!"

"Thinking it all over impartially," Polly went on, "I must say we haven't been much of a success at evidence shifting and book tossing. All we've really accomplished is to immobilize

Paul Harmsworth—who now doubtless hates us twice as much, and is further convinced of our guilt—and *not* get any books thrown away, at all!"

"What about that first lot, this afternoon?" Asey wanted to know.

"Oh, you'll probably *never* believe that one!" Polly said. "Those were John's own schoolbooks, and his childhood books. I bought them myself at the auction—they were part of a lot. I didn't want them, but neither did I want other people to have them. They were personal things. Like his collar buttons, or his pipe, or something. You know, if you've known people and their possessions, sometimes auctions—well, it hurts you to see things that meant something to someone sold to just anyone. I wonder if you know what I mean?"

"I think," Asey said, "that I do. I never liked auctions."

"Those books bothered me. I loaded them into the picnic hampers we'd brought along to take the china back home in, and drove over and dumped them in to the far end of the pond. I'm not crazy about auctions myself, and I felt like getting away from that one then. It was during a lull, when Sharp was selling corned beef, and Chris pointed out to me that we'd need the hampers for the china, and that I'd better dispose of the books as soon as I could."

Charles's vigorous yawn broke the silence that followed.

"Don't, Charles!" Polly said. "If you get me started yawning, I'll never stop! What are you going to do with us, Asey? I wish I could see your face!" she added. "I have a firm and horrid suspicion that you don't believe a word we've told you!"

"I think what's botherin' me," Asey said honestly, "is that you didn't ask Quinton Sharp what was in the trunk, after you'd opened it an' knew. If he'd said it was filled with old bound Harper's, you'd have saved yourself a heap of trouble. Not to speak of gasoline."

"But if he knew," Polly said, "and if they—oh, no! If he

knew the Harper's were in the trunk all the time, then where would the books from the sea chest be? Asey Mayo, you can't be thinking that the first lot I dumped into the pond—you can't think *those* were the chest books!"

"You can see," Asey said, "how the thought might have flickered around my mind, can't you?"

"But those were books I *bought!* Those were *John's!* And you can check up on that easily enough!" Polly said earnestly. "We can get them out of that pond in a *jiffy,* and *prove* they were old schoolbooks—oh!"

"Looks like he's got you, don't it, Miss Polly?" Charles said sympathetically. "Because even if we proved they was schoolbooks, like you say, we can't prove they wasn't in the chest, can we?"

The end of his sentence turned into another vigorous yawn, which Polly caught and transmitted to Asey.

"I think," Asey opened the door of the beachwagon and got out, "that we'd better call it a day before we three fall sound asleep right here in the middle of the road. I'll keep the books, an' see what Quinton Sharp has to say about 'em, an' you run along home. By the way, Chris Bede hasn't been tearin' around with you on this book tossin' project, has he?"

"Chris? Oh, no!" Polly said quickly. "No, indeed! What made you ask?"

"I thought I caught sight of him," Asey said.

"Oh, I'm sure you didn't!" Polly said. "Don't you think he must be mistaken, Charles?"

"Yessum."

"I mean, he's at the doctor's," Polly said. "Chris did altogether too much running around at the auction this afternoon, and got his ankle hurting—he was badly shot up in China, you know. He was practically going to spend the night with Dr. Cummings."

Asey thought back to the collection of patients who'd been

waiting in Cummings' office. He hadn't paid very much attention to them, but he remembered noticing that there hadn't been a man there under fifty.

"Cummings had a lot of experience with wounds in the last war," he said casually. "He was over in France for three years."

"Chris says he's marvelous," Polly said. "He's so frightfully busy now, of course, you practically can't reach him on the telephone. But when Chris finally got him, he said he thought he could do something about that muscle that hurt so."

"Chris phoned him, didn't he?" Asey said. "Why, sure!" he went on as Polly nodded. "*I* remember! I was there at the time. Just about nine o'clock, wasn't it?"

Polly didn't hesitate. She fell for his little trap, hook, line, and sinker.

"It was practically *exactly* nine," she said. "I remember the clock striking—you remember too, don't you, Charles? You were there in the living room, helping to move the highboy."

"Oh, yessum!" Charles said. "Yes, Miss Polly. I remember. Just nine, it was. Exactly. Yessum."

"I'm sure the doc fixed him up." Asey well knew that Cummings had done nothing of the sort. He and the doctor had left the office around eight. At nine, he had been being biffed with a length of lead pipe while Cummings waited among the rhododendrons. "Well, you two get along—by the way, where did you leave this fellow Harmsworth?"

Charles gave him the explicit location on the East Weesit road.

"We really didn't *hurt* him, sir," he added. "What I mean, sir, he may feel he got awful shook up, but I didn't *hurt* him none at all. I hope you'll explain to him, sir, that Miss Polly and me, why we wouldn't hurt the hair on a fly's head, sir! But Mr. Harmsworth hadn't ought to have made all them cracks about us and the Madam, sir, and not let us explain anything about them books, or what we was trying to do, sir!"

"As a matter of fact," Asey said, "I'm not so much upset about your havin' immobilized him as glad that you located him for me. You saved me a lot of work—golly, I got that cop of Riley's to untie, too! I forgot all about him. Well, you an' Charles run along home—an' you *stay* there, too!"

"Oh, we certainly will!" Polly said. "We've had enough for one night, haven't we, Charles?"

"Yessum!" Charles said. "Yes*sum,* we certainly had enough!"

"We know when we're licked," Polly continued. "We'll just go home, and sneak in quietly so mother doesn't hear us, and *stay* there, that's what! Don't you worry about *us,* Asey! We've shot our little bolt and learned our little lesson! We absolutely wouldn't dream of stirring out of the house again. Not after all this!"

Asey moved the roadster so that the beachwagon could get by, and grinned as he watched Miss Madison and her aged retainer depart for home at a brisk clip.

He didn't for one moment believe that Polly Madison had any notion of returning home—and staying there. While Charles's statement about having enough had sounded both genuine and heartfelt, Polly had protested altogether too loudly and too much.

She would probably go home—a sort of token return, he decided. Then she would turn to Charles and inform him that they were setting right out again. And Charles would say "Yessum" with just as much enthusiasm as if she'd presented him with a half share in the Madison Soap Works.

Asey shook his head.

He wished that after people had convinced him of their own integrity and of the truth of their story, they wouldn't go and spoil it all!

Why had she lied about Chris Bede? The mention of his name had set her off, put a different note in her voice. Chris must have been up to something, and Polly must have known it. She'd jumped to the conclusion that Chris had been in some trouble or other at nine—could she perhaps have known that he was over at Solatia's? At all events, she'd promptly placed him in the doctor's office at that time. She'd alibied him like a shot.

And thereby, of course, she'd thrown her own story completely off. For if she lied so glibly about one thing, she could lie just as glibly about something else.

"Yup," Asey murmured, "I think you'll drive home, wait what you think is a safe time, an' then I think you'll go larrupin' off after your boy friend an' try to find out what's gone sour. An' I think, just for the pure, undiluted fun of it, that I'll trail along after you an' pull a confrontin' act, just like Hanson does. I'd ought not to have given you the reins for a single second. I'd ought to have brought you right up standin', as Hanson would have, an' pretended I didn't believe a word you said. I was too dum easy, an' you think I'm soft."

A few minutes later, he looked at where he had tucked the roadster away in the bushes near the entrance to the Madisons' driveway, and nodded his satisfaction. For an offhand camouflage job, that was pretty good. He'd challenge anyone who hadn't seen it driven into its hiding place to find that roadster.

Keeping in the shadow of the high stone wall, he walked toward the driveway gate, and waited.

The Shack *did* rather look like a wedding cake that someone had thrown down on the ground and stepped on, he decided. The white building seemed to sprawl all over the place, and the odd little spires and gables and bay windows gave it an elaborately frosted appearance.

Someone was upstairs—he could see the slit of light around the side of a window.

And there was another light downstairs in one of the wings.

Charles would have impressed Polly with the need for caution, Asey thought. Charles would have suggested that they pretend to retire, just in case Asey Mayo decided to follow them and check up. Then, after a period during which anyone should have become convinced of their intention to remain at the Shack forever, and never stir an inch from the place, then the pair would sneak out, and go after Chris Bede.

Asey sat down by the driveway post, leaned back against it, and grinned as both lights in the house went out simultaneously. Teamwork, he thought.

The turf was soft, the wind from the outer beach was gentle and cool, and in spite of the unyielding stone behind his back, he found that he had to prod himself every now and then to keep awake.

He decided, rather regretfully, to get up. He couldn't afford to take the chance of falling asleep. And if Polly and Charles could manage to keep their respective eyes open, so could he!

As he got to his feet, he heard a sudden crunching of gravel.

A car was coming down the curving driveway.

He flattened himself against the gatepost as the beachwagon, without headlights, slid past so close to him that he could have reached out a hand and touched the driver on the cheek.

He had his own roadster out of its hiding place and was following the taillights—for the beachwagon's lights had been snapped on after it left the immediate vicinity of the Shack— before it occurred to him that the driver had been the vehicle's only passenger.

The driver, furthermore, wore glasses.

And Polly hadn't.

And Polly had turned the beachwagon with a firm, sure hand. She'd driven away at a good brisk clip.

But the current driver was hesitant, and wandered all over the road.

"I wonder," Asey muttered, "if this could be—I wonder! Is it Polly tryin' to be foxy, or is this maybe Mrs. James Fenimore Madison herself?"

At least, he thought, if it was Mrs. Madison and if she was as gas conscious as her daughter claimed, whatever errand she was on should mercifully be brief. If *she* had a large number of old books to toss into a pond or to strew along a road, she should get very rapidly to the point!

Except that she wouldn't get anywhere very rapidly if she continued to drive at that snail's pace, he mentally amended. He had to keep his foot on the brake to prevent his bumping into her. And if she put out her lights suddenly, he would surely crash her, for he had kept his own off, and was driving by hers.

He had about decided to drop behind, to be on the safe side, when the beachwagon put on a terrific burst of speed and spurted ahead.

Asey put his foot down on the accelerator to match it, but instead of responding, the motor choked weakly, spluttered, and died away entirely.

A quick snapping on of the dashboard lights confirmed his dark suspicion.

He was out of gas.

He looked up from the little illuminated needle pointing so dolefully at "Empty" just in time to see the beachwagon's tail-lights swerve off the road and come to a standstill, perhaps three-quarters of a mile on the road beyond him.

"To make me get out!" Asey opened the car door. "To make me run!" He began to run. "At this point! An' uphill every *step* of the way!"

He had perhaps a hundred yards to go when the beach-wagon started up, turned, and set off at a furious pace back in the direction of the Shack.

"Hey!" Asey yelled, and waved wildly as it sped past him. "Mrs. Mad—"

He broke off. There was no use yelling, she wouldn't stop, and she was too bad a driver to take the chance of jumping out in her path to stop her.

And it *was* Mrs. Madison. A good driver like Polly couldn't even pretend to make as bad a turn as that!

He hesitated a moment, and then walked on toward the spot where the beachwagon had been. If she'd stopped, she must have stopped for some purpose, and whatever the purpose might have been, she'd accomplished it in a hurry!

A long whistle of amazement issued from his lips as he reached the place.

It was a gasoline station.

A filling station.

"Huh!" he muttered. "*What* was Mrs. Madison, the wife of the late soap tycoon, doin' in a gas station whose owner closed it up last evenin' an' went home to bed like a sensible man? *What* inspired her to come here? *Did* she want to reassure herself that there still *was* gas pumps? Huh, if it was me, now, under the present circumstances, I'd understand my goin' to a gas pump, even if the station's shut up for the night."

He sat down on the concrete curbing.

He was out of breath, he was sleepy, and his head was throbbing again. The Madisons and everyone else might have started in with an exhausting afternoon at the auction of John Alden, he thought as he raised his hand and touched the lump on his head, but none of them had had anything even remotely resembling his interlude with the biffer and his length of pipe. Or the lad who knew the rope trick. Or Mrs. Turnover. Or those Harper's.

To a disinterested observer, he might present a fine picture of a tired tramp. The wonder of it, he decided, was that he was still going.

"Gas, Riley's cop, Harmsworth," he said, as if he were reciting a list. "What in *time* was she doin' here? Gas, Riley's man, Harmsworth—oh, well, gas comes first! Let's figger, now!"

There were plenty of houses, summer people's houses, nearer

than the Madisons' Shack, but few of them were occupied this lean year. He could hunt up one which might be inhabited, or he could walk back to the Shack.

But had anyone enough gasoline to lend him with which to drive the Porter back to his own home? He doubted if they had, and besides, the siphon process would be long and tedious. Even if he milked the Madison power mower, the results probably wouldn't justify the effort.

He could phone Ellen from the Shack, but could she be roused from bed and cajoled into bringing him gas before this station opened?

This place, he recalled, was near the landing where the fishermen and the quahauggers came in. Probably, for the benefit of their trucks, it would be opened early.

He leaned back against a gas pump and wearily surveyed the first dull glow in the east.

"Came the dawn!" he said. "Came the d—oh, for the love of Pete!"

He jumped up suddenly and looked more carefully at his surroundings.

The metal gas-pump covers were not merely closed. They were padlocked.

The miniature Cape Cod house that served as the station's office and store was not simply closed up for the night.

It was shuttered.

It was boarded up.

And across its door was a sign. As the light increased, he realized that it was not a new sign. It was weather-beaten, and the paint was peeling.

"Closed," it said in rude capitals, "for the duration. Gone to war."

Asey grinned.

"Go on an' figger, Codfish Sherlock!" he said to himself. "If you couldn't figger why she come to a gas station that was just shut up for the night, maybe you can figger why she come to one that's closed for the duration, an' has been for some time!"

One sure thing, he thought. She hadn't come *for* anything! His grin broadened.

If she hadn't come *for* anything, perhaps she had come to *leave* something!

"It couldn't be very much," he said thoughtfully, "an' it couldn't be very big or very bulky. She didn't have the time—huh!"

He went to work.

Half an hour later, he gazed with triumph at what, beyond any doubt, she had left.

Three large wooden duck decoys, and two small ones.

And each bore the name "John Alden" carved on its side.

Seven

DR. CUMMINGS helped himself to a piece of bacon from the platter in front of Asey, took a reflective bite, and absent-mindedly reached out for the slice of toast which had just popped out of the toaster.

"Three big duck decoys, two little duck decoys, and all with John Alden's name carved on 'em! Three big ones, and two little ones! Three big, and two little!"

"The way you keep saying it over and over," Jennie told him acidly, "you make it sound like flocks and flocks, instead of only five—and please, can't you keep your fingers off Asey's breakfast? He forgot to bring his ration book home with him, and I had to trade two jars of put-up strawberries for that bacon you're pilfering!"

"I had my breakfast five hours ago, at the same time the rest of the world that hadn't spent the night cavorting after murderers had *its* breakfast," Cummings returned. "It is now noon, and my lunch time, and I'm hungry. But I'll confine myself to toast and jam, if you'll bring me some more jam, and some more bread, and maybe a bit of old cake, or an egg, or something. Asey, are you sure it was Mrs. Madison who left those decoys there?"

"Uh-huh. She'd popped 'em into a box at one side of the little house," Asey said, "an' then stuck a couple more old boxes on top of that one."

"Why in the name of all that's reasonable and sensible," Cummings demanded, "did she leave them *there,* in that abandoned gas station?"

Asey grinned and asked if the doctor could think of a better place.

"It's the last place *I'd* ever think of goin' to look for anything, doc," he added. "I wouldn't even *go* there, let alone go there to look. Neither would anyone else. I thought it was pretty smart of her, myself. If someone had only put Solatia Spry in a box there, she'd most likely never have been found for the duration."

"How'd you get home?"

"I hailed a kindly milkman," Asey said. "You'll be interested to know he was the same kindly milkman who give Gardner Alden a lift over here yesterday. He's one of them honest, chatty souls with a long memory—he felt kind of embarrassed when he couldn't remember if Gardner had on a tie with gray an' blue stripes, or one with blue an' gray. He corroborated Gardner's story down to the bone, though. He'd even wangled out of Gardner the reason why he was comin' over here to see me— on account of his bein' worried of what Harmsworth might do to Solatia to prevent her from gettin' to the auction."

"Asey Mayo, after the night you put in, d'you mean to say that you came bumbling home with a lot of *milk?*" Cummings demanded.

"Oh, no. He dropped me off at the first available phone up the line beyond the gas station, an' I called Ellen, who come over an' administered first aid. Not a crack out of her, either, at my bein' so dumb as to run out of gas. You'd have thought it could happen to anyone. I come home," Asey said reminiscently, "via Harmsworth."

"When you skimmed lightly through this the first time, you never told me you found *him!*"

"I didn't. I found where he'd been. There wasn't any trace

of him but a piece of what looked like tow rope, an' some of Charles's suspenders—at least, I assume they was Charles's," Asey said. "They might have been Harmsworth's own, of course."

"Who freed him?" Cummings asked. "Where d'you suppose he is now?"

Asey shrugged. "I wouldn't know. By the time I'd got as far as the place where he'd been, I was beyond thinkin'. I didn't even care."

"Did you look into the matter of Riley's cop?"

"I come to the conclusion," Asey said gravely, "that he knew what he was gettin' into when he become a cop, an' that bein' exposed to crime in its various phases was just one of the natural hazards of his job. I decided he could just continue to take it —to tell you the truth, doc, I was too plumb tired to go over to Solatia's, an' I figgered that Hanson would certainly have come by then, anyway."

Cummings took another slice of toast.

"Asey, are you positive it was Mrs. Madison who left those decoys there?"

"Uh-huh," Asey said. "I'm sure it was her. Jennie remembered quite a bit about that lot she bought that had the Currier an' Ives kittens an' the little walnut whatnot in it. Like I guessed, when she got the bid, she sung out that all she wanted was the picture an' the whatnot, an' for Sharp's men not to bother bringin' the rest to her. She remembers that the Madison girl came over to her an' asked if she could have the decoys, an' Jennie said sure, to go on an' take 'em, she had no use for 'em herself. An' the girl took 'em, as far as Jennie knows."

"But if the Madison *girl* took them," Cummings said, "why in blazes should her *mother* be hiding them in the dead of night, or the crack of dawn, or whenever it was?"

"Probably—nuh-uh, doc! *My* bacon!—probably," Asey removed the platter with the remaining bacon out of the doctor's reach, "Mrs. Madison wanted to get rid of them for the same reason her daughter was tryin' to get rid of the books, which she thought might incriminate her mother. Most likely her allonal wore off about the time Charles an' Polly come back, an' she woke up sayin' 'Decoys! Decoys!' to herself, an' without even knowin' or guessin' about them two havin' been out all night, she jumped from bed an' rushed out to do somethin' about them decoys, right away quick!"

"Hm," Cummings said. "Hm. You mean, Mrs. Madison had a brain wave, and decided that anyone who had anything to do with the remains of that lot which contained the fish knife had better not be connected with it in any way. Particularly if the person happened to be her own daughter. Hm. It *sounds* like her, I must say! She's a creature of impulse—of course, all women are, God knows, but she can afford to carry out her whimsies. Does Jennie remember who took the knife?"

Asey sighed.

"That's the more discouragin' angle," he said. "Jennie doesn't even remember there was a knife in the lot, though she called up Nellie an' the girls, an' they're all sure that there was. But they all remember seein' it in one of the pails *before* the auction. They're only too eager an' willin' to assume it was a part of the lot when Sharp actually sold it, but they have to admit that they didn't actually see it then, that he never held it up, or showed it off, or even mentioned it, at all."

"Then it probably had already been stolen," Cummings said. "Sharp is a great enumerator. He wouldn't have let a good knife like that go by without pointing it out!"

"That's my feelin'. But I think we're stymied on the knife department, doc, whether or not it was in the lot when the lot was sold. Anyone at the auction, or anyone just passin' by, could have swiped that knife either before the sale begun, or after Jennie bought the lot."

"Makes a nice mental exercise, doesn't it?" Cummings remarked. "Anyone at the auction could have taken the knife, everyone was at the auction, therefore anyone and everyone had the opportunity of filching the knife which killed her. Therefore anyone and everyone killed her. Hm. Wouldn't it be refreshing to have fate work in an orderly fashion and provide you with proof that someone was just as eager to buy that fish knife of John Alden's as they were, say, to buy his antiques and his china!"

"If we did find out anythin' like that," Asey said, "it would only be Gardner Alden, buyin' it in memory of his dear old white-haired grandmother. The pink sea shells one. You know what keeps disturbin' my mind, doc?" he got up from the table and lighted his pipe. "It's that no one ever mentions Solatia's havin' been there!"

"Oh, merciful heavens, Asey, are you still trying to beat your brains out against the stone wall of her *not* being there?" Cummings demanded. "Of course she was there! *I've* proved it to you several hundred times—look at the *facts,* man, look at the facts! Someone was waiting for her to come, someone pounced on her the second she arrived, killed her with the knife they'd already stolen, put her in the chest. Not being a complete idiot, the murderer took care that no one else saw her, or the actual murder! You certainly," he added with some heat, "have seen enough of this sort of business to know that a murderer *avoids* a large audience, whenever possible!"

"Yes, doc, but—"

"I have seen murders," Cummings made a long reach and took the last piece of bacon, "that ran the gamut from simple pitchfork stabbings and arsenic poisonings to flintlock pistols and belaying pins. And a flowerpot of geraniums dropped by a wife with great effect and precision from a second-story window onto the head of her husband, an unpleasant man who happened to be passing at the time. I've seen all kinds, and so have you, and I'll give you a thousand dollars cash if you can remember one instance where a murderer sent out invitations beforehand. Or even called up a few of his dearest and most intimate friends and asked 'em to drop in for the event!"

Asey grinned.

"Ah, well," he said, *"who* knows? Maybe it *was* done with mirrors, like you suggested last night!"

"Why don't you call Sharp and ask him about the knife, and about those books Polly Madison found in the trunk, and if he remembers any more about the time Solatia came to the auction? He was sure he saw her, wasn't he?"

"I called him first thing, when I got back here this mornin'," Asey said. "An' Jennie called him a dozen times while I was catchin' up on my sleep, an' I called him again just before you come. Nobody answers—doc, what about Chris Bede? Did he come to your office?"

"I never set eyes on him, and he never called. My wife has certain peculiarities," Cummings said, "but she is magnificent with messages. If she'd even thought it was Chris who called, even if he hadn't given his name, she'd have put the fact in parentheses after noting the call and the time—you ever happen to see my phone message lists?"

"Don't know's I ever did," Asey said.

"'Woman called at 9:02. No name, no message. (It was that blonde with the nose who hired the Harding cottage year before last; I recognized her voice. She's got Snow's place this year and she has a boil and can't sit down, because her maid told someone at Red Cross yesterday. Will call later, probably didn't want to tell me where the boil was.)' No," Cummings said, "she can't keep accounts to save her life, but she *can* take messages! Hm. I suppose everything works out for the best, doesn't it?"

"I come to much the same conclusion after I finally found them decoys," Asey said. "While I'd run out of gas, still an' all I'd found—where's my—doc, did you take that bacon?"

"Why, Asey, did *you* want it?" Cummings asked solicitously.

"You'd got up from the table and were smoking, and I naturally assumed you were all finished! Dear me, I'm awfully sorry, but there's virtually nothing I can do about it now—sugar ginger-bread, Jennie?" He removed two slabs from the plate she brought in. "Fine! Nothing I like any better to top off my lunch with than hot sugar gingerbread!"

"I should think you'd be ashamed of yourself, stealing Asey's bacon and eatin' up all the food in the house!" Jennie sounded profoundly irritated, but Asey knew she would have been a lot more irritated if the doctor hadn't touched a thing. "Now, I've got to know what you plan to do, Asey! I can't have anything happen again like last night, when everything went to wrack and ruin for your not turnin' up! I could've *cried* over that cheese soufflé, and the steamed pudding boiled into a *rock!* Now you tell me just *exactly* what you're plannin' to do today, and just *exactly* what time you'll be home!"

"Wa-el," Asey said, "I'm goin' over to Solatia's, hopin' that Hanson come an' rescued the cop, an' assumin' if he ain't come here to talk with me yet, he must still be over there, fine-tooth combin' around. I'm goin' to try an' locate Paul Harmsworth an' have a few words with him. I'm goin' to find Quinton Sharp an' ask him some questions. An' I'm goin' to pay a call on the minister of the Congregational Church."

"Gracious!" Jennie said in surprise. "Gracious goodness! You're goin' to *call* on him of your own accord, after all the trouble I've had bullyin' you into just goin' to church with me once in a while? Oh." She sniffed. "*I* see! I s'pose you only mean you're goin' to call an' ask him some old questions, too!"

"Uh-huh. I want to see if he really did sit next to Al Dorking every minute at the auction," Asey said, "an' also if he knows for a fact that the sea chest was full of books when Dorking flipped the spring lock with his knife an' slammed the lid down before the auction began. I'm also awful interested to know what kind of—"

"Dorking's lying to you!" Cummings interrupted with his mouth full of gingerbread. "I told you so when you first told me about that!"

"Why, doc?"

"Why is he lying? Because—oh, well, I suppose someone *could* have unlocked it again afterwards, if they'd happened to have had the key," Cummings said. "I suppose Gardner Alden or Mrs. Turnover *could* have had one of their dear old grandmother's keys handy. That possibility hadn't occurred to me, I'll admit. Is that another one of your projects, to find out about a key?"

"If I can prove that Solatia Spry wasn't in that chest up to the start of the auction," Asey told him, "I'll derive considerable satisfaction from that one fact. I won't even ask for gramma's keys. Then, after the minister, I'd like to sit an' ponder on who biffed me, an' let the air out of my tires, an' who tied me up, an' what Chris Bede was up to, if it was him I seen prowlin' around last night at Solatia's. An' I'm sort of toyin' with the notion of goin' over an' chattin' with that other antique dealer —what's her name? That Miss Pitkin."

"Eunice Pitkin?" Cummings leaned back and roared with laughter.

"What's so funny about that?" Asey wanted to know.

"Well, I can see where you'd feel you should question her," Cummings said, "but you might as well save your precious gas, Asey. I know Eunice. She's one of my patients. She's short, and blonde, and wide-eyed, and she just misses lisping by the skin of her teeth. And she hasn't the strength in her right arm to cut a lamb chop, if one materialized by some miracle. And she couldn't by any stretch of the imagination wield a fish knife the way that one was wielded. She broke her right arm this spring, you see, and messed up the cartilage. And she's completely helpless and clumsy with her left hand. No co-ordination at all. You'll simply be wasting your time on Eunice—although

I'm sure Eunice would adore seeing you. She's forty-three, and she coos. How many more calls do you intend to make?"

"If he makes only one more," Jennie observed tartly, "that'll take him over into next week, and I want to know about dinner tonight! What time will you be home here, Asey? I've got to know!"

"When all the miscellaneous items I been talkin' about is settled," Asey assured her, "I'll start for home. An' I'll phone you before I start, too."

"And then," she said, "I s'pose you'll manage to run out of gas on the way?"

"I think I'm safe now," Asey said. "Ellen put a five-gallon can of gas in the roadster. She didn't mention it, an' I didn't mention it, an' neither of you ask me any rude questions about it, because I don't know any answers. You couldn't prove by me that that gas can didn't float down from heaven on a parachute, with angels fillin' it as it dropped. Now, are you comin' with me, doc?"

"I'm on my way to the hospital," Cummings said. "Probably people are sending out posses to track me down and drag me there, right this minute—want to know an interesting fact about Mrs. Turnover, Asey?"

"She was a lady knife thrower in a circus, maybe?" Asey asked hopefully.

"At a bright and early hour this morning," Cummings said, "Mrs. Turnover dropped into the hardware store to buy some crowbars."

"Crowbars? What on earth for?" Jennie asked. "She's the last person I'd ever think of as buyin' *one* crowbar, let alone *some!*"

"She's taking up the floor of John Alden's shed, she told the hardware girl. Of course they didn't have any crowbars, but she bought a few assorted ersatz implements. In her estimation, Asey," Cummings said with relish, "you are God's gift to the detective world, a man who could just take a brief gander at an old sea chest and know that her grandmother kept pink shells in it. You're one of the finest men she was ever privileged to meet. She says her nephew, who rarely approves of anyone, concurs. He also thinks you are highly amusing."

"An' I s'pose," Asey said, "that her dear brother Gardner thinks I'm a peach, too. Huh! You makin' it all up as you go along, doc?"

Cummings shook his head. "I pick up little tidbits as I ply my rounds," he said. "Several people, for example, asked me if I knew why you and Mrs. Turnover were throwing things out of John Alden's windows in the middle of the night, and Old Baker at the Inn told me sorrowfully he didn't know what to think of you after seeing you joy riding with Ellen in her wrecker. He said it was real late when the two of you passed his house—both of you, furthermore, were laughing like mad. I dare say the minister'll give you a good talking to, if it's found out that you spent the remainder of the night pursuing *both* Madison women. You'll probably never be able to hold your head up again—by the way," he added with a touch of professional curiosity as he followed Asey to the door, "how does that lump of yours feel today, anyway?"

"It's dwindlin' all the time," Asey said. "By tomorrow, it ought to be down to a baseball, like you said. So long, Jennie. Don't worry about dinner. I'll let you know when I'm comin'. I'll be seein' you, doc. You got a rough idea of where I'll be in case you got any desire to hunt me up."

"Oh, I'll keep your itinerary in mind!" Cummings assured him ironically as he got into his car. "Without any doubt, if I can't locate you in one place, I'll be sure to stumble on you in another. Probably with two more lumps. Or looking like another Gordian knot. Or pursuing a few more women." He snickered. "Maybe Eunice Pitkin!"

"Who knows?" Asey said. "You might even find me helpin'

Mrs. Turnover to turn over her shed floor with a lot of ersatz crowbars!"

Turning his roadster into Solatia Spry's driveway some fifteen minutes later, he discovered that her yard was filled with cars.

At least it contained four, and that was more than he had seen parked in one place since the auction, the previous afternoon.

He recognized the official, two-tone blue police car, and knew that Hanson had finally arrived. But the other sedan and the two battered beachwagons weren't vehicles which he knew, or connected with anyone in particular.

The place was curiously quiet, he thought as he got out of the Porter and walked toward the house. Usually you could hear Hanson a mile away, even when he was talking in a low voice.

"*What* goes on here, kiddies?" he murmured. "*Has* this whole mob of people been bound an' gagged? *Did* this contingent meet up with the biffer? *Why* can't I smell Hanson's cigar, for goodness' sakes!"

He grinned reminiscently at the side door, stepped with caution into the entry, and listened for a moment.

The house was perfectly still.

"Hanson!" Asey used his quarter-deck bellow. "Hey, Hanson, where are you?"

No one answered, but he heard a rustle, and then the sound of footsteps.

"Hanson! What in time!" It *was* Hanson, approaching him on tiptoe. "Hey, what goes on here? Playin' Quaker Meetin'?"

"Ssh!" Hanson said.

"What's the mat—"

"Ssh!" Hanson shook his head severely, and beckoned to him. "Sssh!"

More than a little mystified by the whole hushed proceeding, Asey followed him through the house, and into the front parlor.

Riley was there, sitting bolt upright in a straight-backed chair. Riley's man, the one who had encountered both the biffer and the rope trickster, sat next to him.

Two local men whom he knew, both of them wearing what Jennie would have called funeral faces, sat over by the fireplace. Standing between them, with one elbow resting on the mantel, was Gardner Alden.

And over on the horsehair sofa, sobbing quietly but with a certain fixed determination, was a short, blonde woman.

"What in time," Asey said, "is the mat—"

"Miss Pitkin!" Hanson said in a whisper. "That's Miss Pitkin!"

"What's wrong with her? What's wrong," Asey added, "with *all* of you? I don't know's I ever seen a more melancholy little group! What are you so sad an' despondent about, anyway?"

"She did it!" Hanson whispered.

"Who did what?"

"Miss Pitkin! She killed Solatia Spry!"

"If you could speak up a wee mite, Hanson," Asey said, "I could probably hear you. Who did what?"

"Miss Pitkin." Hanson continued to whisper. "She killed Solatia Spry!"

"You sure of it?" Asey inquired.

"Of course I'm sure! She admitted it!" Hanson barely breathed the words.

"Then why," Asey said, "don't you come right out an' say so in your regular voice? Why whisper?"

Hanson pointed toward the sofa, where Miss Pitkin was still sobbing.

"I know, I see her there," Asey said. "But if she's guilty, an' if you're sure of it, then why be so everlastingly secretive about it?"

Hanson went through an elaborate pantomime, at whose conclusion Asey shook his head.

"I'm awfully sorry," he said. "I just don't get it! If she's guilty, I'm mighty glad you got her. But now you got her, I don't see why you let her sit there sobbin' while the rest of you all sit there an' watch. You ain't plannin' on lettin' her keep this up indefinitely, are you?"

"Miss Pitkin," Gardner Alden said in a low voice, "has been exceedingly hard to handle, Mr. Mayo. She admitted her guilt, she agreed to write a full confession, and then she dissolved in tears. If anyone has spoken above a whisper, she's screamed and said that if she was distracted by loud voices, she simply wouldn't be able to write a single word. Then she's sobbed some more."

"She hasn't screamed at me none," Asey said, "an' I ain't whispered. What's the jist of this, anyway? Will someone take a chance, an' speak up an' tell me?"

"When Riley and I came about an hour and a half ago," Hanson paused and looked nervously toward the sobbing figure on the sofa, "I walked in and found her in this room, Asey. She tried to duck me, but I grabbed her, and all these letters you see on the table fell out of her pocket. Just as I was taking a look at 'em, Riley called out he'd found Jimmy," he indicated the other cop, "bound and gagged outside by the bushes. Riley never expected to find Jimmy out there, you understand. He just thought he'd take a look around before he came in. Well, after he found Jimmy, then he found Mr. Alden, bound and gagged out by the back door!"

"So!" Asey said. "So! I gather that was your bicycle I seen here last night, Mr. Alden?"

Gardner, tight-lipped, nodded stiffly.

"I accused her of tying them both up," Hanson went on. "She's so small, I didn't honestly think she really could have, see, but I thought if I accused her anyway, I'd probably find out the truth quicker, see? You know how it always is, Asey."

"Uh-huh." Asey well knew how it always was. Hanson bellowed out accusation after accusation at the top of his powerful lungs, and from the "I-never!-I-never!-I-only-I-*only*'s" that he got in response, a reasonably true picture of the situation ultimately developed. It was an extremely exhausting process for everyone but the indefatigable Hanson himself, and it wasn't very subtle. But it undoubtedly brought results. "Uh-huh. An' Miss Pitkin admitted she done it, huh?"

"She admitted it right off the bat!" Hanson said. "Then I took a look at the letters—that's her motive, see, those letters she wrote to Solatia Spry."

"You mean, she killed Solatia Spry because she wanted to get them letters back?" Asey asked.

"No, no, no! *They* show why she *wanted* to kill her, see? And then after she killed her, she realized that she had to get the letters back, see?"

Asey nodded, and privately decided it had taken an incredibly long time for Miss Pitkin to achieve such a realization.

"This," Hanson went on rather pompously, "is one of those murders that wouldn't have happened last year, or the year before. This's something on a *new* line, see?"

"Wa-el," Asey drawled, "I don't know's I'd call murder by stabbin' anything particularly *new,* Hanson! I s'pose if you looked into the matter far back enough, you'd find out that the first feller who happened on a nice pointed bit of branch most probably stabbed one or two of his friends with it before the point got too dull."

"You don't understand, Asey! It has to do with rationing, see?"

"With *ra*tioning?"

"That's right. This Miss Spry was the chairman of the ration board, and it seems like she and this Miss Pitkin was in the same business. Antiques. And Miss Spry wouldn't give her any gas to get around and get antiques with, see, or any tires for her car. Get it? She was in a position where she had her rival dealer hamstrung. I read through some of those letters, Asey, and I tell you, they've been having it hot and heavy for some time! Pitkin here, she'd asked nice, then she'd asked a little tougher, and then she'd got good and sore, see? The last letter was threatening, pure and simple. And there was something in it about this auction yesterday, too. I didn't spot the significance of that part, but Mr. Alden did. You tell him, Mr. Alden."

Gardner cleared his throat.

"She's been in correspondence, apparently, with Solatia's rich client in San Francisco," he said. "The man who'd told Solatia to buy John's things for him at any price. It is my impression that Miss Pitkin told him that she could secure the things far more cheaply than Solatia could—that she'd take less commission, or even none at all. Then, you see, she held that over Solatia's head."

"Huh," Asey said. "You mean, if Solatia didn't crash through with gas an' tires, Miss Pitkin was goin' to cut her out with her rich client by what amounted to a bit of underhanded price cuttin'?"

"It was all insinuated rather than actually stated in the letters," Gardner said pedantically. "Whether or not Miss Pitkin actually had been in contact with this collector, I don't know. I shouldn't feel justified in stating that as a fact. It's entirely possible, of course, that she may have been making it up out of whole cloth in order to bully Solatia into giving her the extra gasoline and the new tires she wanted. Speaking for myself, I rather doubt that she had any dealings—"

"She admitted it!" Hanson interrupted. "When I accused her of trying to louse up Miss Spry's deal, she admitted it! You heard her! She admits everything, Asey. She admits tying up Jimmy and Mr. Alden, and stealing these letters—or trying to. She admitted the works. She never even tried to get out of it, or hedge, or anything."

Asey looked thoughtfully from Riley's cop, Jimmy, to Gardner Alden.

Then he surveyed the small figure on the couch.

In all the times he'd seen the rope trick, he thought, he'd never seen a small Cub Scout tackle a full-grown air-raid warden.

"I s'pose," he said casually, "she admits to sabotagin' the beachwagon, too?"

Hanson wanted to know what beachwagon he was talking about.

"Solatia Spry's. If Miss Pitkin admitted to doin' everything else, she's most probably responsible for lettin' the air out of Solatia's tires, too."

Asey spoke to Hanson, but his eyes never left Miss Pitkin. He'd noticed that she'd stopped sobbing, and he had an idea that she was listening intently.

"I never knew about that!" Hanson said.

"Didn't you? An' the phone wire," Asey told him, "was also cut."

"I never knew—" Hanson began, and then stopped abruptly. Miss Pitkin was stirring.

With a quick movement, she twisted herself up from her prone position, and sat up on the horsehair sofa.

Asey watched with interest as she smoothed her blonde curls back into place, straightened out her skirt, and patted down the collar of her blue dress.

Then she smiled sweetly at him.

"That's the only thing I *did* do!" she said, and Asey realized that Cummings had described her mode of speech with amazing accuracy. She didn't quite lisp, but if you didn't listen sharply, she sounded as if she did. "I cut her phone and let the air out of her tires. I did that yesterday afternoon."

"Did you, now!" Asey answered because no one else in the room seemed capable of making any response whatsoever. "Was you sore about John Alden's things, or sore about the gas an' the tires?"

"The gas and tires. I didn't have a dog's chance with John's stuff, and I knew it," Miss Pitkin returned. "Not with Mrs. Madison, and Paul Harmsworth, and Gardner Alden! No, I came over here yesterday—oh, it must have been around one o'clock—to make one last effort to bully her into being decent. I'd tried every way I could think of, and this was a last resort. You see, I'd pretended that I'd written to Maxim Harvey—he's the collector who wanted John's china so badly—and I decided if I was going to succeed in scaring her that way into doing anything for me, I'd have to do it before the auction started. D'you understand?"

"Uh-huh. An' did you?"

Miss Pitkin smiled her wide-eyed, guileless smile at him.

"No. She said I was lying, which was true enough. She knew, because she'd been talking to Harvey on the phone that morning. I knew then that I was licked. I pretended to drive away, but I only went down the road a bit. Then I walked back and waited till I saw her go down to her garden," Miss Pitkin said, "and then I went and let the air out of her tires, and cut her phone wire with a pair of her own garden shears. I didn't think it would get me anywhere, heaven knows. It was just the way I felt about her. And that's all I ever did."

"You told me," Hanson shouted, "you told me that you'd write a confession! A *full* confession of the whole business!"

"It's a woman's privilege to change her mind," Miss Pitkin told him gently. "I changed mine. I decided I'd make a full confession, verbally, to Asey Mayo instead. And I've just made a *full* confession to him!"

"When I asked you if you did things, you kept nodding!" Hanson roared. "You said you killed her! You admitted killing her!"

"When anyone bellows at you like a bull, it's always easier to agree with them and shut them up than to disagree and make them bellow like *two* bulls," Miss Pitkin said. "Besides, I was terribly, terribly confused. You confused me by—"

"You wept! You cried! You—"

"Oh, I always cry when I'm confused, and don't know just what else to do," Miss Pitkin said easily. "Always. It gives you time to think. I didn't have anything to do with any binding or gagging people, or with killing Solatia Spry! Heaven knows I've wanted to get rid of her often enough, but not actively, you know. I mean," she turned to Asey, "I don't think I ever exactly wished that someone would kill her. I just wished she'd move away, or go on a long, long journey. Or something like *that.*"

"You mean to sit there and tell me now that you *didn't* kill her?" Hanson demanded.

"*Yes,* I sit here," Miss Pitkin said, "and tell you that *no,* I didn't! You ask the most utterly impossible questions—no one could give you a straight answer! All *I'm* responsible for is the car tires and the phone."

"Prove it!" Hanson said promptly. "Prove it! *Prove,*" his voice rose, "*prove* you didn't kill her!"

"I'm sure I can," Miss Pitkin returned, "but if you don't stop yelling at me in that tone of voice, I'm *darned* if I will!"

"Attagirl, Eunice!"

Every head in the room turned toward the newcomer standing in the doorway.

He was a tall man in a crumpled blue suit; he was smiling cheerfully, and his head was as bald as a billiard ball.

"Attagirl, Eunice!" he strolled into the room and unconcernedly perched himself on the corner of a marble-topped table. "Don't let him bully you. You *didn't* do it, and you *can* prove it!"

"Who are you?" Hanson swung around and glared at him belligerently.

"If you ask Eunice, she'll tell you I'm probably the best maker of reproductions in the antique business. If you ask Alden, there," he indicated Gardner, "he'll tell you I'm a dirty faker and a rotten crook. Ought to be in a jail this minute."

"Say, what are you talking about? What do you mean? Who *are* you?" Hanson demanded.

"I mean that I once sold Alden a reproduction, and I told him it was a reproduction, and he didn't believe me and thought it was an original. When he found out I'd told him the truth, he became very angry. The name," he added, "is Harmsworth. Paul Harmsworth. I'm glad to find you, Mr. Mayo." He grinned at Asey. "Your cousin thought you'd be here."

"What's all this business to you?" Hanson asked suspiciously before Asey had a chance to speak.

"Solatia was a good friend of mine. I feel rather strongly about her being killed. She hasn't any family, and I thought it would be proper for me to see that arrangements were made about her, and all. I also thought," Harmsworth said, "that I'd like to find out who killed her."

"Oh, you did!" Hanson looked at him fixedly. He was, Asey noted, in what Cummings always referred to as a pre-confront mood. "You were here last night, Mr. Harmsworth, *weren't* you?" he asked.

"Yes, I was. I—"

"Aha! It was *you*," Hanson said, "who bound and gagged Alden and my officer! You're more of a size for that sort of thing! You did that!"

"No," Harmsworth said, "I didn't. Matter of fact, Captain," he gave Hanson a tactful jump in rank which Hanson didn't trouble to correct, "*I* was bound and gagged, myself. Not here, but—"

"Where?" Hanson interrupted. "Who did it?"

"If I'm not sufficiently moved about the affair to make the effort of reporting it, or lodging any official complaint, what does it matter where or who?" Harmsworth said. "I was over here, yes, and I think I ran into the person you're after, because all the air was let out of my tires, and—"

"*She* did that!" Hanson pointed to Eunice Pitkin. "She's the one—"

"No, she's not the tire-air letter-outer," Harmsworth said. "She was home with her mother, her father, her sisters, and her aunts—you were, weren't you, Eunice? I told you to stay there."

"I never moved from the house last night," she assured him.

"Good!" Harmsworth said. "Now, before you run off on any more tangents, Captain, let's settle a few facts. I went to the auction with Eunice. I sat with her during it. I went home with her to look at some glass she wanted me to tell a dealer about. My helper was with us all the time. In other words, there are two witnesses to prove that Eunice had nothing to do with Solatia's murder."

Hanson looked a little abashed for a moment. Then he recovered.

"What about those letters?" he said with triumph. "When I came here, I found her stealing letters she'd written to Solatia Spry! Threatening letters! You can't get her out of that one!"

Harmsworth didn't even try. "I was afraid, Eunice, that you couldn't resist the impulse to come here and take those!" he said with regret. "And God knows you never should have touched her beachwagon! That was unworthy of you. But Mayo will probably understand that you acted on impulse, and he'll cool off this da—er—the captain, here."

"Harmsworth," Gardner Alden said suddenly, "just what were you and your helper talking about on the bus yesterday morning? Just what did you mean when you spoke of the possibility of Solatia's not getting to the auction, or not getting there in time?"

"Really want to know, Alden? Joe and I were discussing *you.*"

"Me?"

"You," Harmsworth said with a smile. "You, and how much

of your bragging was hot air—now don't be tiresome and say you didn't brag. Fully a dozen reputable people have told me you'd been bragging how you'd see to it that *no* one got in the way of your buying up John's things. Coming on the bus, Joe and I discussed what someone like you might do to prevent someone like Solatia from attending the auction. We wondered how to circumvent you without going to the police. The—"

"Afraid of us, were you?" Hanson interrupted.

"No, Captain, not in the least. But the only police officer I ever remembered seeing in this town was a traffic cop, and I had no desire to try and explain to any traffic cop my fears of what Alden might do to keep Solatia away from the auction. Anyway, Alden," Harmsworth turned back to him, "your bragging disturbed me to such an extent that I hired a car and drove over here and warned Solatia to watch out for you, just as soon as I arrived."

That tallied, Asey thought, with what Ellen had told him.

"I didn't realize that you were on the bus," Harmsworth continued. "Joe thought he spotted you getting off the New York train, but I guess you were ducking us. If I'd seen you, I certainly should have had a few words with you. Now, I'd like to talk with you privately, Mr. Mayo, if I could."

"*I'm* in charge here!" Hanson said.

"I know you are, Captain, and I'm sure you're right on your toes." Harmsworth's irony was so bland that it sailed right over Hanson's head. "But this is a personal matter I want to discuss —okay, Mr. Mayo?"

"Sure," Asey said. "First, though, I want to clear up a few things, like why Mr. Alden come here on his bike last night. When I left you at the Inn, Mr. Alden, I thought you was goin' straight up to bed."

"You may recall telling me that there was no reason why I shouldn't return to New York? And I believe you overheard me telling my nephew," Gardner said smoothly, "that I'd see him before I left? Well, Mr. Mayo, after going to my room and consulting a timetable, I found that I'd have to leave too early to see Al this morning. So I started out to see him last night."

"I see," Asey said. "I don't s'pose you could have phoned him, maybe?"

"He's very anxious to enter my office," Gardner returned, "and there were details to be settled which I hardly wished to discuss from the Inn's only public phone in the lobby—it has no door. So I took a bicycle and started over to see him. When I passed by the house here, I noticed a flashlight moving in an odd fashion, as if two people were struggling to get possession of it, and then I heard someone call out—"

"That was me, see?" Riley's man told Asey. "I yelled, see? That was when this guy that'd sneaked up on me got me with the rope."

"I came to investigate," Gardner said, "and—er—in the language of our friend, the guy got me, too. That's all there is to my being here. I remained tied up until the police arrived, and Riley set me free."

"While you're in this narrative mood, Alden," there was a glint in Harmsworth's eyes, "tell me something—why *did* you pay three thousand for that chest yesterday?"

"I know all about that!" Hanson said promptly. "It reminded him of his grandmother. She used to keep trinkets in it. It was a nice thing for him to do, I thought—hey, what's the matter, Harmsworth, are you choking to death?"

"You know that gadget that flaps in the back of your throat?" Harmsworth spoke in a strained voice, and avoided looking at Asey. "Mine's peculiar. Sometimes it flaps the wrong way. Sorry to upset you with it. So that was your grandmother's chest, Alden! Well, well! A pretty sentiment, a very pretty sentiment indeed, sir! Uh—ready, Mayo?"

"Just one more thing I want to know about." Asey pointed to the two local men who were sitting by the fireplace and who had never once uttered a word. "What're Cobb and Patterson doin' here, Hanson? They weren't bound up too, were they?"

"They're members of the ration board," Hanson explained. "I called 'em here to see what they knew about the fight between Solatia Spry and Miss Pitkin, but they didn't even know there'd *been* a fight. They say as far as they know, Solatia Spry gave Miss Pitkin the same amount of gas she had herself, and neither of 'em rated new good tires."

"I don't know why Solatia never told me that!" Eunice Pitkin said. "I wouldn't have cared if I'd known we had the same. I thought she had more—"

"See here, you!" Hanson broke in. "Don't try edging toward the door, because you can't go! Neither can you, Harmsworth! I want both of you!"

"Hanson, listen to me!" Asey summed up what Cummings had said about Eunice Pitkin's arm. "Besides, they both have witnesses! Now, I haven't had a chance to tell you, but I got bound up here last night myself—hey, Jimmy, you heard me speak to you when I rushed away, didn't you?"

"I never heard nothing," Jimmy said simply. "I just went to sleep."

"Well, anyway," Asey said, "the roper wasn't the same feller who biffed me earlier, Hanson. You might as well resign yourself to the fact that for the last eighteen hours or so, people have been flockin' to this house in droves. So be patient an' reasonable, an' take it easy. Let Miss Pitkin go if she wants, an' let Mr. Harmsworth discuss his business with me!"

Five minutes later, out in Solatia Spry's rose garden, he turned and faced Paul Harmsworth.

"Now," he said briskly, "what about last night? What did you run into, beside flat tires an' Harper's Magazines?"

"Frankly, I came here after Eunice's letters. She's not a bad sort, and I knew she wasn't guilty, but the minute we heard about Solatia, Eunice started going mad with worry about those letters she'd written. She wanted them back."

"Uh-huh. It's an impulse I recognize," Asey said. "Go on. What happened?"

"I was standing out front, wondering if I had the nerve to go on in and take 'em," Harmsworth said, "when someone yelled out *your* name!"

"That was doc, an' I'd just been biffed."

"I didn't linger to find out any details. I didn't want to run into you," Harmsworth said. "I lit out in such a hurry, I lost my bearings entirely. When I finally found my car, the tires were flat. I hailed a man in a truck and asked him to phone Ellen, and then I thought twice, and pumped them up myself."

"Decided it was wiser not to be found around here, huh?"

Harmsworth nodded. "Later, I decided I was a jelly, and that I *would* get those letters, as I'd promised. I came back, and almost stumbled over that cop and Gardner Alden, tied up. I did not," he said, "untie them. Alden dislikes me intensely, and he'd at once have asked why I was there, which would have been a most embarrassing question to answer. And I hesitated to go in and leave them tied up outside, for fear I'd be accused of the tie-up job if anyone came and found me. Then I decided suddenly I was a complete fool, and left."

"Why?"

"It occurred to me that Eunice had an alibi, and that those letters didn't matter a whit. I drove over to the beach," Harmsworth said, "and sat there and tried to think who could have killed Solatia, and why, and why I couldn't figure it out. I can always figure out book murders from the first page! I'm good at them!"

"It's a matter of extraneous odds an' ends," Asey said. "You run into more of 'em this way than you do in books. An' nobody presents you with pointed descriptions. You got to figger out for yourself if the New York lawyer an' his fat sister an' his big-nosed nephew an' the antique lady an' the semi-antique man," Harmsworth chuckled at Asey's description of him, "an' the rich Madisons is all lyin' in whole, or in part, an' if so, which part."

"And the auctioneer," Harmsworth said. "Don't forget the auctioneer, or the rich Madison girl's fiancé. Well, on my way back to the Inn, much later, I ran into the rich Madison girl and her henchman. They were throwing away those Harper's. I tried accusatory tactics, somewhat on the order of Hanson's." He grinned. "They didn't work, as you seem to have discovered. I had the hell of a time getting myself loose, and I decided during the process that I never should have sent my helper back to the city. I decided that even the rankest of amateur detectives needs a stooge to untie him—go on and laugh at me, if you want to, for even attempting to detect!"

"Your night as an amateur," Asey said, "don't sound a whole lot different from mine. We went to the same places an' seen the same people, more or less, only you missed a biffin'. Didn't you find out anythin' nice an' useful?" he added. "I got the impression you had some contribution to make to the cause."

"As I went up the steps to the Inn," Harmsworth said, "I suddenly found myself thinking with startling clarity—at that point, I was so physically tired I could hardly put one foot before the other, but my mind began to click. I realized I'd been confusing myself with issues like trying to get back Eunice's letters to Solatia, when they didn't matter because she had an ironclad alibi. I'd been wasting time asking myself all sorts of impossible questions about the Madisons, and Gardner Alden, and John's fat sister, and that nephew, when *they* were all alibied, just as Eunice and I were."

"What d'you mean, alibied?" Asey asked.

"Why, you see, Mayo, we were in groups, there at the auction. The Madisons came together and sat together near me. Dorking came with a minister, and sat with him. Mrs. Turnover came with another fat lady—I think it was her landlady—and sat with her. I was watching for Alden, and kept him in my sight from the moment he came. I know we were all in our seats some time before the auction began—Sharp made a couple of false starts before he actually got going. And—"

"Tell me," Asey interrupted, "did you happen to see either Gardner Alden or Al Dorking near the sea chest before the sale?"

"Yes, I was going to mention that. I got the impression that Dorking was trying to make Gardner bite at that chest—it's an old technique, you know, pretending you're terribly interested in something to get someone else steamed up into buying it. I do it. Solatia was wonderful at it," Harmsworth said. "She's even caught me. Well, I was curious enough to go take a look inside that chest myself. Nothing in it but books, though. Just books."

"You don't remember just what kind of books, do you?" Asey inquired casually.

"What kind? They were just books, old books. Books aren't my line, you know. I wouldn't have known if they were valuable or not. Now," Harmsworth said, "this is the way the thing hit me last night as I went up the Inn steps. Eunice's tire and phone work would keep Solatia from driving to the auction in her beachwagon, or phoning for help. So she probably walked —she was a walker, too. She could walk my legs off me any day in the week. Always used to remind me," he added reminiscently, "of those pictures you used to see of Englishwomen in the country. You know, tweeds, and stout shoes, and a stick. Brisk and wiry. Now, I know how she could walk, and I know she'd have got to John's long before the intermission. You begin to see my point?"

"Dimly," Asey said. "Go on."

"Say that she got there before the intermission. Now, everyone who might have been involved with her murder was in their seats," Harmsworth said, "from *long* before the *start* of the auction, *until* the intermission. Everyone, that is, but Quinton Sharp, and Chris Bede. Sharp was all over the place—a couple of times he had one of his men take over while he went to hunt up certain things. Bede was all over the place, helping Sharp's men. See? Now, in books—" he hesitated.

"In books what happens?" Asey said.

"Well, in books," Harmsworth said, "the young girl always does crazy things to shield her fiancé, if she thinks he may be suspected. I wondered if Polly Madison wasn't trying to get rid of those Harper's because she thought they might incriminate Bede in some way—after all, Mayo, she couldn't be shielding her mother. She and her mother never stirred from their seats!"

But Polly *had* stirred, Asey thought to himself. Not very long before the intermission, to judge the timing from Gardner Alden's hand-washing episode, Polly had driven clear around the pond to throw away two hampers full of books.

"So," Harmsworth went on, "after thinking that out, I walked down the Inn steps, got into the car, and drove to the Bedes' house. It's on Main Street, two doors below John's, you know. He'd pointed it out to me."

"What was your idea in goin' there?"

"Oh, I had some wild plan of rousing Chris Bede, and shouting accusations at him quickly—funny how that's the first method that occurs to you! I see the fallacy of it now, after Hanson. It's like blitzing with cardboard tanks."

"What time was all this?" Asey asked, more from a sense of duty than because he really cared a great deal about Harmsworth's adventures in detecting.

"Just before dawn. And what d'you know, Mayo? As I drove up the street, I saw Bede's roadster turning into the driveway! Then I watched and saw a light go on—it was one of the ground-floor windows that looks out on the open side porch. I wondered what he'd been up to, and why he was creeping home at that hour, so I sneaked up on the porch and peeked in. He was taking out some papers that he'd apparently buttoned inside his shirt. He put them on the bureau, and then went to bed. After he got to sleep, I made a long reach from the porch to the bureau—I never went in for that sort of thing before, but I know now that I'd make a dandy burglar—and took the papers. Here."

With quiet pride, he drew a sheaf of envelopes from his pocket, and held them out to Asey.

"All those letters in the gray envelopes," he continued, "are acrimonious ration-board items from Mrs. Madison to Solatia, and I don't think they amount to any more than Eunice's bickerings. But that white letter on the bottom is very interesting, and I think it's worth all my effort. Take a look at it. It's a written order from Chris Bede to Solatia, asking her to buy for him at any price John's fish knife—he says she knows the one he means—because he expects he has to report to an Army doctor on the afternoon of the auction, and so won't be able to bid on it himself. He wants the knife in memory of John, with whom he spent so many pleasant days fishing, and whom he loved so much, and all that."

Asey read the letter through thoughtfully.

"Huh!" he said. "More pink sea shells! But Bede didn't have to report yesterday afternoon, an' so he was there at the auction in person. But he didn't bid on the lot that had the knife—Al Dorking or Jennie or someone'd remembered it, if he had. Yup, I wonder if maybe he didn't just swipe that fish knife in memory of his old fishin' companion, before the sale begun."

"That's what I decided he'd done," Harmsworth said. "The motive stuck me for a time, I'll admit."

"Motive?"

"Bede's motive for killing her. Then I decided if you were a penniless second lieutenant marrying into the Madison family, you might want a little cash on hand to hold up your end at the start. And there was John Alden's money, kicking around somewhere. And Solatia was a good friend of John's—and she told me yesterday," Harmsworth said, "that half the world had found an excuse to drop in and ask her if she didn't know where John kept that money. She actually didn't know, so she truthfully couldn't tell anyone. But people felt sure she *did* know, and it irritated them profoundly when she said she didn't."

"When you think it over," Asey said reflectively, "there seems to be a lot more people who wanted that money of John's than people who actually wanted to kill her, don't there? Huh!" he started walking slowly back toward the house, and Harmsworth fell into step beside him. "Tell me, when Solatia didn't come to the auction, why didn't you go after her?"

Harmsworth seemed taken aback by the question. "Why, I kept expecting that she'd come, of course!"

"But," Asey persisted, "if you thought that Gardner Alden or anyone else might be tryin' to keep her away from the auction, an' if she never came, why didn't you go look into the matter? Why didn't you investigate the situation?"

"Remember that *I* was taking an active interest in that auction, too!" Harmsworth told him. "*I* was buying things! *I* had to be there!"

"Uh-huh," Asey said gently, "that's what I was drivin' at."

"But see here, Mayo! Gardner was the man I worried about in connection with her, and he was there in front of my eyes! And—look, you're not insinuating anything about *me,* are you?"

Asey paused by Solatia's beachwagon, and surveyed it for a moment before answering.

"I'm only thinkin'," he leaned over and looked at the milk bottle and the pair of white pumps in the front seat, "that you worried about what Alden might do, an' he claims he worried about what you might do, an' Sharp was worryin' about pretty near everything under the sun, before the auction started. You was all worryin' about Solatia. But none of you cared enough or worried enough to leave, an' go find out what'd become of her, did you, now?"

"All right, I'll admit it!" Harmsworth said. "What d'you think I'm staying in this Godforsaken town for, when I have a million things to do other places? It's because I'm so bitterly ashamed that I didn't go find out what Eunice had done to this beachwagon, and bring Solatia to the auction myself! And seeing this thing through is the only way I can salve my conscience! Look," he went on as Asey started toward the house, "your mentioning Sharp reminds me—Solatia said he'd driven her crazy, asking her where John's money was hidden. And he was *funny* about that chest, Mayo! He didn't want to sell it. He looked furious when it was brought out, and I think he'd have refused Gardner's bid, if he'd dared."

"The price," Asey said, "would've been enough to make anyone look funny. I dare say I'd have looked a little odd myself, if I'd been there."

"But even before Gardner bid, he looked queer—by the way, d'you believe that yarn about Gardner's grandmother? You know," Harmsworth said, "that nearly threw me, when Hanson said that! I've seen Gardner kicking around auctions and sales and dealers' rooms for years, and I'd say that far from feeling any sentiment for his grandmother, he probably stole her cough medicine, regularly."

"I think I'm beginnin' to be convinced," Asey said, "that the old lady kept pink shells in the chest, at least, an' maybe—"

He broke off as he opened the front door of Solatia's house, and found Gardner Alden, Eunice Pitkin, and Hanson, all crowded into the tiny front hall.

"It's really *old* Canton," Eunice was saying, "and the glaze —oh, Mr. Mayo, can you squeeze in? Hello, Paul—that umbrella stand *is* an unusual piece, isn't it? And then that lovely carved teak piece to make the division for canes and umbrellas! Isn't that interesting, Captain Hanson?"

"Yeah," Hanson said. "Yeah, sure is—Asey, what're you going to do now? You're not going!"

"I want to make a few calls," Asey told him. "I'll see you over at my house later. Okay? So long, everybody."

He heard Harmsworth's caustic comment as he strode down the walk toward his roadster.

"Very perfunctory, isn't he?"

"Oh, he gets these ideas," Hanson answered. "He sees something nobody else notices, and off he goes! Sometimes I think he's bats. But the hell of it is, he gets there—"

Hanson was overestimating him, Asey thought with a grin as he drove away.

He hadn't any brilliant and inspired ideas at all.

He simply wanted to see Quinton Sharp!

"I'd ought to have phoned an' seen if he was home yet," Asey murmured. "Oh, but if he was out all mornin', he must be home at his place now!"

But Sharp wasn't at his house, and a brief inspection of his bungalow showed that his bed hadn't been slept in, either.

"Huh!" Asey left the bedroom and returned to look more closely at the disordered mess of papers he'd noticed on the dining-room table.

Then he laughed aloud.

Nothing very fatal could have happened to Sharp, he decided, noting that the morning paper was there in the clutter, and that Sharp had taken time out to do the crossword puzzle!

He poked curiously around the rest of the litter. In addition to Sharp's morning mail, it consisted of a list of John Alden's auction sales, and an insurance inventory, dated several months before, of the contents of John Alden's house.

"Wa-el," Asey said philosophically to himself, "I had the readin' of all this comin' to me sooner or later, an' who knows, maybe it might anyway prove I'm bats, like Hanson seems to think!"

An hour later, having read through both lists four times each, he marched back out to his roadster with a springy step.

The minister next, he decided.

"Maybe books'll be enough in his line," he murmured, "so's if he seen 'em in the sea chest, he'll remember what they *were!"*

Ellen's extra tin of gas gave him such a sense of security that he recklessly took back roads, and wove around the outskirts of the town instead of cutting through to the center by way of the highway and Main Street.

At a turn in one of the lanes, he braked quickly to avoid crashing into a car parked in the ruts directly ahead of him.

He started to lean out and hail the driver, realized the car was empty, and then he jumped out of the roadster and hurried over to the man standing on the edge of a clearing in the pines.

Quinton Sharp, white-faced and trembling, turned and looked at him.

"I knew I couldn't ever get away with it—here!" he thrust into Asey's hand the round coffee tin for which he had apparently been digging a little grave. "Take it!"

"What *is* it?" Asey demanded.

"John's money," Sharp said wearily.

Eight

"John's money—you mean, John *Alden's* money?" Asey demanded.

Sharp nodded, and for a moment, Asey thought the man was going to burst into tears.

"Where'd you *find* it?"

"I didn't *find* it! John *gave* it to me! The week before he died," Sharp said. "He called me in and *gave* it to me! But you won't believe me. Nobody will. John told me to take it to the bank and deposit it at once, and I didn't. Now if I do, you and the rest'll say I found out from Solatia Spry where his hoard was, and then killed her after she told me! And I didn't tell anyone about it because John said not to. And I wish," he concluded unhappily, "I was dead!"

Asey took him by the arm.

"Come over to the car an' sit down, an' pull yourself together, an' let's get to the root of this. Now," he shoved Sharp into the roadster, "why did John give you this money?"

"He said not to tell."

"When he said that, he didn't know that Solatia would be killed, an' that it would matter," Asey said. "Why'd he give it to you?"

"Well, it was really that I shouldn't tell anyone about *him,*" Sharp said. "He told me he'd had a couple of heart attacks, and it was senseless to think you'd live forever, and he'd made his will and knew my brother—he's executor—would carry out his wishes about selling everything, and since I'd probably be the one to auction off the things, he wanted me to promise to do it fair and square."

"What'd he mean by that?"

"John said he thought maybe his brother or his sister, or maybe some dealers or collectors, would try to bribe me— Gardner *did,* too. I told you about that. He offered me a lot more than the five hundred in this tin, Asey," Sharp said. "He offered me a thousand, and would've raised it, too. But I'd told John I'd have an honest auction, and get as much as I could for the Hospital Fund, and I did!"

Asey nodded. "Tell me," he twisted the lid off the coffee tin, and peered curiously at the bills inside. "Huh—wrapped in cellophane! Tell me, when did the possession of this hit you in the face, as you might say?"

"Two seconds after you opened that sea chest yesterday afternoon!" Sharp told him. "It was all I could think of. John's money over in my desk drawer! Honest, I hardly knew what you and that cop asked me! The minute I came home, I wrapped the bills in that cellophane, put 'em in the tin, and took it to the beach and buried it near my fish shack. You know what happened, Asey? Before my back was hardly turned, two little kids came running up and said 'Mister, did you leave this?' "

Asey chuckled.

"I decided," Sharp went on, "to wait till dark before trying to hide it again. About nine o'clock, I went down to the shore again, started to bury it—up came the Coast Guard with one of those guard dogs they have! I damn near lost a leg."

"Ever think of the old dodge," Asey said, "of mailin' it to yourself, day in an' day out?"

"If you mailed a package to yourself more than once in this town, old Walters'd sic Doc Cummings on you!" Sharp said. "Well, then I took the tin home and put it in the bottom of a trunk in my attic. And at ten-thirty last night, out of a clear sky, over comes my brother's wife for a piece of old black lace she needs in a rush for something—and up she goes, straight to that trunk! If you could've seen me, trying to keep her from seeing that tin! Because she'd have grabbed it and opened it before you could say Jack Robinson. She's the kind that has to know what's *in* everything!"

"Wa-el, they claim lightning never strikes twice—"

"That's what *I* thought!" Sharp said. "After she left, I put the tin back into the trunk. I was a happy man. At eleven-thirty, she's back—she takes the *trunk!*"

"Why?" Asey asked weakly.

"Says this costume she's making for her little girl's dancing-class recital needs lots of other things from that trunk, and she can't be bothered making more trips, and the costume has to be finished by noon. I couldn't head her off, Asey!" Sharp said. "I told her I was too tired from the auction to move trunks—so she took it down herself! I couldn't stop her!"

"So," Asey said, "you trailed her home, an' spent the night keepin' guard over the trunk!"

"How'd you know? That's *just* what I did! I guess she was tired herself, because she left the trunk in the car—it was like a steamer trunk—and then she locked the car! And I sat out by their garage till my brother came around seven this morning, unlocked the car, put the trunk on the garage floor, and drove off. And did I get that tin out in a hurry—and I felt awful, Asey, sneaking about with it!"

"An' then you brought it here?"

Sharp shook his head. "I buried it over at the far side of town in a field I own. I went up to town and got the mail and the paper—"

"An' brought 'em home," Asey said, "an' done the crossword while you had some coffee. I know, I been to your house. Then what?"

"I set out to see you—Asey, you know what was happening

in that field when I passed by? The Army'd come, and men were digging fox holes and slit trenches—I'd said they could, but it was so long ago, I'd forgot!"

"So you dug up the tin again?"

"Right in the middle of a mock war! This," Sharp waved toward the clearing, "was the end! I gave up, here, when you came! Now, what're you going to do with me?"

"Oh, I believe you—don't look so stunned! You couldn't make up a story like that! An' you couldn't lose so much weight over night just from actin'," Asey said. "You've dropped ten pounds since yesterday. Now, tell me things, quick. What was in the trunk you threw in with Mrs. Madison's Hitchcock chairs?"

"Old bound magazines. Harper's, I think. Nobody'd buy either them or the old trunk separate, so I threw 'em at her, and got a good thirty dollars out of her."

"Fine," Asey said. "Now, that fish knife of John's—"

"My God!" Sharp said. "Was that knife—was that *his?* Asey, I been so worked up about the money, I never thought about that knife! I gave it away—"

He stopped short.

"Who to?"

"Well, I gave it to Chris Bede," Sharp said slowly. "He told me before the auction he'd top any bid on it, and I told him he could have it. He and Polly Madison were nice to John, you know. Polly drove him around a lot, and Bede went fishing and sailing with him."

"Did you give it into his hand," Asey said, "or tell him to take it?"

"Told him to help himself—I bet someone beat him to it, Asey, if it's that knife that killed her! Chris is all right. Nice fellow."

"Uh-huh. Now, Sharp, this is the one I really care about. What kind of books were the books in the sea chest?"

"What kind? Why, old books!"

"What *kind?*" Asey repeated. "Old novels, or old bound magazines, or what?"

"Why, I don't know," Sharp said. "Just old books—I had 'em out, too. I looked around inside the chest to see if it might have a false bottom, or something, where John might've hidden his money. That's why I was so surprised when Gardner bid so much for that chest. *I* knew there was only books in it! Just books."

"Think," Asey said. "What *kind?*"

"Old books," Sharp said helplessly. "Like old schoolbooks. Old books in dark cloth bindings. They *must* have been old schoolbooks!"

"How many?" Asey was thinking back to Polly Madison and the hampers of old schoolbooks that had gone into the pond.

"Oh, sixty-seven. I don't know, Asey. The chest was full."

"One more thing. Did you see Solatia at the auction?"

"I keep thinking I did," Sharp said, "and then I think I didn't, that I only *thought* I did!"

"Yes, or no?"

"I guess no."

Asey thought for a moment. "Sharp, what'd keep you from goin' to an auction? I don't mean how could you be stopped by someone, but what'd have kept you, yourself, from goin' yesterday, say?"

"Gee, I don't know! Only thing ever made me hesitate," Sharp said, "was once when I tore my pants. But I pinned 'em up with safety pins, and got a big laugh. That what you mean?"

"Wa-el, I don't know's it'd apply to the person I was thinkin' of. Did you check your sales with John's inventory?"

"About half. That money," Sharp said, "has taken up a lot of my time!"

"Anythin' missin' as far's you got?"

Sharp shook his head. "Chris helped me keep sales, and he was pretty accurate. You think anything *is* missing, or got missed at the sale?"

"Was Solatia," Asey countered with another question, "known as a great walker, would you say?"

"Sure, she was always tramping around. She was a great golfer, you know, too. Sometimes she'd carry a golf club with her when she walked, and whack a ball along."

"Huh! Who'd you say John might've given money to, if he thought he was seriously ill?"

"Maybe Solatia, maybe Chris, or the Madisons, maybe—oh," Sharp said, "he had a lot of friends around town. You got an idea, Asey? You look funny."

"I feel funny. Sharp, do you trust me?"

"You ask the damnedest things! Sure, I trust you."

"Lend me this tin, an' the money?"

"Sure," Sharp said. "Take it. Why?"

"I'm thinkin' of promotin' a treasure hunt," Asey said, "an' I like authentic props. Hang around your house. I may phone you an invitation later, after I've chatted with the minister."

"The *minis*ter?"

"I'm pinnin' my hopes on him," Asey said. "Now, go get your car out of my way—an' promise me somethin', Sharp. Promise me you'll never sell another lot of books that you don't look at each an' every title. This way's too hard."

"But what difference do the *titles* of those books make?" Sharp demanded.

"All the difference in the world—never mind movin', after all. I'll go the other way, I think," Asey said. "Don't look so confused. Next time you dig up this tin, you can keep it, but you'll please not mention it till then!"

He found Chris Bede sitting on the front steps of his house on Main Street.

"Hi, Asey!" he said cheerfully, as he limped down the walk to the roadster. "I've been waiting for you—*did* you swipe the letters from me last night?"

"No. *Did* you get the knife?" Asey returned.

"I went for it, but it'd gone. I was too busy to tell Sharp—I thought it would probably turn up in some other lot."

"Why'd you tie me up? In fact," Asey said, "what got into you last night?"

Chris shook his head. "Mind if I sit in the roadster with you? I'm paying for my activities today, right through the ankle— well, Asey," he sat down and lighted a cigarette, "it began with that cop. He started to wave a gun at me, and habit was too strong. I automatically got him. Then Gardner Alden appeared, and what could I do? I had to take him. And then you! I recognized you, but at that point, I certainly wasn't going to untie you and say gee, I was sorry, I'd just come to steal some letters, and I hadn't *really* got the knife that killed Solatia, it only *seemed* so!"

"I see your point," Asey said. "Tell me, what in time did you even bother tryin' to get them letters back for? What come over you, an' Polly Madison, an' her mother—strewin' books around, an' hidin' duck decoys, an' all!"

"Hasn't anyone told—" Chris paused and drew a long breath. "No, I can see they haven't! And it *would* look silly, I suppose, if you didn't know. It's—er—about the sea chest."

"What about it?"

"I could wish," Chris said, "that it wasn't me who had to break this to you, even gently. Perhaps I'd better give you a brief résumé of the terrain. The auction's over. Everyone's running around wildly with a lot of stuff. I'm running around with Mrs. Madison's priceless china in one hand, and a rabbit hutch in the other, and two lobster pots on top of my head. Sharp's been called to the phone across the street, at Whittaker's, because Gardner Alden is using John's phone for a long-distance call. People are asking me where is their blue vase. And—er—"

"An' what?"

"Two of Sharp's feeble-minded boys stop me and say where shall they put the sea chest that Mr. Alden paid so much for. After I tell them where I'd like to put them, I say, 'Put it in the beachwagon!' I mean, Sharp's beachwagon. I point to it with my third hand. They go away. Someone else asks me where is their breadbox and did I see a little lost girl. Polly Madison asks me if I'll drive the first load home while she and her mother stand guard over the rest. She says Charles will help me. Charles cannot be found. Someone wants to know if I've seen an and-iron. You're following all this closely, I hope?"

"Sometimes," Asey said, "I get this dreamy feelin' that I actually *went* to that auction! Go on."

"Polly says Charles is lost, but that her mother is guarding things and will doubtless locate Charles. Polly says she and I will drive the first load home. We start off. We go about a mile. It's been a long time since I've seen Polly alone. I stop the car."

"Uh-huh."

"We are rudely brought back to earth by another beachwagon cutting across our bows. It's Sharp's beachwagon. It's driven by Al Dorking. Al wants to know what we mean, driving off with his uncle's chest. I say he must be after two other people. He gets out, I get out, and by God, there *is* his uncle's chest in our beachwagon!" Chris paused. "You mean, nobody's even hinted at this?"

"It's a new angle," Asey said. "A very interestin' angle, I might add."

"The Madisons and I," Chris said, "felt it would fascinate the average cop. Well, Al and I put the chest into Sharp's beachwagon. I apologize for Sharp's feeble-minded boys who made the error, and Polly and I drive on. Later, we hear what happened to Solatia. Polly remembers the books she threw in the pond. I remember the knife I didn't get. Charles says if anyone accuses the Madam or Miss Polly or me, he'll say *he* done it. Mrs. Madison says Polly and I have our life before us, Charles can't make any more sacrifices for the Madisons, and she'll say *she* did it. Polly and I say neither of 'em'll do any such thing. *We* will. We were pretty dramatic there, for a while."

"I wonder," Asey said thoughtfully, "if there's anythin' more disarmin' than nice, gay, pleasant people like you an' the Madisons, Chris? When the Alden family talk about themselves an' each other, it's family snapshots that accent everybody's faults. You an' the Madisons—an' Charles—are just cabinet photographs."

"I know. Nice people *are* more suspicious and sinister than anybody else, aren't they?" Chris said. "Having more imagination, they're capable of more. More villainy, that is. I tried to work up some villainous deductions I could hang around Al Dorking's neck, after figuring Solatia might have been killed after the auction. But they didn't work. They backfired, in fact."

Asey wanted to know what he was talking about.

"I hunted up Gardner Alden, yesterday evening," Chris said. "Got him as he was going into the movies—odd pictures for him to see, too. Two-gun Blaney and some slapstick. He told me when he'd got through his long-distance call, after the auction, he found Sharp, who'd got through his call, and the two of them went for Sharp's beachwagon, intending to drive it and the chest to your house. They found from one of the feeble-minded boys that Dorking had driven off in it, after us, and so they at once took another car and put out after Al—I gathered that Gardner doesn't waste any affection on his nephew, and thought he'd been trying to steal the chest. Gardner and Sharp caught up with Al just two seconds after he'd left Polly and me, with the sea chest safe and sound in the back of Sharp's beachwagon. They fol—"

"Whoa up!" Asey said. "How'd Gardner know that Al had left you just two seconds before?"

"I asked him that, too. He knew," Chris said, "because he and Sharp saw us as we drove off. And that fouled my dandy idea that Solatia had possibly been killed after the auction, not before, and that Al Dorking had done it. Because Gardner and Sharp followed Al all the way to your house. Closely. Gardner wasn't convinced till he talked with Al at your place that Al was acting in his interests, and not with any fell idea of swiping the chest."

"So the other car in my yard," Asey said, "was what Gardner an' Sharp come in, not Al, an' the other was Mrs. Turnover's. Huh!"

"Well, if you should find out definitely that Solatia was killed after the auction, Asey, don't bother with Al. He hadn't the time. Just come after Polly and me. We did."

"How much time did you have, exactly," Asey inquired, "after you parked, an' before Al come?"

"Oh, I don't know, Asey, I honestly don't! Long enough to have killed Solatia if she'd been handy—though I *can't* imagine what she'd have been doing on the East Weesit road if she hadn't come to the auction! And long enough to have ripped the books out of the chest, and put her in, I suppose. But if you accuse us, you'll have Charles and Mrs. Madison in your hair. And if you knew 'em as well as I do, you'd shy from the situation."

"Why would you think that you an' Polly might be accused?" Asey asked curiously. "I mean, I grant you the opportunity of killin' her, in a broad sense, but why? You two ever have any quarrel with Solatia?"

"Solatia," Chris said with a frown, "had a habit of taking a very personal interest in Polly's love life. And mine. Before I went into the Army, Polly and I weren't speaking, all because of some gossip Solatia started. That sort of thing couldn't have bothered us now, but it rankled for a long time, and it's a good motive on paper. Kidding aside, Asey—"

"Yes?"

"If you do have to land on us, pick me, will you?" Chris said seriously. "After all, I was around that chest more than anyone. I used to sit on it and drink coca-colas when I got tired of moving rabbit hutches and lobster pots. And you can't prove I *didn't* take that knife!"

"True. Chris, what would have kept you from goin' to the auction? I don't mean like your havin' to report to a doctor, but why wouldn't you have wanted to go?"

"Mostly the rather repulsive thought," Chris said, "of seeing John's things picked over by a lot of unpleasant people. That really *would* have kept me away, I think, if I hadn't felt that Mrs. Madison was going to run into a lot of lusty competition, and ought to have some other male than Charles around to keep a watchful eye over her, and see she didn't get gypped."

"You think maybe that repulsive thought of people pickin' over John's things might've kept Solatia away?"

"Never!" Chris said simply.

"I see. Well," Asey started the car, "you run along, an' ride herd over the Madisons for me, please. Don't let 'em throw anythin' else away anywhere. In strictest confidence, I'll tell you that John's money has been found—"

"No! No! Who found it?"

"Wa-el," Asey said, "it ain't literally been brought to light, but I know where it will be found." Which was true enough, he thought. He intended to lay it away himself. "I'm goin' to dig it up later. I'll let you know when."

"Gee, I had a whack at trying to locate that, myself," Chris said. "The Madisons don't seem to mind my being poor, but I feel the difference in our surtax brackets very keenly, and I couldn't help thinking what a difference some loose cash would make! Er—I gather you're holding us in abeyance, Asey. Could I," he hesitated as he got out of the car, "could I ask who's next on your list?"

"The minister," Asey said. "So long!"

But Dr. Cummings hailed him before he reached the end of Main Street.

"What's new, Asey? How're you doing? Got anywhere?"

"Wa-el, yes an' no, as you might say," Asey told him. "A few miscellaneous items has got unearthed."

"Like what?" Cummings got into the roadster and sat down. "Tell me!"

"Wa-el, seems Miss Pitkin was tryin' to steal letters she'd written Solatia in a ration-board row, an' Hanson caught her in the act. And Harmsworth stole letters from Chris Bede that Chris had stolen from Solatia's last night—Chris was the rope-trick boy. Seems Chris longed for John Alden's fish knife—in a nice, sentimental way, like Gardner's pink shells—an' Sharp says he gave the knife to Chris, but Chris says the knife was gone before he got it. Seems Harmsworth always solves book murders, an' don't like the way you can't figger this. An' it seems Quinton Sharp spent the night tryin' to hide a tin no-body'd let him hide, an' the tin was full of John Alden's money, an'—"

He paused as Cummings got out of the roadster, crossed the street to his own sedan, removed his car keys and his ubiquitous black bag, and got back into the roadster.

"All right, let's get Sharp!" he said.

"Let's not." Asey explained the matter. "Then I found out that the sea chest hadn't come direct to my house—want to hear about that?"

"All right, let's get Dorking," Cummings said when Asey concluded his recital.

"Nope, doc, he didn't have time, an' besides, Gardner an' Sharp followed him all the way."

"Why in the world didn't Sharp, or Gardner, or anyone tell you about it?"

"Wa-el, I didn't ask 'em," Asey said, "an' I don't s'pose they

felt it mattered. If you assumed she was killed at the start of the
auction, so she wouldn't get a chance to bid, then what happened to the chest later probably didn't seem important."

"D'you mean to tell me that the moving of that sea chest
has *no* bearing on this case," Cummings demanded, "and that
you have merely told me all about it in order to add to my state
of confusion?"

"Nope, it has some bearin'," Asey said. "Polly an' Chris was
parked there on the East Weesit road, an' I don't think they
know what might've gone on at the tail of that beachwagon—"

"I suppose Solatia Spry walked out of the woods," Cummings said with elaborate irony, "and was killed there behind
the beachwagon—oh, Asey, sometimes I think your mind is
faltering! *What* would Solatia be doing there? Who, with the
world before them, and specifically the East Weesit pine woods,
would follow Solatia and kill her behind an inhabited beachwagon, remove a chest from inside it—no, Asey! No!"

"Sounds crazy, don't it?" Asey agreed. "Doc, why wouldn't
you have gone to the auction, if you were Solatia?"

"I *would* have gone if I'd been her! Why," Cummings said
irritably, "do you ask idiotic questions like that of me? I don't
know why I wouldn't have gone, if I'd been *her!* Why wouldn't
you do something that was *your* business that *you* set out to do?"

"I s'pose," Asey said, "if I was settin' out on behalf of Porter
Tanks, an' I got a wire from Bill Porter—Doc!"

Before Cummings had a chance to open his mouth, the roadster was parked in front of the station, and Asey was halfway
into the telegraph office.

"And I suppose," Cummings greeted him when he finally
emerged, "that you've found a lovely telegram from Bill Porter
to Solatia, saying not to make tanks—I mean, not to go to the
auction?"

"Nope, but I found a lovely telegram to Solatia from Maxim

Harvey, doc," Asey said. "That's her rich client in San Francisco. It came yesterday around one o'clock."

"*No!* What'd it say?"

" 'Make no purchacheth Alden thale. Planth changed. Letter followeth.' "

"*What!*"

"The telegraph girl, who's replacin' her brother in the service, is Miss Eunice Pitkin's kid sister, doc, an' she lisps. 'Make no purchases Alden sale. Plans changed. Letter follows.' "

"I get it!" Cummings said. "I get it! Solatia's been bragging that she could top anyone's bid. Then she gets this wire! Hm. *I* wouldn't have wanted to go to the auction, then, if I'd been in her boots! *I'd* have gone for a nice long walk by myself!"

"An' Solatia got the wire," Asey said. "It was put right into her hand. Miss Pitkin's sister says she tried to phone it, but Solatia's phone seemed to be out of order—Miss Pitkin herself havin' cut the phone wire. So she planned to take it over to the auction an' give it to Solatia in person, but then she saw Solatia walkin' by, an' went out an' handed it to her. Uh-huh, doc, that's what I think Solatia did, too. I think she took a nice long walk by herself. I think I would have. I don't think I'd have enjoyed goin' to the auction an' not biddin', not after all the squabbles an' such. Huh."

"Huh, what?" Cummings asked.

"I was thinkin', if you wanted stuff at an auction that you couldn't afford to buy, an' if you was sore with a rival lady dealer you think is goin' to get the stuff, an' besides you hate her because she won't give you tires an' gas, an' if you was sore enough to flatten her tires, an' cut her phone wire—now, I wonder, doc!"

"Asey, d'you mean you think that telegram isn't genuine? You think it's a fake?"

"An' if you had a sister who worked in the telegraph office—

of course," Asey said, "Harmsworth has connections all over the country. So does Alden. I dare say the Madisons an' Mrs. Turnover most probably could think of someone they know in San Francisco who'd send a telegram for 'em. Most probably you an' I could. Let's look into it!"

When he came out of the telegraph office an hour later, Asey found the doctor holding an impromptu clinic from the seat of the roadster.

"There," Cummings said, "that's all! Rest of you'll have to come to the office and get stuck with a bill—what'd you find out, Asey?"

"Maxim Harvey never sent that wire," Asey started the car, "but it's a genuine wire in that it got sent from San Francisco. Someone's got a friend—"

Cummings had no opportunity to ask who the someone was until they drew up, five minutes later, in front of the parsonage.

"Who—"

But Asey had jumped out and was making a beeline for the minister, hoeing in his garden.

"I wonder," Cummings heard him say, "if you could tell me what kind of books was in the chest, the sea chest from John Alden's that we found Miss Spry's body in later?"

"Why, yes, Asey. I regretted Mr. Alden's bidding that large sum, you know. I thought," the minister said, "I might offer a few dollars—"

"They *was* hymnbooks?"

"Yes. Old, but we could have used them. John Alden's grandfather was a deacon, and I suppose those books must have come into his possession some time, perhaps when the new church was built."

"I understand," Asey said, "that there's been some agitation about the church's havin' a new coat of paint?"

"Why--why, yes. Er—"

"Have it painted," Asey said, "an' charge it to me. I'll throw in all the new hymnbooks you want, too. Thank you, sir. Come on, doc!"

"That poor man," Cummings said, "will head the line in my office tonight, still suffering from slight shock! Where now, Asey?"

"I'm goin' to drop you off back at your car—"

"Oh, no, you're not!" Cummings said. "I refuse to move! I know you've got this thing, and I'm not going to miss the finale!"

"I'm goin' to drop you off at your car," Asey repeated, "an' as you ply your rounds, you're goin' to spread the news for me to a few selected folks that I've found where John's money is."

"You don't know where that money is, Asey Mayo!"

"The money that's goin' to be found is John's," Asey said, "an' I know where it is, doc; it's right here with me! I really want you to do some news spreadin', please. An' I don't know how long I'll be over at the Madisons'."

"What d'you want with them?"

"I got to find somethin'," Asey said.

"What?"

Jennie informed the doctor that it was golf clubs, when he put the question to her later in the afternoon, outside John Alden's house.

"He come back home with the Madison girl's golf clubs. I don't know *why,*" she said. "He wouldn't tell me. *I* don't know what he's up to! He's got all that crowd in there!"

"Who?" Cummings asked.

"Oh, both the Madisons, and Chris Bede, and that fat Mrs. Turnover's runnin' around like a hen with her head cut off," Jennie said. "And Al Dorking, and Hanson, and his cops, and Eunice Pitkin, and that bald Harmsworth, and Clinton Sharp and his brother, and that bandy-legged chauffeur of the Madisons'—Charles. And Gardner Alden."

"What're they doing?"

"Well, Asey's got these directions he says are for findin' John Alden's money," Jennie said, "but they're *not!* He made 'em up himself, and I seen him sittin' at the desk figgerin' 'em out. I tell you, *I* don't know what he's up to, but *I'm* not goin' to spend a hot afternoon runnin' around pretendin' to dig up money he wrote the directions for findin'!"

"I knew he had some scheme up his sleeve," Cummings said, "but I don't get this!"

"They're all pacin' around so solemn!" Jennie said. "*They* don't know it's all a fraud! So many feet from the junction of this eave and that drainpipe. So many," she broke off to wave at Al Dorking, who had appeared at the front door, "so many inches from something else! It's all nonsense—you suppose Asey sent Dorking for us? Maybe we'd better go in!"

They entered to the accompaniment of shouts, yells, and shrill screams.

"What's the matter?" Cummings grabbed Charles as he ran through the hall.

"I don't know, sir! We was out helping Mr. Mayo pace off distances, and then Mrs. Turnover yelled—"

"What for?"

"She yelled to her nephew. Al Dorking. Mr. Mayo'd just called out something, and then Mrs. Turnover yelled and told him to run through the shed and get away—and there was an awful crash—"

Cummings and Jennie raced for the back of the house.

They paused in the doorway of the shed.

Before them, with one leg through the floor, was Al Dorking. He could neither stand nor sit, and Cummings judged with professional accuracy that the fellow was in agony.

In his right hand, he held a cane.

"That's John Alden's cane!" Cummings said involuntarily.

"You knew he had one?" Asey was at his elbow. "You knew, doc, an' you never told me? Oh, doc! Keep still, Dorking! Don't wriggle, or you'll go through more. We'll get you out, an' prob-ably your leg ain't broken, it just feels that way. First, give me that cane," Asey tiptoed with caution across the shed floor and snatched the cane from Al's hand, "an' then let's remove your gun. There! That's why I done this so elaborate; I didn't want you to let loose reckless with that gun!"

"Wasn't I fine?" Mrs. Turnover was glowing with pride. "Wasn't I *fine* when I yelled out for him to run through the shed because then you couldn't catch him? Didn't I yell that out *beauti*fully?"

"That was first-rate," Asey said, "an' well timed, too. Just like I told you, three seconds after I yelled at him to stop. Yessir, you was fine!"

"*I* knew the floor out here was rotten," Mrs. Turnover told Jennie. "I knew, because I started to go through, myself. I told Mr. Mayo about it. And he was *so* smart, he said that was the way we'd get him! He said he was just casually going to leave the other cane *in*doors, and we'd all go *out*doors, and pretend to hunt John's money, and then he rather thought someone would sneak in and try to steal the other cane, see?"

"No," Cummings said, "I don't see any of it—Asey, we've got to get him out. That board's acting like a pincers. His circulation—"

"Because of the *money* in the other cane," Mrs. Turnover continued. "And it all happened as Mr. Mayo thought it would! He'd left the cane so he could see if anyone touched it, and when Al took it, he yelled out what was Al doing, and to stop! And then *I* yelled out for Al to run through the shed because then he couldn't be caught—I *really* did that *beau*tifully! Al thought I was honestly trying to help him escape, and so he ran here, and went right through the floor, just as Mr. Mayo planned! Of course," she added confidentially to Jennie, "*I* really set Mr. Mayo on his trail, you know. *I* told him about Al's debts, and how he always wanted money. I *told* him his mother was always afraid he'd come to a bad end. You might really say I was the *inspiration* for all this!"

"Bede, Hanson," Cummings said, "grab that board easy and see if you can lift it without its digging into him—watch out you don't go through, too. I suppose, Asey, he was the biffer, too?"

"Uh-huh. When he told me he'd been in the Army," Asey said, "he forgot to add he'd been a commando—grab him, Riley, as they lift."

Cummings sighed as Dorking was lifted up. "Charles, go get my black bag from my car. Sometimes this gets so tiresome, Asey. You catch, I patch!"

An hour later, in Asey's kitchen, Jennie said she still didn't understand everything.

"I mean, I know he was crazy for money, and in debt, and had tried to find John's—but why'd he kill Solatia Spry?"

"Dorking was sore because he couldn't find the money," Asey said, "an' he was sore with Solatia because he thought she knew where it was, an' wouldn't tell him. An' he was sorer with her because just as he thought he was beginnin' to make some headway with Polly Madison, Solatia told Polly he was a heel, an' Polly stopped seein' even what little she had been seein' of him. So he thought he'd get even with Solatia, an' had a friend of his send her a fake telegram from her rich client, sayin' not to buy him anythin' at the Alden auction."

"Did he admit that?" Cummings asked.

"Yes. He wouldn't tell Hanson who sent the telegram for him—said the friend thought it was a joke, and didn't know anythin' about it. Anyway, he felt he'd paid her back plenty, an' when he spotted her on the East Weesit road, after retrievin' the chest—which was full of hymnbooks up to that point— why, he stopped an' asked what happened she hadn't come to the auction?"

"But you told me Dorking didn't have any time to kill her!" Cummings protested. "You said people were watching him every minute, from the time he got the chest till he got over here!"

"Gardner told Chris Bede he saw the Madisons' beachwagon leavin', an' Al turnin' Sharp's beachwagon around to start back," Asey said. "He seen Al turnin', but it wasn't the Madisons' beachwagon departin' in the distance. It was somebody else's. Gardner thought so, because he asked Al later if that was the Madisons' beachwagon he'd seen leavin', an' naturally Al said yes. It'd have been awful silly of him to say anythin' else, at that point. Anyway, Al told Solatia it was too bad she stayed away from the auction, an' I guess from the way he said it, Solatia had a sudden flash of suspicion. She asked if he sent that telegram, and he said he couldn't imagine what she meant. She was sure she'd been tricked by him, then, an' raised her cane to strike him. And Al grabbed the cane—an' that's why she got killed."

"Why?" Jennie said.

"Because the cane come apart, an' it was full of money," Asey said. "John Alden's hidden money. You see, John had given Solatia that cane before he died—but she never knew there was money hid inside it! Dorking admitted it was as much of a shock to her as it was to him. Only he acted. He grabbed the fish knife he'd swiped before the auction, an' killed her. He wanted the money that bad. His debts, it turns out," Asey added, "was considerable more than the picayune little sum he told me."

"And then he took out the books, and put her in the chest —why in blazes did you make such a fuss about the *titles* of those books?" Cummings asked.

"Wa-el, first off," Asey said, "I wondered how she got into the chest, an' then I wondered who put her in, an' then I wondered who took the books out before they put her in—"

"All I asked about were the titles," Cummings said. "Not the mental processes of your sometimes unfathomable mind!"

"N'en I wondered what you'd do with the books," Asey continued calmly, "an' it occurred to me it made a powerful lot of difference what *kind* of books you had to dispose of. Novels would be hard. You couldn't just leave sixty-odd novels by the side of the road, stickin' out like a sore thumb. I thought it over, an' I decided hymnbooks would be the easiest kind of books I knew to get rid of."

"Why?"

"Because you'd just leave 'em in a church," Asey said. "No fuss, no effort, no bother, no burnin', no drownin'—just take 'em to the nearest church an' stack 'em neatly under a rear pew. That's just what Dorking did, too. He marched twenty feet up the road to the little church on the East Weesit lane, an' stacked 'em under a rear pew—Hanson found 'em, before I come home."

"But that chest was locked at the sale!" Jennie said. "And *think* of the awful time you had gettin' it open, an' findin' a key to fit!"

"But Dorking *had* the key," Asey said. "That's one little fact he kept from me. See, he thought he'd inveigled his uncle into buyin' the chest, an' he wanted to be around to laugh when Gardner opened it. So he kept the key. He had it with him. An'—"

"Did he?" Cummings interrupted. "I mean, did he inveigle Gardner into thinking there was money hidden in the chest, or was that pink shell yarn genuine?"

"Genuine. But Dorking didn't know Gardner'd been sufferin' a streak of sentiment. Dorking thought he'd played a fine joke on him."

"Hm," Cummings said. "If he wanted to give his uncle a start when the chest was finally opened, he certainly succeeded! Rather clever, wasn't he? He was alibied before the auction by the minister, and after it by what was apparently the Madisons' beachwagon just leaving him. And I suppose the chance of those hymnbooks being found very soon was reasonably remote."

"I don't think," Asey said, "I'd ever have considered huntin' John Alden's books in the East Weesit church, myself. No more than I'd hunt decoys in a fillin' station—"

"How'd you know about the canes, anyway?" Jennie demanded.

"Oh, I looked in Solatia's beachwagon and seen a pair of pumps in the seat—not old pumps you'd be takin' to a cobbler's, but new pumps you might have put on to go to an auction with. I remembered when we found her, she had on stout walkin' shoes. An' Harmsworth said somethin' about her stridin' around with a stick, an' then I noticed a lot of canes in her hall, in a Canton stand. An' then I run through an inventory of John's things, an' come on an item that'd been crossed out. It was a pair of silver-headed canes. Seemed like John had had the canes when the inventory was made, an' then he'd got rid of 'em, an' crossed 'em off the list. He'd done it himself, because he'd initialed the crossin' out. I wondered if he'd give the canes away, an' thought of Solatia as a likely person to give 'em to. An' then," Asey said, "it occurred to me that everyone had thought of every conceivable place an' possession of his that might contain money, but nobody'd thought of canes!"

"Well, who *would* think of 'em!" Jennie demanded.

"I would," Asey said. "Sooner than secret drawers, or the backs of pictures. Anyway, I wondered about 'em, an' I wondered what could've become of Solatia Spry's cane, if she usually carried one when she walked. An' it all begun to fit together. I figgered she'd been carryin' one, it was one John gave her, an' then because it was all conjecturin', I decided to locate the other cane, if I could, an' waggle it around as bait.

An' Al Dorking bit, as I guessed he would. That's why he was at Solatia's last night, you know, doc. Tryin' to find if she had the second cane."

"I know you said he was the biffer—but look, we *saw* him coming out of the movies!"

"Uh-huh, he did what I thought Gardner'd done, he went in an' come out—he'd seen the pictures before, an' could discuss 'em fluently, as he did. Dorking knew," Asey said, "that there was two canes, an' havin' got the contents of one, he wanted the contents of the other. That's why he snuggled up to Mrs. Turnover with directions about that chimney box that he knew wouldn't pan out, because he'd already looked there. He wanted to get into his aunt's good graces, an' get her confidence—he suspected maybe *she* might have the other cane, see? An' when I dropped in on 'em, Dorking realized he'd done a mighty bright thing."

"Why so?" Jennie asked.

"He had the protective colorin' of a fat lady who was funny," Asey said. "It threw him into a completely different light. He was the fat lady's nephew. An' what your fat aunt accuses you of is funny. That's all there is to it, an' I'm hungry enough to eat a horse, Jennie."

"But what about the other cane?" Jennie said. "Where'd you get that?"

"John gave it to Polly Madison, like I suspected," Asey said. "But lackin' a cane rack or an umbrella stand, she'd stuck it into her golf bag an' forgot about it. She never dreamed there was money in it. Dorking probably looked around at the Madisons', too," he added, "but Polly said it'd slipped her mind. She never spoke of it, an' he didn't spot it among the golf clubs, which was probably just as well for Polly—stay an' have some clam chowder with us, doc. Clams ain't rationed, an' Jennie'll probably let you have all you want. She—Jennie, are those hot biscuits?"

"What do they look like?"

Asey eyed her. "Clam chowder, hot biscuits, strawberry short-cake! Jennie, I feel a touch. What's comin'?"

Jennie said with asperity that she couldn't imagine what he meant.

"It's just a regular meal, that's all, and it only happens just by the merest chance to be all the things you like! I haven't any ulterior motives! And *don't* you dare say it's because I want to be taken to the auction in Orleans tomorrow, because it is *not,* and I never mentioned it or brought the matter up!" she paused. "I don't suppose you *would* think of going, would you?"

"I'll take you," Asey said when he and Cummings had stopped laughing, "but I wouldn't think of going myself, Jennie! I've had all the going I want. I'm gone!"

Available from Foul Play Press

The perennially popular Phoebe Atwood Taylor whose droll "Codfish Sherlock," Asey Mayo, and "Shakespeare lookalike," Leonidas Witherall, have been eliciting guffaws from proper Bostonian Brahmins for over half a century.

Asey Mayo Cape Cod Mysteries

The Annulet of Gilt	*288 pages*	*$5.95*
The Asey Mayo Trio	*256 pages*	*$5.95*
Banbury Bog	*176 pages*	*$4.95*
The Cape Cod Mystery	*192 pages*	*$5.95*
The Criminal C.O.D.	*288 pages*	*$5.95*
The Crimson Patch	*240 pages*	*$5.95*
The Deadly Sunshade	*297 pages*	*$5.95*
Death Lights a Candle	*304 pages*	*$5.95*
Diplomatic Corpse	*256 pages*	*$5.95*
Figure Away	*288 pages*	*$5.95*
Going, Going, Gone	*218 pages*	*$5.95*
The Mystery of the Cape Cod Players	*272 pages*	*$5.95*
The Mystery of the Cape Cod Tavern	*283 pages*	*$5.95*
Octagon House	*304 pages*	*$5.95*
Out of Order	*280 pages*	*$5.95*
The Perennial Boarder	*288 pages*	*$5.95*
Proof of the Pudding	*192 pages*	*$5.95*
Sandbar Sinister	*296 pages*	*$5.95*
Spring Harrowing	*288 pages*	*$5.95*
Three Plots for Asey Mayo	*320 pages*	*$6.95*

"Surely, under whichever pseudonym, Mrs. Taylor is the mystery equivalent of Buster Keaton."   —Dilys Winn

Leonidas Witherall Mysteries (by "Alice Tilton")

Beginning with a Bash	*284 pages*	*$5.95*
File for Record	*287 pages*	*$5.95*
Hollow Chest	*284 pages*	*$5.95*
The Left Leg	*275 pages*	*$5.95*

Available from bookshops, or by mail from the publisher: The Countryman Press, Box 175, Woodstock, Vermont 05091-0175. Please include $2.50 for shipping your order. Visa or Mastercard orders ($20.00 minimum), call 802-457-1049, 9-5 EST, Monday–Friday.

Available from Foul Play Press

The perennially popular Phoebe Atwood Taylor whose droll "Codfish Sherlock," Asey Mayo, and "Shakespeare look-alike," Leonidas Witherall, have been eliciting guffaws from proper Bostonian Brahmins for over half a century.

"Headed for a lazy week at the shore? Pull up a sand dune and tuck into one of Phoebe Atwood Taylor's charming Cape Cod mysteries. These period how-dunnits recall simpler, more carefree times, and sparkle with the Yankee wit and salty idiom of Asey Mayo, a local handyman who knows something about police work and everything about everybody's business."

– Marilyn Stasio, *Mystery Alley*

Asey Mayo Cape Cod Mysteries

The Annulet of Gilt	288 pages	$5.95
The Asey Mayo Trio	256 pages	$5.95
Banbury Bog	176 pages	$5.95
The Cape Cod Mystery	192 pages	$5.95
The Criminal C.O.D.	288 pages	$5.95
The Crimson Patch	240 pages	$5.95
The Deadly Sunshade	297 pages	$5.95
Death Lights a Candle	304 pages	$5.95
Diplomatic corpse	256 pages	$5.95
Going, Going, Gone	218 pages	$5.95
The Mystery of the Cape Cod Players	272 pages	$5.95
The Mystery of the Cape Cod Tavern	283 pages	$5.95
Out of Order	280 pages	$5.95
The Perennial Boarder	288 pages	$5.95
Sandbar Sinister	296 pages	$5.95
Spring Harrowing	288 pages	$5.95

"Surely, under whichever pseudonym, Mrs. Taylor is the mystery equivalent of Buster Keaton."   – Dilys Winn

Leonidas Witherall Mysteries (by "Alice Tilton")

Beginning with a Bash	284 pages	$5.95
File For Record	287 pages	$5.95
Hollow Chest	284 pages	$5.95
The Left Leg	275 pages	$5.95

Available from bookshops, or by mail from the publisher: The Countryman Press, Box 175, Woodstock, Vermont 05091-0175. Please include $2.50 for shipping your order. Visa or Mastercard orders ($20.00 minimum), call 802-457-1049, 9-5 EST, Monday – Friday.

Prices and availability subject to change.